THE CITY OF LIGHT

The Last Shadow Epic, Book Five

by

AJ Cooper

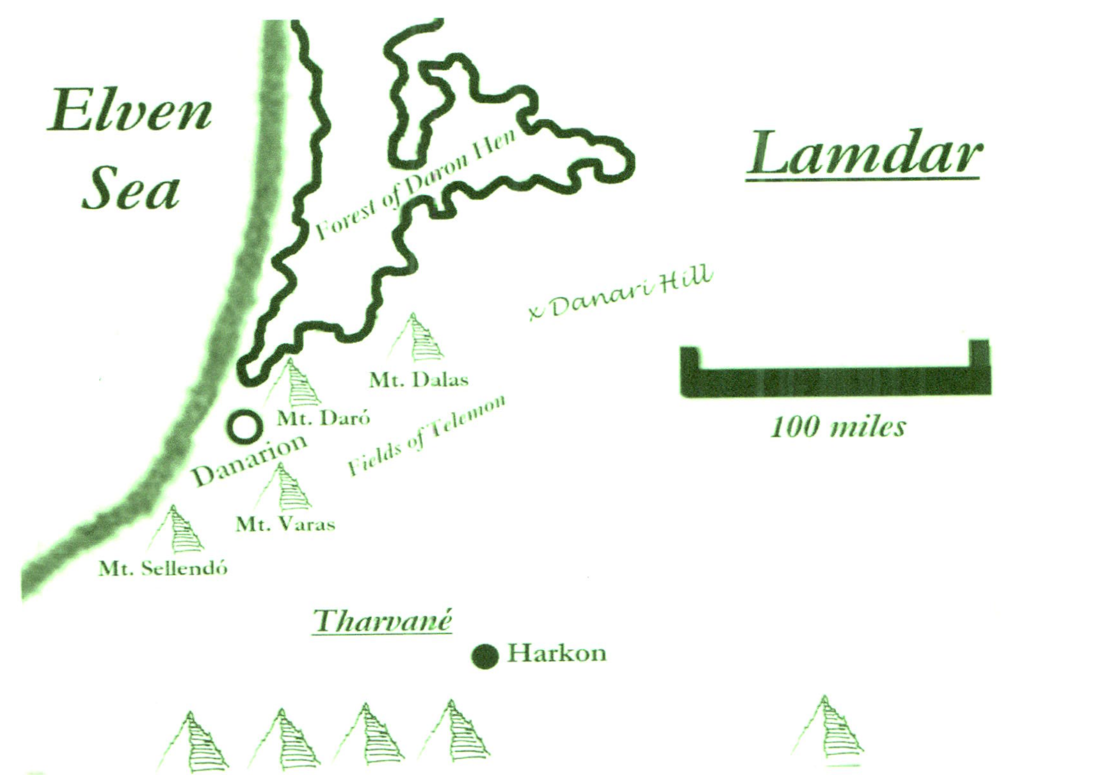

Elven Sea
Lamdar
Forest of Daron Hen
x Danari Hill
Mt. Dalas
Mt. Daró
Danarion
Fields of Telemon
100 miles
Mt. Varas
Mt. Sellendó
Tharvané
Harkon

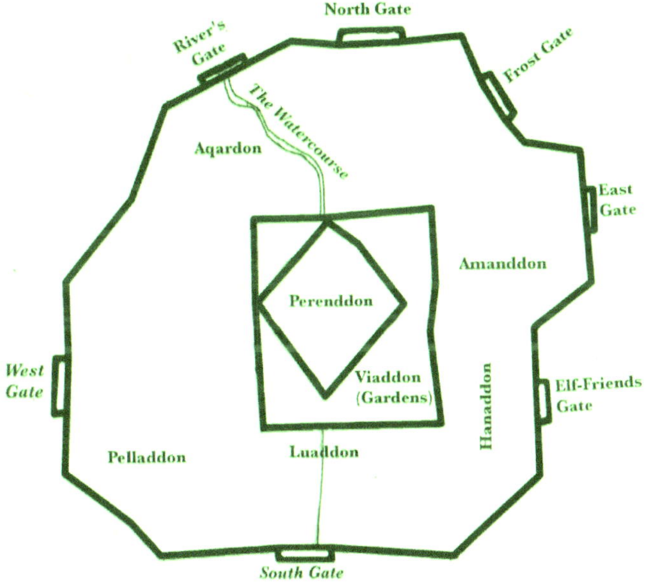

Danarion, the City of Light

Chapter One:
Green Fields, Green Hills

The sun dawned on a land living and breathing, and pulsing with life.

The sun dawned on green fields and villages on hilltops. It dawned on vineyards and wheat fields. It dawned on a land of abundance, and in view of that light, all thought of the perilous journey and all thought of what had preceded it was gone from Reev's mind.

"Mount Dalas!" howled Fortunato astride Tyra Jade, and as Reev, riding two-a-saddle behind Lord Calion, rounded the waters of a gushing river, through mist and fog emerged a titanic peak capped in snow, from which smoke was steadily emitting.

The ground began to descend, and a vast valley opened up as far as the eye could see... the Fields of Telemon, the princess Yanenré had called it.

"Welcome!" she cried to Reev's left, "to my father's kingdom. Welcome to Lamdar..."

~

Farmers provided food every night they stopped, as they progressed due southwest, through fields so green Reev thought each individual blade of grass was young and at the height of its life. Food they never lacked, nor new wine from the vineyards just barely fermented. No Servant of Seymus they saw, nor rokahn nor Imperial soldier, in this world of plenty, which darkness did not seem to touch, where neither hunger nor signs of want could be seen. The Shadow had not fallen in Lamdar, and Reev thought it never would.

Days into their journey, and the sun was at its height, and warm was the air, and from the south was blowing a hot dry wind, when a great mountain appeared titanic in size, its peak jagged and hollow yet covered in white snow.

"Mount Daró!" Fortunato howled from Tyra Jade, their guide or so it seemed, and his words reminded Reev that Fortunato had been here once before, and what's more, was considered an elf-friend, an ally or perhaps even a citizen of the Elven World.

The countless thousands of galloping horses began to descend down a bowl shaped valley. There were glistening ponds and lakes, and forests of spruce and hemlock. There was the smell of mountain flowers, a good and propitious wind, when the elves on horses began to slow, and then come to an abrupt stop.

The party had been traveling for the better part of a week, at an easy pace.

Reev looked about, alarmed that they had halted the ride. Nenré came riding forth on her white horse, her magic staff in hand, and then wheeled around to face the army. "The borderlines of the city," said Nenré.

"The city?" Reev said.

Nenré smiled, and it seemed from her expression that she thought she was being patient. "Yes, Sage, the city," she said, "for during the Time of the Elves, its *waris* and houses and small shrines stretched to where I ride."

Beyond her, Reev saw, were spruces and hemlocks in view of Mount Daró, a rugged forest or so it seemed.

"For once," said Nenré, "the capital of elvenkind was the largest city in all Varda, and from it the light shone on the world. No darkness was allowed within. No darkness is allowed within it now."

"What darkness do you think we bring?" said Reev.

Nenré's affable expression vanished, replaced with a solemn frown. "There is one of you here who practiced works of darkest darkness. There is one of you here, who accompanied you, Sage, who took on the black mantle of the warlock. He turned away from his evil deeds, yet not even one who now serves the gods, but once was stained by darkness, is allowed into the City of Light."

Reev turned to Xan, riding on a speckled horse that the elves had provided. Xan's surprised expression turned to a grimace. "The Sage trusts me," he said. "You should trust me too. I have put aside the wages of the warlock. I am now a warrior of the light."

"So you say," said Nenré, "but beneath that cloak you wear is still buried a warlock's tool."

The Skeleton Key… without it, Reev and the six others in his party would not have escaped Galiope alive. It had unlocked a secret passageway they used to flee the Imperials, unseen.

"Cast it before me," said Nenré. "Let it lie, inert, forgotten, and I will let you pass the borderlines by my authority as the King's daughter."

Xan did not stir, nor did his grimace vanish. No, his grimace seemed to darken. He did not reach into his pocket; he did not expose the Skeleton Key to the light of the sun. Reev's heart sank.

"You have made your choice," said Nenré. "And there is still something of a warlock in you."

~

They left Xan behind, moving through woods and overgrown meadows. In places there were bits of stone and moss-covered rubble. As Reev, at the head of the army, passed through an especially dense thicket, there was what appeared to be a statue of an archer, its features long eroded by wind and water, its bow covered in flowering purple moss. Reev could only guess at the statue's grandeur when Danarion, the City of Light, was at its height, when its features were sharp and lifelike, and it was coated in bright paint, at the corner of a street or in the courtyard of some rich elf's house.

There was fog and there was wind, a cold gasp of mist and then hot dry, summerlike air. Mount Daró was in view, and the towering white walls of a great city.

~

The city was surrounded by watchtowers, built on many sloping hills. The sunlight reflected on its dazzling white walls, and gates so vibrant in color they seemed to be covered in emerald. Beyond the walls were the city's mounting levels, reaching a peak far beyond where two towers stretched into the sky, and between those two towers, a palace whose roof glittered with gold.

Nenré stopped, wheeling around on her horse, and faced Reev and the others, and the army behind them, with a tearful smile. "The Sage arrives," said Nenré, "at the City of Light. Long awaited, our hope is here."

As they stood there, there was the sound of pealing trumpets, of horns made from goat horns blasting. The gates before them, colored emerald, began to grind steadily open, laying bare Danarion, the City of Light… Danarion, the city of the great king.

~

Where the forest ended and the city began, Reev could not quite tell. Indeed, it seemed to him, after he had dismounted from Lord Calion's horse and walked forth with Gastreel at his side, that they had not truly left the forest when they passed through Danarion's gates. Along the ancient stone street, headed due north, in the hazy light of the sun, spruces and hemlocks were bunched up against the wood-gabled homes, and leafy deciduous trees, whose green foliage hid well the private yards and gardens, offered shade and protection from the wind. On the street, headed north, there was no stain of excrement or mud, but pure gray stone on which pine needles had fallen and turned red, and beside which ran channels of water where the citizens of Danarion could remove whatever unwanted waste they had accrued.

Indeed, it was not a forest or a city, but both, and Reev marveled at a people so close to nature, who though they lived richly and sumptuously, had one foot in civilization and one foot in the wild.

As they progressed north, there were small squares and markets — every one, it seemed, centered on a tree or a stand of rosebushes — and amid these squares, besides farmers hawking wheat or flowers or new wine, were cats wandering about, black or silver and gold. They seemed to neither fear Reev, like the feral cats near Norwood, nor rush to him like housecats would. Like the people of Danarion, it seemed they had one foot in the wild and one foot in civilization. Their eyes, of gold or brown or green, enchanted Reev as he passed them by, as the forest-city continued, and the street became a broad avenue.

It pierced, south to north, and the trees diminished. There were great stone buildings now with domes of faded bronze, the sides of the buildings covered in thick ivy. Reev thought then of the Library of Dendérion back in Galiope, how it had made him feel an ant and not a man, and now these buildings — set in a similar style — each twice the size of St. Sigmund's back in Galiope, made him seem less than an ant, but a mote of dust instead.

"Luaddon!" Nenré cried, the only one of them still astride a horse. Reev looked back; the army had vanished behind them, and Lord Calion was nowhere to be seen. Gastreel was at his left side, and Wrinn was at his right. Spyke and Fortunato were walking amazed a few steps behind.

And Xan… *Xan.* Reev hoped he had found lodgings, but Reev

supposed he had made his choice.

Before the towering monuments and buildings hewn of stone, as the sun's light glittered on the bronze domes and gray obelisks, there was a great wall, and a gold door. Beyond were the towers Reev had seen before, and the palace.

The palace of the elvenking... Reev, from Norwood, was headed there.

Nenré grabbed the reins of her horse and wheeled him around. "Sage," said she, "never before has a human passed through this door. Never before has a human entered into the inner citadel. Never before has a human been granted audience with our ruler the king. And more than an audience shall you have, Sage, as you soon will see."

The door shimmered as it opened, and shafts of sunlight bathed all in gold. There was a warm and gentle wind, and the scent of flowers. The skies were clear and blue, and beyond a garden fair and white was the house of the elvenking.

~

In the palace's highest level, a feast had been prepared. It had been waiting for this very moment, and when Reev stepped into the light there were gasps among the courtiers.

"So this," an elven woman said from the shadows, "is what he looks like."

On a table was spiced lamb wrapped in flatbreads, and pots of soup hot and cold. There was sweetbread and bread of a savory kind. There were stewed vegetables thickened with sauce, and bits of beef in bowls of rice.

As Reev stood in the light of the windows, he noticed a great chair on which a figure was sitting, and a smaller chair beside.

Fortunato and Spyke walked off to a table; Gastreel hauled himself to a booth with Nenré, taking fragile steps. Wrinn and Reev were standing in the center of the room, bathed in light, when from one of the corners of the room a starstone brightened into existence, revealing a stage and a wooden lectern.

An elven child, gold-haired and blue eyed, stepped forth into the light.

"Danarion of the Seven Gates," the child said, speaking the common Imperial tongue as was courtesy, each syllable formed by her Elvish accent.

"One gate for leaving and one gate for entering," said the child, "one for hoping and one for fearing. One for the dusk and one for the dawn. One for the way of the sea and the Sage's coming."

The feasters were staring at her transfixed.

"The words of Omré," said the child.

"Who is that?" Reev said to Wrinn, as if Wrinn would know.

The child departed.

"Hail, Annenwé," said the figure on the great seat.

~

There was red wine and white wine, wine that was sparkling and wine that was still, wine sharpened with spices and wine sweetened with honey, beer and ale and firewater laced with resin. And though the feast was joyous, so too — Reev sensed — sitting at a table with Spyke and Fortunato and Wrinn — that underneath the words of the elves and permeating the air was a sense of urgency and alarm.

After the elven child, more took to the stage, a singer singing songs in Elvish, a band of pipers, dancers accompanied by fiddles… and as Reev sat, feasting first on bread and then on steaks and then fish, as puddings and cakes were brought before him, he stole glances at Nenré sitting with her brother Vélerion, and one who appeared to be his twin, save for his grayish hair.

"Our hope, at last, arrives," said the shadowy figure seated on the great seat, "and for as long as he is with us, he shall live well."

It dawned on Reev only then that this feast had been made especially for him, that all this honor had been accorded for him and him alone, and that the only reason Gastreel and Fortunato and Spyke — humans all — and Wrinn, an outsider among elves, were allowed within this palace, were because they accompanied the Sage. And that was what the elves believed him to be.

After cakes came puddings sweetened with sugar, and honey confections flavored with peppermint. Reev had eaten several days' worth of food, and though he was satisfied, his capacity for eating seemed increased here. His stomach did not protest as more and more was eaten, and the wine, served without cease, stimulated his appetite. All care, all worry was gone, in this place of plenty and opulence and love. He was safe, and though the night outside was dark, he looked out the window, and the streets below were lit with torches, and there were lanterns in the whiteness of the garden. Even in nighttime, in the City of Light, the darkness would never fully fall.

And this feast, which had begun in daylight, had passed him by quickly. All care was gone. All fear was nowhere more to be seen. Reev did not want it to end, and yet, as he sat, partaking of the last of the honeyed confections, and drinking the last bit of wine from his pewter goblet, there was motion — a shape taking form from the great seat. The light of the starstones and the city outside glinted in a pair of eyes, and on the gems of a crown.

"The feast, this day, the tenth of the month Yanenré, has satisfied the king," said he. "Has it satisfied the Sage?"

"It has," Reev said.

"Then we shall consider this first feast ended," said the king, "and let it be recorded by the College of Priests, a decree to Lamdar and all its dominions and possessions, that seven weeks of feasting are declared, and all elves shall be light in their labors. Our hope at long last is here, and the dawn soon shall come."

"I shall record it, father," said the man sitting with Yanenré, what appeared to Reev's eyes to be Vélerion's silver-haired twin. "Tomorrow, Sage, you shall be given fine clothes to wear, for you shall be widely seen. Your arrival was unexpected, though it was long foretold. You arrived with the coming of the New Year, this 1470th year of the age of humanity, and on the eve of the funeral of Amané the gods' favored, and her love, Lamadon."

Amané…

"The Lady of the Wood," Wrinn said, under his breath.

The patrons began to stand up from their seats. Reev arose, dizzy from the wine, and steadied himself on his chair.

"To the royal apartments you go," said the figure standing in front of the great seat. "To the place of the king's favor, beside the garden called *Viaddon.*

"*Danen vadilla… Illuné vadilla, Eldari…*"

~

They departed the palace into the garden, the last of the patrons to depart. A group of elves in full plate, with blue capes hanging over their silver armor — the King's Guard, Reev learned — led them past trees and bushes, underneath the soft glow of lanterns, down a cobblestone path, to a row of buildings in the shadow of the palace. Each door was of wood, with silver knobs, and the windows above were cross-hatched and aglow from the light within.

Gastreel and Fortunato, then Spyke, disappeared into the doors, until Reev and Wrinn were alone, standing in the cool air.

From the shadows, beyond the dark forms of the King's Guard, appeared the shape of an elf — and in the lantern's light, a face Reev knew.

His long black hair fell down his tunic. His pale lips formed into a faint smile. He was as fair as the moon, and to his skin was a healthful sheen.

"Vélerion," said Reev.

"Sage," Vélerion said, and when he said the word that faint smile turned to a grin. "We meet again, at long last, after I saw you in the forests of Alonar. There I saw your work for the first time. And now you are in my country."

A wind seemed to blow, and the branches of the white bushes gusted in its wake. Reev saw in Vélerion's eyes a gleam he wasn't sure he liked, a gleam he wasn't sure he trusted.

"Here you are safe," Vélerion said. "In vain, the Dark One has assayed to lay low Danarion. In vain has the Dark One assayed to spread evil to this country. But he shall not prevail. Darkness shall never extinguish the City of Light. And you are safe here, Sage, for as long as you choose to stay."

Safe… and yet, Reev found himself inching away, amid this fair garden, in the light of these lanterns.

"Get rest, Sage," said Vélerion, "for tomorrow at dawn, your work begins… if you are truly the one promised to us."

Reev peered into Vélerion's dark eyes. He so badly wanted to trust those eyes. But he was glad when he turned, and relieved when he laid his hand on the silver knob of the door, and twisted. Relaxation followed when he entered, and when he and Wrinn were alone, there was joy.

Chapter Two: Having Dreams

Wrinn stirred awake at the light of the dawn. The sun was shining through the windows of their upper room, and the cool of the night air was fading. Reev, sound asleep in the other bed, had a look of peace Wrinn hadn't seen in his former master since the night he was first bought. He was laying still, his hands cupped over the silk sheets, and whatever dreams he'd had the night before were surely ones of peace.

As for Wrinn, his initial wonder of seeing the Elf Lands — what would be his homeland, in a just world — had been met instantly with another force. For as he rode, there were nameless whispers, a thousand voices crying out in every direction, uttering a nameless language whose words he did not know. These voices were of a different kind than the voices he knew in the South Weald. These voices, of the trees of Lamdar, were ones bold and loud, and the voices were of trouble.

Reev stirred — gasped. His eyes opened, and the peace was gone. A note of terror touched them, bewilderment.

"Where am I, Wrinn?" Reev said.

"The king's apartments," Wrinn said, and put on a bold smile. It was easier, now that the troubled voices of the trees, shouting in the ears of his mind, were fainter. "We are in Danarion, the city of the great king."

"Ah," Reev said, "and there was something planned for today. What was it? I cannot remember…"

~

Vélerion and his twin brother dressed Reev in a robe of yellow silk, cinched with a white robe belt. They ran a comb through his hair and placed in his right hand a rod of gold.

A moment later, Gastreel and Fortunato, then Spyke, exited the royal apartments dressed for the day. Vélerion's gray eyes sparkled as he looked upon them, and there was the sound of blasting trumpets, dozens at once.

"A day, sad," said Vélerion's brother, "a day, joyous. Amané, the gods' favored, enters into eternal rest. And we shall bid her goodbye into the kingdom of the gods."

Fortunato looked up; birds were soaring overhead. A wind was rustling through the bushes, as more trumpets blasted, and the noise of the city suddenly was deafening.

~

The crowds to Wrinn's eyes were like a raging sea. Just beyond the gate, they had gathered by the side of the broad thoroughfare, which pierced the district called Luaddon and clove it in two. They were rich and poor, in browns and grays or in bright purple or blue silks, but all — Wrinn noted — appeared healthy and well fed, having spent their youth, or so it seemed, in sunshine, in the fresh air. The poorest in Lamdar was better off than the richest elf in Gallia. And not for the first time, Wrinn burned with discontent at a life stolen from him, an inheritance snatched away from him before he was born. He had not grown up in this place of summer and sunshine and plenty. He had labored as a pit fighter for the bloodlust of humans. Then he had labored at a pig farm, and then at an inn.

More trumpets blasted. The crowds seemed to sway. A wind blew from the sky up above, a hot dry wind that blanketed Wrinn in warmth. The snow of Mount Daró seemed to sparkle in the light of the sun, and then far in the distance, a procession began to make its way through the thoroughfare.

More trumpets blasted. The crowds cheered and some of them scrambled to the edge of the street, while children hoisted themselves on their parents' heads and others strained to look over shoulders. Wrinn narrowed his eyes and peered as far as his eyes could see, and he saw Lord Calion mounted on his brown horse, and behind him a pair of elven warriors. Behind those warriors, elves dressed in robes of flame orange were hoisting a stone box, a box Wrinn had seen before in the forests of Gallia — what the elves called Alonar.

It was Amané's ossuary, the receptacle of her bones and the bones of her lover Lamadon. The Lady of the Wood was a woman Wrinn had never met, but Reev had met her in her fullness and struggled to describe her glory. Beautiful, terrible, he had called her, a force of nature that terrified the forces of evil, so strong and so great that, Wrinn wondered, in a battle between Amané and the Dark One himself, who would win.

More trumpets blasted and the very street beneath their feet seemed to quake. The cheers of the crowds rose up amid the daylight, and the voices in Wrinn's mind — though far off — were louder, now. Deafening they were, angry, wrathful, as terrible as Wrinn guessed Amané had been. He struggled to ignore them; he struggled to put them out of his mind. And Wrinn felt somehow that they wanted his attention.

Son of the Forest, the first phrase he understood — shouted. North by northwest.

A face flashed in his mind, two piercing green eyes, and hair like burnished bronze, fair lips, a fair jaw.

And Wrinn was shuddering in terror when the procession reached them — the five heroes in the elves' minds, Wrinn, Gastreel, Reev, Spyke and Fortunato. And Fortunato, as the priests carrying the ossuary turned, grabbed a rose blossom from a bush beside him and cast its pink petals in the path of the ossuary and the elves' stamping feet.

Fortunato, healthy, hale, full of life — garbed in a inky black cloak the elves had provided. He was smiling as the elves passed him by.

But Wrinn was not smiling.

Son of the Forest, the terrible voices were speaking to him, *what evil have you brought to us?*

He turned in the voices' direction. He saw he was facing directly north.

What lay north? Up above-head of towers and high roofs, and the bronze domes of buildings, was the sparkling snow of Mount Daró. What lay at its foothills?

There were more trumpets blasting — and then loud shouts, and scattered screams. Wrinn turned, and saw the Sage, Reev, had fallen to the ground. He was like a gold petal on the ground, in his yellow robe. Spyke, Fortunato and Gastreel had gathered round him.

Amané's ossuary had processed down the street.

And Wrinn, bewildered, alarmed, looked at his friend and remembered his many travails, and thought of the words he had heard in the ears of his mind, *Son of the Forest, what evil have you brought to us?*

~

"The Tower of Warding," said Lord Calion the fair-haired. "No human has set foot within it. Great honor you are accorded, Fortunato and — Spyke — and Gastreel Osiris. Great honor you are accorded, Wrinn, *dra'datsi.*"

The dark stone chamber spread before Wrinn, and in the darkness, the cold of the stone floor, the anger at the word *dra'datsi* was only a gust of fire, not a raging inferno.

"Pity," said Lord Calion, "that this honor is at a time of peril. Pity that the Sage was overwhelmed, when the people of the city first beheld him."

"Overwhelmed," Gastreel said weakly, "by what?"

"We shall soon see," said Lord Calion, and flicked his wrist. He had cast something into a brazier, and instantly it blazed to life, fire burning bright, revealing the body of Reev lying still and breathing upon a stone table.

"I sense him," said Lord Calion, "he is still with us. And here, the forces eager to hinder him are weaker. The Dark One lusts after Danarion, to bring low the city of the great king and make the Light's firstborn love him. But the king's army still has strength. The sun's light still shines on the Fields of Telemon. And the elven people remain faithful."

Lord Calion rounded the table, reached into his robe pocket and procured black powder. He flicked the powder into another brazier and it burst into flame, and then lit a third brazier in the same way.

The room was now as bright as day, and Wrinn could see the expert stonework, the channels cut along the ceiling and the floral reliefs that ran along the walls in gold leaf.

Reev was lying still, but it seemed to Wrinn that Lord Calion was right. He was breathing, though those breaths were halting. Reev was alive, as alive as he had ever been. And Wrinn's fear was lessened, though it was not gone.

"What now?" Gastreel said, and when he had spoken he began to cough.

Reev was healthy, with a lush complexion and a youthful strength. But Wrinn had never seen Gastreel so weak. The wizard, long their guide, the one who had purchased Wrinn for Reev and eventually led him to manumission, had not been the same since he channeled all his power into the Gate of Tedron. The magic portal which had taken them to the Elf Lands had cost Gastreel all his strength, and he was thin, now, and could barely eat. His complexion was ashen, almost gray. His gaze was weak, like the gaze of cattle or some animal. His breathing was labored and seemed to take effort, and along his arms now were the marks that had appeared when he had channeled all his power, and rendered to the Gate of Tedron all his strength.

"What now," Lord Calion repeated Gastreel's words, more softly, "what now, you shall see."

He rounded the table again. He laid his white hand on Reev's forearm, and grazed his finger along Reev's scar.

"A great weapon was used against the Sage," Lord Calion said, "not so long ago. I was there in the forests of Alonar when it was used against him. I removed the splinters of *Serpentax*, the Dark One's own sword, from his flesh.

"But not even the greatest of Healers will be able to fully cure the wound. Only the defeat of Seymus, when he is ground underfoot and cast into unquenchable flame, will mend the wound which hinders the Sage."

"Is that why he fell?" Wrinn asked.

Spyke and Fortunato stirred.

"No," Lord Calion replied. His white hair, hanging down his back, seemed to glow in the light of the braziers. His keen dark eyes turned to Reev, and his hand — once at the wound — moved toward Reev's chest, above his heart.

"Sage," said Lord Calion, "*Ridio!*"

Reev gasped for air and sat up. His eyes were wide as a fish's, and then his ragged breaths slowed to a steady rhythm. The shock began to fade from his eyes, and Lord Calion asked him, "What did you see?"

"I saw," Reev said, "the Lady of the Wood in her glory. I saw… a pair of scales and a lady blindfolded.

"I saw… I saw…"

"What did you *see*?" Lord Calion pressed him. "*Locta!*"

"A tree," Reev said, "I saw a tree."

"Yes," Lord Calion said, "a tree is what you saw, when Amané in her repose passed you by. You saw a tree, and of what form were its leaves?"

"Like flame…"

"And what form was its bark?"

"As white as snow," Reev replied.

"And what was beside it?" Lord Calion said.

"A stone…" Reev's breathing was growing ragged again. "And sorcerers casting into it light."

"The World Tree," said Lord Calion, "its seed sown at the dawn of the Age of Mankind. Three ages there have been, the gold Age of the Gods, the silver Age of the Elves, the iron Age of Mankind."

"There was something else I saw," Reev said.

Lord Calion stepped back.

"What was it, Reev?" Gastreel said.

"A shape," Reev said, "rising out of the sea…"

At Reev's words, the fires of the braziers flickered and flared, and the room brightened and then darkened, and then brightened again.

"Of what form is this shape?" said Lord Calion.

Reev gasped; his eyes grew shallow, the darks of his eyes dilated. "I… I… billowing blackness. Shadow. Horns."

Lord Calion's lips twisted upward, giving the impression of a smile. "*Eldari*," he said. "*Hirda!*"

Reev sat up, then removed himself from the stone table. He took a few staggering steps forward, then steadied himself, laying his hands on the wall. "What must I do now, Lord Calion?"

"A woman, you saw, with a blindfold," Lord Calion said, "beside her a pair of scales. I believe you were sent a message by Amané's spirit. Only one in Danarion walks about blindfolded, our Sibyl, the speaker of truth. And her sigil is a pair of scales. To her you must go, Sage, and do not delay. She shall tell you the meaning of your visions, and the dark shape that you saw rising out of the sea."

"Will you take me there?" Reev said.

~

From the monuments of Luaddon down the great thoroughfare, beside the great buildings and then back into the midst of the forest city, Reev followed Lord Calion. He drew the robe he'd been given a bit tighter, on the face of a cold wind, and realized that after his vision, and in the wake of last night's feast, he had begun to feel disquieted somehow, an illness of the mind he could not place. Following Lord Calion's form, past the spruce and hemlock-crowded streets, he uttered prayers under the breath, and as he walked, he shuddered at the sight of every long shadow, and trembled at the sight of every cloud when it obscured the sun.

Why had they come here, after all? Back home, in Galiope, the situation in the city had become dangerous. The Empire had invaded, and seized control. Their last fortress had been taken away from them, underfoot, and Fortunato had suggested the brash idea of finding safe haven in the Elf Lands.

A City of Light... a land of light? And yet, could the shadow also here fall? Could the Dark One at last succeed at what he had long wanted, and make acolytes out of the Light's firstborn? Reev shuddered at the thought, and as he had that thought, another cloud passed by, obscuring the sun, and as he had that thought, Lord Calion turned, right down a winding cobblestone road, and then right again.

~

Far from Luaddon and its monuments, in the shadow of arches and towers and spires, was a great canal projecting due northwest from the palace. Here there were shops and quiet markets, small shrines and, in the cool damp, gardens where *sindomas* flowers were blooming. Lord Calion had continued on at his easy pace, and, seeing that Reev was flagging, raised his right hand and said, "Hurry up, *Eldari*. We have reached Aqardon."

The walls of Danarion were ahead, and in front of Reev, the vast canal — a man-made river — met the broadness of a great gate.

"What is this canal?" Reev said.

Lord Calion stopped his stride, and turned. "These waters, if you sail a ship west, will take you into the vastness of the Great Sea. The Watercourse is not oft used, though, and its gate has long been shut. The seas have been plagued with pirates since the onset of the Southern Terror. Any ship that travels to Danarion's gate, eastwards, is viewed — for good reason — with alarm."

"And the gate — it holds back the water?" Reev said.

"The gate is shut," said Lord Calion. "Long has it been so, and so it is for your coming, *Eldari*."

"The gate… what is it called?" Reev said.

He was fixated on it, bright and shining gold, seeming to luminesce in the light of the sun.

"The River's Gate," said Lord Calion. "*Hanathroni*."

Reev thought, staring at it, that the gate was somehow of great significance, and a quiet voice told him that he should keep his eye on it, lest anything dark befall it. *Hanathroni*, it was called, a queer word to his Imperial sensibilities, yet on further thought, it lightly rolled off the tongue.

Along the Watercourse they walked, past shops and underneath the *waris*, ceremonial gates, that seemed to predominate this part of the city. At last the buildings and shops and houses vanished behind a stand of bushes, and Calion and Reev were in a great courtyard.

There was green grass, there, and a cobblestone path winding its way toward a stone building. There were elves wandering the yard, all women, all wearing white gowns and blue veils. And When Lord Calion raised his right hand and shouted "*Hail!*" and they looked up, they did not appear at all pleased to see them.

One, the boldest among these women, walked up to them, daintily upon the grass. Her eyes narrowed; her pale lips were pursed. "Calion, *drubi*, why do you bother Her Eminence Callisti?"

"The Sage has seen a vision of the World Tree, and we wish to know if it is now time."

Now time — time for what, Reev wondered.

The bold woman lowered her veil, revealing a pair of catlike green eyes. "Bring unto Callisti an offering, a bowl of wheat and spelt and emmer. Even the Sage must pay the price required of all."

Lord Calion grew dour. "The hour is late, Kydé. You know this. You know what the Sage's arrival in Danarion means, for us and for all our people."

Kyde's bright green eyes darkened. "Wheat, spelt, emmer. If the gods themselves came and asked for Callisti's truth, we would ask the same."

~

"Shall we get it at the market?" Reev said. "Wheat, spelt, emmer," he repeated, and was proud of himself for remembering.

"We must read into Kydé's words the hidden truth," said Calion. "The Sibyl is not interested in meeting you. Otherwise, such a request would not have been made."

But had Kydé not said if the gods themselves had asked an audience with the Sibyl, she would have demanded the same?

Reev, howver, would not argue, and that night, and the ensuing ten nights, they feasted and they drank, and all thought of the failed meeting with the Sibyl was gone.

Chapter Three: Ancient Memory

Spyke had never tasted wine so rich, nor had he eaten food spiced so perfectly and baked so tenderly. Each morsel, each baked good, slid down so smoothly into his stomach and — though he was never hungry — he never was too full to eat. The more food the elves brought before the feasting hall, the more Spyke ate. The more wine they ferried from the royal cellars and Danarion's market-squares, the more Spyke drank, and so his mind was swimming one night — which night was it? — after his arrival in Danarion.

In Spyke's hometown, the seaside city of Perremum, vineyards surrounded its walls and wine was not in short supply. But the elves, it seemed, delighted in wine above all things, wine sparkling and still, wine red and white and pink and gold. Wine — it was what they lived for, or so it seemed.

Spyke did not complain as he took another sip of the sharp fluid — what was it? Red, they had poured into his cup. On the stage — how many nights had they been here? — a band of lyrists were strumming a symphony.

Feasting, joy — the Sage had arrived. And what a choice it had been for Spyke to compete in the Pan-Vardic Games back in Galiope, a choice that had led him into the company of Fortunato and of Reev, the promised Prince of the Dawn, a choice that had brought him here, to the land of the elves, to this endless feast that had not stopped nor shown signs of stopping.

But too much pleasure is wearying, and too much of anything can dull the senses. Spyke was beginning to nod off, to sleep, when there was the flash of something — through the window, light.

As the lyrists' tune rose to a new dazzling height, Spyke was stirred from his pleasure-filled stupor. He got up from where he sat, laid his hand on the table, and took a drunken step around the chairs, past Fortunato and Nenré where they were sitting, to the window where he'd seen the flash. There was darkness — the lights of the city and the lanterns in the garden below the palace. There was Danarion in its nighttime glory — and the flash, again.

Spyke, an Imperial, was at his core a warrior. The ranks of the Imperial Army were where he had been forged. The oath, he took… to serve the emperor and the people. And something else… to give no heed to danger. He would give no heed to danger now.

That light, he recognized, was a flash cast through a mirror, a signal. He could not ignore it. He took another drunken step forward.

~

Outside the night air was cool, verging on cold, but not cold enough for Spyke's tunic to be inadequate. The day's gentle heat was long gone, and the lovingcare of the sun was nowhere to be felt. In this land of plenty, in this city Spyke did not know, he ventured in the dark, knowing he had seen something with his own two eyes, that he had not imagined it.

The moon was shining in the city below, a half moon aglow. The stars were shining. The constellation of the Bull was resplendent against the purple-black sky. In this city, this city that time forgot, which never lacked food nor wine, treated gently by the elements, Spyke began to feel exposed somehow, watched from all corners. And Spyke, suddenly, wished he had brought his Dohorensi board which had been his weapon ever since he left the army. He'd become a master of it, a master like his uncle Koru, and whatever force watched him now would be quickly dashed to nothing, if Spyke laid his fingers round the handle.

He passed through the gate. Spyke's experience at sea had made him an expert at navigation by eye. When he had navigated the rough waters of the Western Ocean, and docked warships on the far shores of the Antipodes, he had learned where things lay on his horizon, how to travel to places he had seen. And the light, cast from a mirror, was beyond the garden, beyond the interior walls of the Inner Fortress, in the city proper. It had been aimed, directly, at the place where the elves and their guests had been feasting, and it was a message similar to that of signal-fires used by Imperial camps… Spyke was sure of it. Light, cast into a mirror, a signal, a summons… and Spyke would uncover it, yes, he would uncover it. He took another drunken step forward.

That feeling of being watched, of something lying in wait, was getting stronger as the broad thoroughfare became a network of streets, and from the windows of candlelit houses Spyke could see elven eyes peering at him. Guided by starlight, like a journey to the Antipodes, Spyke followed his recollection, down a road, through an alley, past barrels and an empty market square, past a narrow road where hawkers were selling trinkets even this late into a night, past a bookshop, past a group of idlers talking underneath the boughs of a tree — a flash… light, cast into a mirror, aimed — to Spyke's right — at the place of feasting. And an elven woman was standing, holding that mirror, while a young girl would periodically aim a lantern at the glass.

"Hail!" Spyke said.

The elven woman gasped and dropped the mirror. It shattered into shards on the cobblestone of the street.

The young girl and the woman backed away. The woman's eyes widened like saucers. Her lip trembled.

"Are you he?" said the woman. "The one promised to us? The one who brings the Dawn?

"And so he comes, not what I expected, older than I had thought, brown-eyed, dusky as the night…"

"I am not he," said Spyke. "I am his companion. As for Reev, I know him little better than anyone else. I accompanied him on his journey here."

"Anyone whom *Velati Sonoren* trusts is worthy of trust," said the woman. "I had hoped to call, Light to light. I had hoped to summon him. I knew he was feasting beyond that window."

"And why did you call him?" said Spyke. "What is your need, milady? Perhaps, I can help."

~

In the refreshing, bracing cold of the night, Spyke followed the woman and the girl down several streets, to where cats were mewing and business was being undertaken in the light of the moon. Sellers were out, selling by starlight toys and trinkets out of their cart, or bottles of wine, or firewater by the glass. The ground began to descend to what appeared to Spyke's eyes an artificial river, then to a group of homes shadowed by pines, and a home with its door open, its lights aglow.

Within that house was a fire, and as Spyke entered, following the woman and the girl, the woman laid tight her hand around the girl's wrist.

The fire, in the center of the room, was crackling in the night. Amid its flame was pottage in a black cauldron, steeping and bubbling — grains, bits of meat, vegetables, salt and spices over the days congealing into one tasty whole.

"Why have you brought me here?" Spyke said. "Why have you summoned the Sage's servant?"

"What is your name, *dilari sonoren*?" said the woman.

"You must tell me yours first," said Spyke.

"My name is nothing," she said. "A poor woman, getting by. The husband of Narsari, rest his soul."

"I'm sorry."

"Omas is my name," she said, "and my purpose in this world is the mother of Rimarvé. That is why I brought you here."

"My name is Spyke," he said, and looked to the girl who had been casting the lantern's light into the now-shattered mirror. Her name was apparently Rimarvé, a name whose meaning Spyke could only guess.

"Spyke," said Omas. "A name that does not easily roll off the tongue. Abrupt. The name of a warrior. You must be a soldier. A fighter. A warrior in service to a nation."

Spyke wondered at Omas's eyes, green like glass, lips perked into something between a smile and a deep frown. Spyke had a thought that this woman was an enchantress, that she had read his mind somehow. And now, he was not glad to have left the feast, but glad that Reev had not been drawn here.

"I am a soldier," Spyke said. "I am a soldier of the Empire… or was."

Omas's green eyes narrowed. Her grip of her daughter's wrist had become viselike. "The Empire, yes," she said. "Perhaps, you will be able to help.

"For in the past days, my Rimarvé has been in danger. At odd hours of the night, she will rise as one possessed, and attempt to fling herself into this fire of mine. At morning she has no memory of it, but when she is overcome by this strange spirit, her eyes are full of something vicious.

"I sought the Sibyl's wisdom. She said unto me something unfathomable, and difficult for my elven tongue to pronounce.

"*The Sixth Anthanian,* she said unto me. And, '*Only the Sage can help you.*' "

Spyke peered at her, then to Omas's troubled girl. "The Sixth Anthanian," he repeated in a low tone, a dark utterance in the night, and when he spoke those words the flames of the fire flared, and the coals burned with new life.

"Omas," said Spyke, "I know how you can help yourself. Put

out this fire, and have no pottage to eat. Buy bread and meat at the market, and wine to drink. If you have no fire, your daughter will not cast herself in it."

The fire's light cast about Omas's face, and she seemed surprised, as if she had not thought of this before. "And the Sixth Anthanian?" said Omas. "Your face betrays you. You know this means something."

"I have done all I can to help," answered Spyke.

~

As Spyke walked back to the palace in the cold of the night, he knew he had not told this Omas all.

For the Sixth Anthanian was in fact a word he had not heard before. But the fact he had not heard of it troubled him.

The Empire's legions that terrified the world were named after the city or region in which they were first constituted. The First Anthanian Legion Spyke had heard of before, the Second Anthanian won an awe-filled victory at the Siege of Keruda. Spyke had served in the Fourth.

There had been a Seventh Anthanian legion in which famed emperors of old had fought. But the Sixth… Spyke had never heard of the Sixth.

This sixth legion, formed in the province of Anthania of old, had to be in existence. If there was a Seventh Anthanian Legion, there was a sixth.

Why then had Spyke not heard of it? Why was there no trace of it in his memory, in the memory of Spyke, once a careerist in the Imperial Army?

He shut his eyes and saw fire, and eyes aglow. He looked up at the constellation of the Bull, and as he did, the stars of the Bull seemed to twinkle. Were they red, rather than white?

Chapter Four:
Prince of the Dusk, Prince of the Dawn

The taste of wine filled Fortunato's mouth, and his mind was swimming. The party was moving from the feasting hall to the balcony above the garden. The party was moving locations, as drunken parties often do.

The bores and the dullards — they had gone to bed. The King — Yanenré's father… Yanenré, whose hand he was drunkenly holding — had retired after having only a spot of wine, leaving his daughter and others by themselves.

In this city of wonders, Fortunato had drunk more than he'd ever had, and he'd eaten more too, yet when he looked in the mirror there was little sign of plumpness or softness to his flesh. He took another gulp from the saucer of wine he was drinking from, and staggered forward.

"Fortunato!" Yanenré called after him, and slipped her hand from his grip. "All in moderation… but moderation is key."

Moderation had not been the order of the day among these elves. No, it had been wine-cup after wine-cup, glass after glass, pastries sweetened with sugar and honey, and meat glistening with fat. Moderation was not in the elves' parlance, of late, now that the Sage had arrived, and the time of the promise was here.

Fortunato had noted a difference from the prior and only time he had been to Danarion — then a city in turmoil and in tumult, then with news of the wide world striking terror in the heart of the elvenking. And though events abroad had never been so ruinous, the wars never so wide-reaching or violent, though the world it seemed would fall, the day the elves had longed for, for millennia, had come at last, the Sage accompanied by his friends arriving on the holy ground where Solarias once trod.

"Fortunato!" Yanenré cried out. "Get a hold of yourself!"

He had fallen and was gripping the edge of the balcony, looking down into the white of the garden below. The wine of the elves was powerful, and took away all care and all fear. Fortunato had never drunk so much, or drunk anything of such potency, ever before. "It is your fault, I declare," said Fortunato, "the fault of your people, that I am staggering about like this. Seven weeks of feasting… what kingdom in Varda has so much wine, or so much food, that they can afford seven weeks of feasting?"

"Quiet," Yanenré said. "Our day has come. We will rejoice while the Prince of the Dawn is with us. We will don clothes of mourning, and girt our swords and shields, when he is gone."

"Will he be gone?" Fortunato said. "We will leave?"

"He must defeat the Dark One," Yanenré said. "He must crush Seymus underfoot and bring about the Enemy's doom. He must leave, for the Dark One is not to be found here amid light and life."

Leave… Fortunato did not want to leave. But at the end of seven weeks of feasting, when he'd grown plump and besotted, he wondered if it would be too much for his constitution to bear. Now, though, he delighted in the wine and in the tastes of the breads and pastries and rich meats. Now, he loved the feast.

And in the moonlight, standing far off, he realized he rather liked the sight of something too. In her robes Yanenré was, white and flowing, and her red hair glowed amid the night sky. Her blue eyes were blue as the sea, her pink lips as pink as roses. She had not aged a day or night since Fortunato first met Yanenré in the forests of Gallia… what elves called Alonar.

"Fortunato of Ríva," said Yanenré, "I was glad to see you accompanying the Prince of the Dawn, our hope. You impressed Lord Calion greatly on our first meeting. You shall be an asset to the Throne of Solendir."

Would he be something more? He almost said it as Yanenré the princess turned, joining the bores and the dullards in their quiet beds.

He would have her, he realized. That, he vowed, as she turned and departed through the door.

He took another deep sip of red wine.

~

Reev had drunken only lightly, and he had guarded his sips. He had often swallowed and then spat the wine back into his cup, as Wrinn drank more and more and as Wrinn's cup was continuously refilled. As the feast ended, Reev noted a motion of shadow in the corners of the room, a shape — the gleam of something, as if beckoning him.

He felt drawn in that moment in the emptying room, a fish caught in a hook, a bear unable to resist bait. That gleam — what was it? — and as the feasting hall emptied, he followed the shape, and the gleam, through a door, and a dark hallway.

In the light of the starstones Reev realized he was following an elven figure. There was a robe of silk, green in color, with the shape of eyes and stars dyed on the fabric. There was a belt inset with gold and rubies, and on fair hands silver bracelets, and diamond rings.

"Hail!" Reev tried to say, but his voice stopped him. Another door seemed to open of its own accord, and Reev followed the figure through, to a room with a silver floor and a glass dome, lit by starlight, yet seemingly as bright as the sun.

The figure turned, and Reev saw that on his head was a gold crown inset with stars and moons.

Amid this feasting, amid these endless days and nights — or had it been weeks? — Reev realized he had never seen with his own two eyes Yanenré's father the king.

For the glory did not come from his robe that was worth the price of entire kingdoms, or his rings or bracelets the same, nor from his crown that seemed fashioned by the gods themselves, but by his brown eyes as commanding as an eagle's, his long brown hair lined with the crowning gray of age, his imperious pose, and the presence that caused Reev to wish to fall to his knees and declare "Your Glory!"

"Your Glory!" Reev declared, but he did not fall to his knees.

"Sage," he said, "call me no such thing. I see that you stayed your knees. You shall not kneel to me.

"For the king of the elves is just a steward. The first Sage was the true king of the elves, and when the armies moved they followed him, not the elvenking they swore to serve. My armies are at your beck and call, Prince of the Dawn, and at your name the armies move.

"Do not kneel, do not bow. For the call of Antheleon the first Sage, the Prince of the Dusk, was the same as yours. And where he failed, you will succeed."

Reev from Norwood… he was saying all these things about Reev from Norwood.

"The Dark One hates you but he also fears you, like he fears and hates the Light's firstborn."

"I want to defeat the Dark One," Reev said, desperately. "How will I do it?"

"Tell me, Sage," said the elvenking, "about the necklace you bear. A gold coin, on its face a mountain." He drew nearer, took the metal in his hands and flipped it. "On the reverse, the likeness of a man."

"I am a Telantine," said Reev, "that is what I learned. A people and not a thing, a place and not some descriptive word. I am from Telantis, though I do not know where Telantis is."

"Yes, that is what the wizard Gastreel told my hostler Imrari," the elvenking said. "A riddle at last solved, solved with the Sage's coming, as is fitting. 'He shall be *Telantari*,' the books of prophecy declared, but what is *Telantari*? The wisest of the elves, the most learned, the soothsayers and even the Sibyls tried in vain to uncover it. *Telantari*, he shall be, a thing of *Telantas*. But what is it? And where is it?"

"I do not know," said Reev.

Would he mention that Fortunato, another in his company, was a Telantine?

"You do not know where Telantis is, or where this coin was minted," said the elvenking, "nor have our scholars found any trace, after hours and days of scouring. But perhaps, in some hidden place in Varda, in some dark corner, knowledge endures unheard by elven ears."

The silver of the room seemed aglow, and the starlight was dazzling. A silver light appeared in the elvenking's eyes, and he seemed to stiffen, and to grow.

"My daughter Yanenré met you amid the trees and glades of Alonar, Sage. And on the first day of the month of Yanenré, her namesake, at the start of the year, she meets you outside Danari Hill, and accompanies you into Lamdar.

"Fortune… the favor of the gods. You are safe, unharmed, on this 1470th year of the Age of Humanity. You are safe, unharmed, and that cannot be said for all in your company."

"What do you mean?" Reev said.

"Did you notice, Sage, that Gastreel was absent from tonight's feast?"

Reev had thought the meats and breads and wines for endless days had been too much for Gastreel's old constitution to bear. He had striven to keep faithful to the most innocent of explanations, the ones that did not break his heart. But he had not been the same since those scars had appeared, when he had used his physical body to invigorate the Gate of Tedron.

"He is at the Healing House with the *Amandori*, the chief healer," said the elvenking. "His wounds are grave and he shall not recover. When you depart he will not go with you. He will enjoy his final years in light and life, in comfort, in peace and in the gods' favor."

The thought was hard to bear, and the idea of going on without Gastreel was terrifying to his mind, but worse than that was an old man, wounded and wearied, a husk of his physical form, forcing himself onward for the sake of his pupil.

"I am glad," Reev said, "that he has found healing. I am sorry that coming here sapped all his strength."

"His body is frail," said the elvenking. "His spirit is a torch, like the star-gems of old. He is not the Gastreel we knew, but stronger."

It seemed true to Reev. Gastreel had walked frailly and taken fragile steps, but his voice was booming, powerful. There was strength in him yet.

"How will I defeat the Dark One?" said Reev.

"How?" said the elvenking. "Not like Antheleon, the Prince of the Dusk. He gathered up all the armies of the elves, then a thousandfold more powerful than they are now. He marched to the Dark One's land, and battled the hordes of rokahn before the Throne of Skulls. He dealt the Dark One's forces a wound, and shattered to pieces the blade *Serpentax*. But he fell on the fields of *Tiras pal Erdot*."

"So how?" said Reev.

"More wisdom than I possess," said the elvenking, "more knowledge than I the king now have. But the prophecies declare that it is you, the Prince of the Dawn, that shall complete Antheleon's work."

"We must find out," Reev said, "now…"

"So eager are you," said the elvenking. "So eager…"

The brightness of the silver was beginning to daze Reev, and the room was beginning to spin. He felt something all about him, a hot breath in the night. He felt himself strike the floor.

~

There was shadow, there were eyes.

Were those pointed shapes the forms of horns?

He had gone from the city, and was in a narrow wood.

The hot breath breathing on his neck was like that of a wild animal.

"A pity," a voice said, gravelly and stinging like hot cinders, "he is no longer a child."

He turned in the dark woods, and saw a dark form, tall and brazen, wearing clothing the color of smoke. Tall, proud, the figure was, with shaggy black hair, in his right hand a butterfly blade, in his left hand the Skeleton Key. In Ivan Xandrast's eyes was hellfire.

~

"Again," said Lord Calion's voice. "Again, he falls."

"The Sage is in a dire state," said the voice of another, soft, strong, female — Yanenré.

Reev's eyes were closed, and he struggled to open them, but he could hear the voices, and he could feel the room spinning all about.

"Is he truly the one promised?" said the voice of the elvenking. "Of such small constitution? The Enemy's attacks so oft lay him low."

"He is the one promised," said Lord Calion. "He saw a vision of the World Tree."

"So it is time," said the elvenking. "Time to make our move…"

"He must initiate things," said the Lord Calion. "Then, there will be no doubt as to his identity…"

Reev shot up from his stupor, eyes open, breathing like a fish out of water. He gasped, and saw he was again in the infirmary in the Tower of Warding, surrounded by elves. It was night, probably the same night as the party.

"I'm sorry," he uttered. "I'm sorry… I—"

"Calm, Sage," said Lord Calion. His hair, so fair it seemed white to Reev's eyes, was as it had been in the forests of Gallia. But a silver circlet now rested upon his head.

And in the light of braziers, Lord Calion's fingers were visible, and on them were rings, inset with gems whose size seemed to wax or wane with Reev's focus or inattention. Reev had a feeling that there was magic in those rings, and that whatever powers Reev had witnessed of Lord Calion—healing and wisdom and foresight—he had only seen a little of what Lord Calion was capable of.

"Another vision, you saw," said Nenré. "It troubles you. I can see it in your eyes."

Reev had seen a vision, indeed, far worse than the one before it. He had seen Ivan Xandrast working evil in the forests outside the city, and his heart told him that it was not his imagination.

"What did you see?" said the elvenking.

Reev would not tell anyone what he saw. He would not abandon Ivan Xandrast to the forces of evil. And what would these high-minded elves think of Reev, if they knew he had love for a warlock? "I will not tell you," said Reev.

"And we will not pry," said the elvenking. "What the Sage allows, we allow. What the Sage tells, we listen. And what the Sage commands, we do."

It was a terrible responsibility. He had a thought, of the failed visit to the Sibyl, and he wondered if she could have freed him from this darkness had she not rejected him.

He had another thought, one that frightened him and saddened him, one borne of doubt — *Am I truly who these people think I am?*

Chapter Five: Who Has Walked

The autumn was leaving, Wrinn knew. In his walks in the parks and gardens with Fortunato, he could feel the trees' wistful longing for the summer's warmth and abundant sunshine. The trees in Danarion were mostly conifers, spruce and hemlock, but there were broadleafs scattered throughout the city fading to brown and gold that foretold the imminent future, if it were not apparent by the increasing cloud cover, the chilly nights bordering on cold, and of course the calendar.

In all, though, as he rose one morning after another night of wild drinking and feasting, he thought the autumns in this blessed land were not overharsh, and whatever winter had in store in the coming year, this blessed land that the gods favored would treat him kindly.

It was his birthright, or so it should have been. Instead, born afar — he cursed — as he exited the apartments and entered the fresh air, he was called *dra'datsi*, an outsider, and could never be one of the elves as long as he lived, for he had been born outside the ancestral land.

Fortunato was walking off into the distance. Wrinn felt an urge to join him, then something stopped him — a cold wind.

A cold wind, and a word, a voice in the wind, one whose origin he knew, *"You are not dra'datsi, Son of the Forest. You are our shepherd. And you will not tend to us. Will you come to us when you are called?"*

They were drawing him away, and though Gastreel and others had insisted he not leave the city bounds, let alone the borderlines, he thought that maybe the trees had a point, that they worth listening to, that perhaps the green growing things of the world were as important as those who walked about on two legs.

"Come to us! Help us!" said the voice. *"You have brought darkness here… Will you not come to our aid?"*

Wrinn did not know the way, but the trees would guide him to where they wanted him to go. He was the Son of the Forest, at least in their eyes. Would he not do his duty? Would he not use the gift the gods had given him?

~

Wrinn passed around the inner walls in view of Mount Daró's sparkling snow, through streets overgrown with trees and hanging gardens, underneath a sky that was growing cloudy and threatened rain. He felt the trees afar, calling him, guiding his steps, as he pressed down ancient stone streets, beyond market squares and wineries and gardens that lay open to view. Though in some places, autumn threatened gloom, here the winter did not seem so threatening. People of all ages and ranks walked about, in this happy land, in light coats and robes. The world of mankind was iron; here was silver, under the light of gold.

Beyond fortresses and towers standing tall he pushed, until the stone streets were a rabbit's warren. Then, there was a gate, and beyond, the forest full and true.

Wrinn pressed on.

~

He was amid the spruces and hemlocks, and as the trees' voices grew louder, so too did Wrinn's senses of their growing alarm and trouble.

His shoes trampled on the soft earth, and as he ventured through a forest that had once been a city, he could see the telltale signs, bits of ruined stone covered in moss, and more — voices, memories, flashing through the air, and the inescapable sense that he trod where countless millions had before.

When Nenré had spoken of the "borderlines," he at first had thought it impossible that a city could be so large, but apparently he had been wrong. The elves built their cities differently from humans, and where humans lived in crowded homes and lean-tos, packing themselves in as small a space as possible, climbing to the heavens, the elves let nature take its course.

"Nature…"

The ancient ones could read his thoughts. He could feel their longing for him. He could feel their adulation, their belief that he alone could help. But they were wrong. For he had two legs, and he could hear their voices, and that was the extent of his powers. He could not rescue these ancient trees from whatever danger they believed they were in, or imagined they were in.

He was out of the borderlines now. It had to be past noon. Still the trees called, still they urged him on. And he did not disobey.

With spruces and hemlocks and thick growth brushing against his trousers, he knew he had gone far beyond what Gastreel would ever allow, and that if Reev knew where he was and what he intended, he would urge him to stop.

Yet the voices were not growing only in strength and in desperation, they were growing in number, until the countless throng, he imagined, was like the stars in heaven.

The skies above were slate gray. At some point Wrinn became aware that the cold stinging sensation on his arms was a constant, misting rain. He had traveled perhaps three miles beyond the borderlines, and was rounding the top of a verdant green hill.

He had reached the summit. He looked below. And beyond a green field dotted with *sindomas* blooms, under the slate-gray sky, was a dark green forest stretching into the horizon. At its vastness, Wrinn's heart quickened its pace, and his breath became a cold gasp in his lungs. At the sight of the green horizon, a terrible feeling settled in on him —a thought. *The forest is evil.*

"*Evil!*" a voice said to him. "*How dare you, proud shepherd… when your grandparents' grandparents first were born, we were here. Do you know who has walked here, among us, before?*"

"*Help us, Son of the Forest! Rescue us from our peril!*" said another voice. "*Enter in!*"

Enter in — he would, he thought. "I will come to you," said Wrinn, and though his heart had trembled, though he had thought of evil when he first seen it, he was their shepherd, wasn't he?

He thought of roots risen from the earth, strangling him and burying him under a bog. He thought of marshy ground like quicksand swallowing him whole.

"*Come here! Come here! Enter in!*" said the trees of the green horizon.

Then there was despair. "*Protect us! The son of darkness comes!*"

Wrinn drew his quarterstaff, even as there was the sound of a twig crunching underfoot.

His heart felt ready to explode as a human figure emerged through the bushes and green vines, and then he uttered with a sigh: "Xan, thank the gods it's you."

It seemed Xan had left all vestiges of civilization behind him. His black hair had grown matted, tangled and greasy, and he was now sporting a beard. His eyes had a mad look that Wrinn hadn't seen in him before. He smelled putrid, and even before he had crossed the distance between him and Wrinn, the odor was overpowering.

"Xan," Wrinn said, and this time he did not thank the gods.

His eyes had a yellow look, in the light of the slate gray sky, in the stinging of the misting rain.

"Wrinn," Xan said, as if he were merely guessing at his friend's identity. "I haven't seen you in weeks."

Wrinn could see that the Skeleton Key was dangling from Xan's rope belt. The Skeleton Key had allowed Wrinn, Reev and the others, to flee the City of Galiope, but Wrinn wondered if it had not been worth the cost.

"Wrinn," said Xan, "a human name and not an Elvish one."

"I was a slave," Wrinn said, "remember?"

Wrinn felt himself begin to back away, and it was not because of the odor.

"You were staring at the ancient wood," said Xan.

"I was," Wrinn said.

"A wood, sacred to the elves, wherein only the purified are allowed to enter," said Xan. "Did you go in?"

"No," said Wrinn. His grip grew a bit tighter around his quarterstaff. Xan was a master swordsman, but Wrinn had overcome him before, in Gallia.

Why was he thinking such a thing about his friend? Xan's butterfly blade glinted amid the soft gray light.

"The Forest of Daron Hen is not to be trod upon lightly," said Xan. "To do so is a crime."

"*He lies…*" A tree's voice had hissed in Wrinn's mind.

"Did you enter in?" said Xan. "Do not lie to me!"

"I would not lie to you, Xan!" Wrinn snapped. "I am not fond of lying!"

"Say," said Xan, "how old are you, Wrinn?"

"Nineteen," Wrinn said.

There were specks of blood on Xan's tunic.

"Curses!" Xan howled.

And Wrinn ran off, and Xan did not give chase.

Chapter Six:
In Wine, Truth

There was a point where wine and feasting became a chore, Spyke realized. Perhaps, it was after the fourth or fifth straight week, or perhaps after too many mornings of headaches and nausea, or perhaps after the tenth time one had loosened his belt. Even the elves no longer had radiant visages when they were drinking wine and eating rich meats, but seemed to gorge on them out of newly acquired habit.

Indeed, the celebration was wearing on Spyke's constitution, and though the wine was better than any variety had tasted in the Empire, and the food was higher in quality than at any emperor's banquet, there was such a thing as too much.

Across from him, sitting at the table, Fortunato had an ill look as he eyed a giant bowl of sweet pudding, and to Fortunato's left, Wrinn was barely touching his lingonberry flatcakes, though the young man's appetite for wine and strong drink seemed bottomless.

An elven serving girl came by with a pitcher of wine, and before Spyke could protest, she had filled his cup to the very brim. "Enough!" he started to say, but the elven girl was walking away.

Spyke had had about too much of this. He had come here to serve — to put his Dohorensi board to good use. He had come here to serve the gods, and the Prince of the Dawn, not to celebrate for endless weeks.

But perhaps, if something had been promised to him, or to his people, for millennia, and it had at last arrived, endless weeks of feasting and drinking might be warranted. Could he blame them?

There was a gagging sound up ahead — an elven woman in the center of the feasting hall dropped her goblet of wine and began to vomit.

"The Lady Valensé has had too much!" called out the Prince Vélerion from the corner of the room.

The elven woman had drunk herself ill. As a part-time medic in the Imperial Army when the Priests of Sollust were not available, Spyke was well trained for such a circumstance. He hurried out of his seat and ran swiftly to her.

He noted in the light of the starstones the strange shape of the mixed food and wine which she had purged. It looked, to his mind, like the Imperial numeral six.

There was another sound of heaving, and a man had sat up from his table. He had spilled his wine glass on the table, the elven man, and had keeled over to vomit.

And in the strange light of the room, the ways the starstones inside and the moonlight outside conspired together, Spyke thought he was wearing an Imperial soldier's helmet, though on closer inspection it was just his hair.

The numeral six, an Imperial soldier… in wine, truth.

Spyke remembered the woman he had met in the streets of Danarion, the woman whose child kept lunging near fires. He remembered her words, meaningful beyond what she had thought, the Sixth Anthanian Legion.

Spyke knew of the Fifth Anthanian, and the famous Seventh, but never a Sixth. But the logic of numbers meant there was one.

All this could be madness, but it could also have to do with the task that Spyke had vowed to carry out, the service of the gods and the Prince of the Dawn.

In wine, truth. In drunkenness and gluttony, Spyke had been stirred to act.

~

He retreated to his quarters and got out a slip of paper. With the ink and quill provided by the elves, he began to write, carefully forming each letter as he had been trained.

To the Archivist in the Conciliar Library:
Greetings, from Vitto Khandulis.

He would use his legal name in official correspondence.

A soldier of the rank of legionary, a member of the
reserves. A servant of the emperor.
This is my request to you: Send me a copy of all
documentation regarding the 'Sixth Anthanian
Legion.' Mark it posthaste to the city of Danarion,
at the Royal Palace, in the lands of the elves.
Send the emperor, and the people, my regards.

He folded the letter and fetched one of the standard-issue envelopes he always brought with him out of his pack. In the heat of the candle, he melted the wax seal a slight bit. Then he stamped it with the signet ring he still carried.

The light treason he had committed in Gallia, fighting against the Empire, had surely not been noticed. At least, it had not been noticed yet.

~

The endless drinking and feasting had turned to a dance. Elves were gathered about, and music was playing on viols and harps. Fortunato was among them, and though he did not consider himself a skilled dancer, he certainly enjoyed whenever there was a chance to do so. His eyes scanned for Nenré throughout the room, but he could not find her. He could see no sign of her.

As he stepped about and did a light twist, to the tune of the drums and the stringed instruments, he noted an elf staring at him in the corners of the room. He was the spitting image of Nenré's brother Vélerion, yea, his twin, Avernathi. His hair looked silver in the light.

"*Quilenthi*," said Avernathi, "why don't you settle for us a matter of dispute? It has become a parlor game in Danarion, to guess which elf shall die."

"What do you mean?" Fortunato said, and he had stopped his dancing.

Avernathi sidled up to him. He grasped Fortunato's left arm and the white cord. "An elven woman gave you this *hafri*, this love-band. But the penalty for love between a man and an elf is death."

Fortunato blushed, and wondered if he should remove it. Again, he searched, for Nenré, and he wondered who had seen her give it to him in the forests of Alonar.

~

Spyke rose with the sun. With his letter in hand, he tracked down the king's steward in the palace's vestibule.

The elf, whose long brown hair flowed, seemed to still be growing accustomed to the presence of humans in these halls, humans being creatures that were long considered unclean.

"My good man," said Spyke, "I must have this letter delivered."

Spyke strained to think of the closest Imperial town to Danarion, and then he remembered that the west had fallen, that the western capital of Zarubad was under Imperial control.

"My good man," said Spyke, "I must have this delivered at once to Zarubad."

"To *Abollalion*," said the steward.

"Pardon?"

"Little Hell," he continued, "where elves were once sold as

slaves — souls for a price.”

Spyke didn't know what to say.

“Nonetheless, the command of the Sage is my duty, and the commands of his friends an obligation, for as long as you dwell in the High House,” the steward said. “I will send a ship, at once, to deliver this letter, even to *Abollalion*.”

“Tell him to deliver it to the cursus publicus,” said Spyke. “Tell him to say that he marks it urgent.”

And along a horse relay that spanned the Empire's network of roads, a hundred miles a day, useable only by the military, the letter would be carried, borne to Imperial City and its Conciliar Library… an answer, *What is the Sixth Anthanian Legion?*

Swiftly, would he receive that answer. A career in the Imperial military had its privileges.

Chapter Seven:
The Ancestor

One crisp autumn night, a gaggle of elven girls fitted Reev with a long blue tunic.

"*Thó velati,*" one said.

"You are a prince," she repeated herself, "even the Prince of the Dawn. So we had thought you should dress like one."

The tunic fit Reev well, and its fabric was soft and gentle against his skin. It was of finer weaving than any clothing he had ever possessed. "Who made it?" he said.

"Queen Rhioné spun it for you," the girl continued.

Reev looked out behind him. The balcony overlooking the city, down the corridor from the feasting hall, allowed him to glimpse the breadth of the urban expanse. And though the atmosphere within the palace was joyous, there was a storm brewing within his heart. He had a thought that something was hunting him, something bent on his destruction. He had seen that shapeless thing, a dark form, the sign of horns. What was it? Was it anything more than a phantasm?

Another thought was percolating in him, if it was all true, if he really was the one promised to defeat Seymus.

And another thought… how could he defeat something that was not made of flesh, which had no mortal form?

~

Within the feasting hall, the feast endured. The chill of the night was gone before the great fireplace that stretched from the floor to the stone ceiling. Fortunato was in the corner with Spyke and Nenré; Wrinn was making a fool of himself, dancing with the elves.

But Reev's trouble was only growing, and his fear, and his doubts about himself were only increasing. He could not share in the elves' gladness and joy when he himself was not certain. How could he, a boy of seventeen, defeat the Dark One? How was it possible?

The gladness of the wine, the richness of the meats, were only driving him away. And though he wished to share in it he knew he couldn't. He could not share in their happiness when his doubt was so great, and when he knew something inexplicable was hunting him.

What, then, was there to do?

Perhaps, it was to find truth where he had an inkling he could. He would return to the Sibyl and gain her wisdom. She would tell him what was hunting him, and whether he should fear it.

~

At night, back home in Galiope, there were certain parts of the city that were off limits. If you traveled down certain streets during the night, you were liable to be robbed or worse. But in Danarion, the clean-swept streets were free of more than dirt and excrement, they were free of pickpocketing and thievery. Reev could walk them at night in this fine blue tunic and not fear for his life.

And so, following the route he remembered, through the inky dark streets, in the cold of the night he walked. He passed by the glittering waters of the Watercourse and as Lord Calion said, he uttered a prayer for *Hanathroni,* the River's Gate, and gave it heed.

Then he saw it; the Sibyl's house.

There were lights in the yard, bathing the green grass in illumination, and there were shapes, elven women, the Sibyl's women, dressed too lightly for the cold. Some had cats perched in their laps.

Something else assailed him then, besides fear of the horned dark shape, a new fear, that what if the Sibyl spoke a truth that would destroy him? What if she said he was not the Prince of the Dawn, not the one promised? What would he do if she said he would not defeat Seymus, or that he was not strong enough? What he was of no value, or what if the truth was something worse?

A memory flashed, Gogg's iron mask in a mountain pass.

"*You… it is you,*" the phantom hissed.

And at the thought, at the memory, he hurried back through the cold, as rain began to pour and the first bitter wind he felt since coming to the Elf Lands seared him through his tunic.

He danced; he ate. He drank in the feasting hall. His teeth were stained purple when he climbed into his bed.

He saw that night, in his dreams, a woman in a white gown. Her hair was a bright gold, her lips luscious and red. There was a necklace about her neck, and on that necklace a star. "Reev, my son," said the woman. "The truth will not hurt you. It will heal you."

~

Morning broke, and Reev remembered the dream. There seemed to be a commotion swirling about the palace grounds, outside the doors of the royal apartments.

He stirred, thinking of the woman and her youth, and of her beauty, and of that star about her neck. He sat up with a gasp and saw that Wrinn was not in his bed.

He rushed, then, out of the covers, as noise echoed outside, and swiftly donned the blue tunic he'd been given. He placed his coin amulet on the outside, across his breast. He swiftly donned his trousers, grabbed Doomblade and his belt and sheath, and fitted them around the waist. Then he rushed outside.

What was going on?

~

There was a party of elves outside the royal palace, elves dressed differently from those Reev had seen before. They were heavily armed and armored, some in full plate and some in hauberks, with long hair of a brown or black variety. A few of them bore standards, upon those standards the sigil of a white lynx on a gray field.

Wrinn soon joined Reev from the yard's far corners.

"Who are they?" Reev said.

"Elves, it seems," Wrinn said. "From Tharvané, some said."

Reev looked at Wrinn quizzically. "Tharvané?"

~

In the throne room, the commotion threatened to become a brawl. The elves of Tharvané were about three dozen in number before the Elven King's throne. At the fore of those elves in armor was a man in a long brown coat trimmed in white ermine. At his side was a broadsword. His pointed ears stuck out beyond his long gray hair.

"I've told you this a dozen times, Lord Albenhas," the Elven King said, his green robe shining in the morning light, his crown of stars and moons glistening. "I dispatched a message to every grand shrine in Lamdar."

"But you did not send a messenger to me," said the gray-haired elf, presumably Albenhas, "not to me personally, to my castle at Harkon, that the Sage has arrived."

"Will I do for you what I did for no other provincial lord?" the Elven King said. "And look — " He gestured to Reev. "Here he is. You may see him for yourself."

Lord Albenhas turned, and Reev wondered at the richness of that coat of his, how finely spun, without blemish. The ermine trim had black spots, the appearance of eyes. And Albenhas's cold gray eyes startled him as they looked upon him, at first with wrath, then with curiosity.

"This is he," said Albenhas. There was the workings of a smile on his face. "So small, so slender. But I suppose the gods sometimes use the little things of this world to shame the large."

The smile came to fruition. His teeth were white like snow.

"An honor, *velati sonoren*," Albenhas said. But the smile was fading. In the end, it could not compete with his wrath.

He turned, and it was as if Reev was no longer in the room.

"My people did not get the message," said Albenhas, and the joyful tone was gone. "They have been working these seven weeks, not feasting. Are not they the sons, the daughters, of Luvé?"

"I have had about enough of this, Albenhas," said the Elven King.

"*Lord* Albenhas," he snapped.

"You left your grand shrine untended," said the Elven King, "and so your joy shall not be full. You did not keep a watchful eye, that the joyful day had at last come upon you. The fault is your own."

Lord Albenhas, of Tharvané, snarled and turned. He made a signal, and his men departed with him.

Reev could see Fortunato in the corners of the room.

~

"I am sorry, Sage," the Elven King said to Reev. "Politics, what may I say?"

He and Reev were alone in the throne room. The chair of gold or silver glittered in the morning light.

"Who was that?" Reev said.

"The Lord of Tharvané, the province southeast of here," said the Elven King. "The Lord of Tharvané and the king have often clashed. He and I are no different.”

“Where is Tharvané?” said Reev.

“Ride a few days southeast by Elvish horse,” said the Elven King, “and you will find its cold jungles at the foot of the Dragonteeth. Far from Danarion’s light it is, a den of heresy and dissensions.”

“Heresy?” Reev said.

“Each generation in Tharvané seems to rebel in a new way,” said the Elven King. “First, they wished to bring offerings of wheat and apples to the priests rather than gold, saying to them it was more precious. Another generation in Tharvané forbade the people from marrying and drinking wine before the king intervened. Of late, they make images of the gods to ‘focus their worship,’ and I have relented.”

“Why did you relent?” Reev said.

“*Tharvané tona luné*,” said the Elven King, “*xanoren xanen*.”

“Tharvané without light, forever,” he repeated himself in Imperial.

~

“Did you hear the uproar?” Fortunato said to Nenré on the upper balcony.

She smiled and that smile sent his heart aflutter. There was a glass of wine in her hand, and at the sight Fortunato’s tongue felt dry.

“What uproar?” Nenré said.

“Elves came and confronted your father,” Fortunato said. “Elves of Tharvané.”

Nenré chuckled. “Ah, Tharvanians,” she said. “And what did the *Tharvanians* say?”

She said the word *Tharvanian* with a contempt that only a princess could muster.

"Do you hate them?" said Fortunato.

"Why would I hate someone so far beneath us?" said Nenré. "Do you know, Fortunato, that in Tharvané the snow sometimes sticks for as long as seven days?"

"Well, you've been to Gallia," said Fortunato.

"And sometimes it rains heavily, there, in the summer, and those cold jungles turn into true ones," said Nenré. Her contempt seemed bottomless. "You have much to learn, love. Repeat after me: *Tharvané tona luné, xanoren xanen.*"

"*Tharvané tona luné, xanoren xanen,*" Fortunato said, but all he thought of was the word she had used. She had called him "love."

Chapter Eight: Go Tell a Workman

"Sit up," said the Chief Healer. "Inhale."

Gastreel took a deep breath.

There was pain in his chest, and pain in the scars that had formed when he had used his body's vitality to invigorate the Gate of Tedron. The Chief Healer's medicines and exercises allowed him to function just barely, but he would never run about or fight again like he had.

This room in the Healing House faced the garden, beyond a glass wall, and Gastreel could see that the ferns and flowers had withered from the autumn's chill. For the first time, a true chill had settled over Lamdar, and though it was not as cold as autumn in Gallia, the spoiled elves of Danarion had taken to wearing thick coats and cloaks when they walked about outside.

"Exhale," said the Chief Healer.

His long blond hair flowed down his orange robe. His blue eyes gleamed. He was an expert, but he could not help Gastreel. Nothing, and no one, could.

Gastreel exhaled.

"Good," said the Chief Healer. "I can see your life and vitality. It remains. You are stable, Gastreel, and I do not foresee you slipping into death."

"If it is my time to go, I am ready," said Gastreel. "I would have wished to see my pupil defeat the Dark One, but the gods shall not grant me all my desires."

"The gods have granted you much," said the Chief Healer. "Wisdom and arcane power, a love for elves and for mankind. The duty to protect the Sage."

"I will protect him," said Gastreel, "even if it costs me my life."

"There shall not be such a cost," said the Chief Healer. He turned, grasped his birchbark staff that was leaning against the wall. He eyed Gastreel, and his blue eyes shone like starstones through a veil, or like the flashing of a summer storm. "Stand up," he said.

Gastreel stood. He was dizzy, and the breath in his lungs was faint.

"Perhaps," said the Chief Healer, "drawing your sword would rekindle your spirit."

Gastreel's mind was scattered. He took another deep breath. From his side, he drew Maderias his sword. "It's strange," said Gastreel, "it is my sword, my blade. It has hewn down mighty foes. But I feel as if I need something much more."

~

Outside the Healing House was the district of Amanddon. Here the Healers operated, the magicians who had powers of curing wounds and healing diseases. In human lands, such a gift was unheard of. Yet the healing magic could not mend the wounds Gastreel had intentionally brought upon himself.

He knew he would do it again, if given a choice. Reev had escaped with his life, and Gastreel could ask for nothing more. Reev had been brought from danger to the one place in the world where the Shadow had not fallen, to the one place in the world not under the Empire's power or under Seymus's control.

Healers male and female were walking about in the brisk air in their orange robes. Gastreel had completed his treatment for the day and so now the day and the night was his. He would avoid the revelry of the feasting hall. He had a thought of visiting the Royal Library and studying elvish history, or going to Pelladdon where the priests reigned and studying the religious texts. But to enter Pelladdon he would have to bathe in a ritual bath and purchase for himself a special robe, then make an offering. The elves took ritual purity seriously.

There was a loud commotion and scattered shouts and screaming. Gastreel looked about, weak from his pain and delirious in his mind.

There were elves on horses roughly riding through the streets, overturning carts — shattering glass as they broke windows with their spears. There were about a hundred, at their fore an elven man with long gray hair, riding on an Elvish horse. There was a furious look on his face.

Gastreel did not know what possessed him, what strength had filled him after so much weakness, how or why his outrage was so strong, but he stepped forth in the midst of the street with his staff in hand, and shouted, "Cease this!"

The elves on horseback stopped, and the gray-haired elf reared up on his steed, giving Gastreel a look of utter contempt.

"What is this?" said the gray-haired elf. "*Iramon iramoren,* a human stands in the way of an elf in the City of Light."

"Not just any human," the Chief Healer's voice echoed behind Gastreel. Before he stepped in front of Gastreel in his brilliant orange robe, Gastreel felt the eldritch breeze which caused a chill all over his body.

"He is the Sage's caretaker, Lord Albenhas."

This Albenhas did not seem to be any less dissuaded from his path of destruction. "The men and women of Tharvané have endured much over the years. We have now had our fill of ill treatment. Their lord shall not abide your people's insults any longer."

"If you choose the path of darkness, Albenhas," said the Chief Healer, "it is no one's fault but your own."

Albenhas cursed and galloped ahead heedless of Gastreel. Gastreel spun out of the way in the nick of time. The Chief Healer was almost trampled as the Lord of Tharvané charged down the street, continuing his path of destruction, smashing windows and overturning carts and anything in their path. Their vandalism would not avail them, no matter what insult they bore.

The elves of Tharvané eventually galloped out of Amanddon's gate.

"Gastreel," said the Chief Healer, "in your retirement you shall abide with us long. A phrase you should learn, if it please you. *Tharvané tona luné, xanoren xanen.*"

"*Tharvané tona luné, xanoren xanen,*" Gastreel said.

The day was now his. A dark force now was gone, though he had not successfully resisted it. But its ruin was sure.

~

It was after a morning tea with the elves, and Reev was growing tired for a reason he did not know. In a daze, he left the solarium, his stomach full of sweetcakes and his tongue still tingling from the honey's sweetness. His exhaustion was drawing him to his bed, or was it something else?

The light filtering into the apartment windows seemed slanted to Reev's eyes. All he wanted was sleep. He quickly removed his blue tunic and his trousers, down to his smallclothes. He hurried into his room and leapt into his bed. Only moments after his head hit the pillow, he fell into a deep sleep.

And he was in the woods outside the city, or seeing a vision of it. He could hear his own ragged breaths. Ivan Xandrast was in the thick brush amid the cloying vines, now withered from the late autumn cold. And he was not alone.

In the dark they were approaching, six figures on monstrous beasts. In the barguests' eyes was the fire of Hell. Their riders, no better, with their hideous iron masks, seemed to startle Xan, despite the infernal darkness that had consumed him.

"Lamech," said one of the Servants. "Thou hast done well."

His voice was like a hissing wind, or like a freezing gale in a winter gulch.

"Nonetheless," the Servant continued, "you are a workman, and a workman needs his tools."

"I threw them away," Reev watched Xan cry. "I threw them —"

"In the Galios River," said the Servant, and strode forth further on his barguest. From the folds of his black robe he drew a case, black in color and covered in dried mud and algae.

The Servant tossed the case before Xan and Xan cried out in horror. There seemed to be a little light left in him, a little part of him that was resisting. Then his eyes turned black like marbles, and he took the case with relish and opened it. There were scissors and daggers and knives of a strange metal within the case, and jewels of an odd hue. There were fetishes made of straw, and a sigil of two serpents eating each other.

The horror returned in Xan's eyes, and his eyes lost some of their blackness. He was resisting, or part of him was. He turned, and Reev could see through the brush, down the road, the elves of Tharvané storming by on horse.

The black color of Xan's eyes returned, and now a gleam of Hell. As he stared at the elves of Tharvané, galloping down the way, a sadistic grin formed on his face.

Chapter Nine:
The Six Who Ride

From his perch in the upper balcony of the palace, Fortunato watched the first of the season's rains. Clouds had moved in from the south, and now covered the sky, a steely gray covering for the firmament. And though the cold season in Lamdar would have its occasional sunshine, from here on, for a little while, there was gloom.

Fortunato had grown up in the town of Ríva in the Empire, amid the baking heat. Winters, he longed for then. But now —in late autumn — he would do well with the baking hot sun of Ríva in the summertime, a swim in the ocean, a dip in the public baths. The snows of Gallia he did not mind. But rain… he did not like the rain.

"Fortunato," said a voice, a voice that now filled him with fear.

He turned to see the Elven King, Nenré's father, and he eyed the *hafri* tied about his left wrist. Did he know his daughter had given it to him? Did he know the things his daughter was saying to him now, when no one was around?

"The slayer of the Fell Smith," said the Elven King. "The bearer of Danenhir."

Fortunato eyed his sword.

"I have good news, on this nineteenth day of the month of Estion."

Good news, he claimed to have, but there were worry wrinkles on the man's face, and he did not seem as happy as he had been.

"The feasting is extended for three more weeks," said the Elven King. "It was scheduled to end on this day. But it shall not be so."

Fortunato felt his body could bear a little more, but he knew people who would not be happy. Spyke was complaining in private to him. Gastreel wanted to get to business. Reev had never been as happy as those who celebrated him. Only Wrinn, of those he knew, would be glad to have more wine. Wine made Wrinn happy to the exclusion of all else.

"I confess I am worried," said the Elven King, "things are not going as has been decreed, as prophesied. And so we shall feast, and hope, and wait."

Something was unspoken in his words, a true meaning left unsaid. The Elven King was beginning to doubt that Reev was the one promised, the Prince of the Dawn.

But Fortunato had seen Reev transformed. Fortunato had seen Reev destroy the Servants of Seymus with heavenly fire. Fortunato had seen much evidence. Could he, and all of them, be wrong?

~

Cutting his way through the brush, Reev made his way through the forest, searching for Xan. He would not let his friend slip into Shadow.

It was raining, and it was deathly cold. Drops of the icy rain were soaking him as he ventured through the gloom, across the moss-covered forest floor. Where had he seen that vision? Where had Xan been standing in that dream clear as day?

Spruces and hemlocks surrounded Reev, and the sound of a frosty wind. The forest that surrounded Danarion was vast, and there was no telling where Xan had gone off to.

But if Reev applied himself diligently, if he searched with his whole heart, perhaps he would find Xan, and heal him from the darkness he had succumbed to.

The forest, though, was vast, and the site of Reev's vision would be difficult to discern. "Xan!" Reev began to shout, above the frosty wind and the sound of the pattering rain. "Xan!"

He knew he invited danger. He knew Xan had returned to his old ways. But he would not see his friend succumb to Shadow.

"Xan!" he said, and there was movement through the brush.

Standing in the clearing was an elf with hair the color of driftwood, and before he turned Reev knew his identity, the crown prince Vélerion.

At his side an *estirion* sword — about his chest a suit of glittering mail. He was dressed for battle.

"Reev," said Vélerion. He did not call him "Sage." "What are you doing here?"

"I ask you the same," said Reev.

In the silver light of the clouds, something like a smile formed on Vélerion's lips. "You brought yourself, and you brought your five friends. Something else you brought, too, something which followed you. It is not your fault."

"What else did I bring?" Reev said.

"Creatures of another realm," said Vélerion, "called in human parlance the Servants of Seymus. Now spurning horses, they ride on creatures of darkest Hell. They are *haraindó*, things to be hated."

"I saw them," Reev said, "in a dream."

"Did you?" said Vélerion, and his gray eyes sparkled. "What did you see?"

And Reev hesitated, suddenly lacking in trust. For he realized he did not trust Vélerion, and something in his heart told him to avoid him. "I was looking for Xan," Reev said.

"The warlock," Vélerion said. The smile grew. "The watchers of the Blue Tower say he left, walking down the road that leads to Tharvané."

"That is what I feared," Reev said.

"Do not worry," said Vélerion, and then he paused. When he at last spoke again, his grin had become dark. "Actually, do. For much rests on you, in fact, all — or so some have believed."

"Are the Servants gone?" said Reev.

"They have fled," said Vélerion. "They are gone. But the fact that they crossed the ancient boundary, the borderlines of the city, means they are growing in strength. They are intent on the ruination of Danarion, the dispossession of the elvish people. They are intent on your mission's failure. Their master is Seymus."

"I know," said Reev.

"Do you?" said Vélerion. "Do you know their power? If you did, you would not come out unaccompanied. It would take an army to defeat them."

Reev disagreed. But he would not give Vélerion any heed. He would not give Vélerion anything. And he sensed that Vélerion wanted something from him. He glanced into Vélerion's cold gray eyes, and then he turned and walked back, toward the city, praying under his breath for Xan, praying that his friend might be saved from this dark path he had found himself on.

Chapter Ten:
What She Requires

The nights were growing longer. The days were growing shorter. Mount Daró, outside the city walls, was now fully clothed in white.

The sea and the beneficial winds conspired, the air lingering from the summer's heat and the massive wall that was the Dragonteeth Mountains far south of here had staved off winter's wrath. But Danarion was so far north it could not help but feel a bit of boreal fury.

Winter was here, though there was no snow at ground level in Danarion and Reev suspected there would never be, the chill outside would only grow. The palace had become a place of hidden tensions, and the looks that the elves gave Reev were becoming unnerving, perhaps hostile. It seemed to Reev that they were waiting for something that was not happening, and yet they would not tell him what he was doing wrong, what they were missing.

In the feasting hall, he sat slumped in his chair, having at last succumbed and having drunk his third wine glass of the night, for it took the edge off the tensions and dulled his senses. There were dancers with streamers and tambourines in the center of the room leaping about and twirling to the sound of stringed instruments and drums, but their movements seemed strained and the audience seemed disinterested. The dark looks from the elven partygoers were only increasing in frequency and alarm. And to the sense of tension was added the thought of looming disaster, the Six Servants of Seymus running free through Lamdar and the Lord of Tharvané threatening revolt.

What do you want from me, Reev wished to say. But something stayed his tongue. Something stopped him from asking what the elves demanded. Perhaps, he was too proud. Perhaps, he thought he was owed an answer without a question.

What day was it, what night? He recalled, the third of Dorion, Solarias's birthday. That made it the fifteenth of Anthanos by human reckoning. Reev wondered if the first snows had fallen in Gallia, if the snow was already up to the Dragonpaw's windows. He wondered how Glenda was doing, and Bala, and Ambrass. He supposed he did miss home, even amid such splendor.

Fortunato wasn't eating or drinking. For the first time, Wrinn wasn't touching his wine. Even they were giving him dark looks, demanding of him something they would not express.

Yet Reev would not ask them. Pride — maybe. Stubbornness — perhaps. He would not ask them for what they wanted. He simply wouldn't.

As he began to ponder, he began to stir, and as he began to stir, the discomfort only began to grow.

There was noise up ahead of him. An elven woman had stood up from her seat. She was dizzy from drink, placing her hand on the chair. She looked about ready to purge her innards. Her drunken eyes turned to Reev. "He is not the one promised," she said, "not the Prince of the Dawn."

There were scattered hisses, and a flash of rage in Reev's heart. It seemed to him the darkest lie.

Yet the elves did not correct her.

The fire flared. The shadows of the room turned and twisted about. The anger in Reev's heart grew, and then twisted into panic, as the shadows of the room in the flaring fire turned to what his mind's eye recognized intently. It was the shadowy shape he had seen hunting him, the thing he had seen in visions and in nightmares unremembered. He had seen it in nightmares he was only remembering now.

There was wild panic.

"He has turned the Lord of Tharvané to dissension by his

coming!" said the woman.

In the corner of the room, Lord Calion was sitting in a chair, observing Reev intently.

"Who is he?" said the woman. "Not the one promised… someone else."

The implication of her words stirred the panic into mad furious fear, and Reev stumbled out of his seat in a daze, then fled with the elves and all his friends looking at him.

~

The truth… he would hear it. It could destroy him, but it would be final.

He had staggered out of the palace, putting one foot in front of the other, dazed by drink and by fear. He knew the city now, its contours and its streets, having lived here for some two months. Danarion was second nature to him, now.

And he ran, away from the fortress, in the dark and stumbling, under the dark mantle of the sky. It was cold, and there was a constant misting rain.

He ran in view of the lights of the palace, down dark streets, and as he ran the clouds unveiled and veiled the moon, a waxing gibbous. He ran, and his run turned to a sprint as he thought of the dark shape, and the accusation which he had heard before, long ago. He ran, and the glittering waters of the Watercourse appeared, and the lights of the palace were far behind him.

He ran, and it was night, but there was soft warm light up ahead, at last, where the truth he could find, for once, forever.

The Sibyl's house was just as he had left it. The grass yard was green, and there were cats wandering about. There were elven women, too, in gowns of green or yellow, of blond hair or brown, with eyes aglow in the light of the starstones.

There he ran, to the women, and though he was in the throes

of panic, they eyed him with utter calm.

"I must speak to the Sibyl!" said Reev. "I must hear her truth!"

A woman rose — what was her name? — Kydé. Her eyes were green, her hair a dirty blond. Fine was her silken gown, dyed a deep cerulean.

"The Sibyl will be happy to speak to you," Kydé said, "but she has made her price clear.

"Wheat… spelt… emmer… bring them unto her, and she shall do as you require."

Chapter Eleven: The Lost Legion

Spyke was in his seat, alarmed and enraged by the elven woman's outrageous accusation. To his mind, such an accusation if false deserved death. The elves in the feasting hall had at first witnessed her words in shock, saying nothing, but after the Sage had fled, the King's Guard entered in their full plate and blue capes. They had seized her by the arms, and dragged her screaming away.

Fortunato and Wrinn were sitting across from Spyke. "I hope he is okay," Spyke said.

"If he is the one promised," said Fortunato, "he will be."

There was commotion through a door; an elf stepped into the light, one Spyke recognized, the steward. His long brown hair shimmered in the light of the fire. He was holding in his hands a packet of papers. His eyes searched the room, and at last laid upon Spyke. In a manner of moments, he had crossed the distance between them.

"Spyke," he said, "your letter has arrived."

What a wonder, what a marvel. The wizards of the north could conjure fireballs and devastate armies and meditate on arcane mysteries, but could they travel the span of thousands of miles in a matter of weeks, from the boreal north to the sunny dry south, and return with such swiftness? The wizards had their marvels, but the Empire had its cursus publicus — a network of horse relays that spanned the ecumene —and so much more. Had there ever been such a nation? One thing he was sure of, there would never be such a nation again.

"Thank you, steward," said Spyke, and stood up from his table. Thankfully, he had barely touched his wine. Tonight would require his faculties. He hoped the Sage would return once he had his answers.

~

In his private room, Spyke took the letter and broke the Imperial seal. The letter unfolded. Its writing was immaculately laid down in black ink.

To Vitto Khandulis,

Greetings from the Archivist of the Conciliar Library. Long live the emperor, the Empire and her people. All documentation on the Sixth Anthanian Legion is copied below.

Spyke's eyes turned to the quoted text.

THE SIXTH ANTHANIAN LEGION WAS A LEGION IN EXISTENCE DURING THE THIRD CENTURY YE, WELL KNOWN IN ITS TIME FOR ITS DEVASTATING VICTORIES AGAINST FORCES MUCH LARGER THAN ITSELF, AND FOR ITS KEY ROLE IN SUBDUING AND CONQUERING THE ANTHANIAN PENINSULA. ITS GRAND LEGATES RECEIVED THE HIGHEST HONORS FROM THE IMPERIAL COUNCIL AND FROM EMPERORS OVER THE DECADES. BUT IN 276, ITS SUCCESS WAS BROUGHT TO A HALT.

A GRAND LEGATE WAS NAMED IN THAT YEAR TO COMMAND THE SIXTH ANTHANIAN BY THE NAME OF SERAPO REX. FOR A TIME, HE COMMANDED THE

ARMIES WELL AND USED HIS WELL-DISCIPLINED TROOPS TO CONQUER THE FURTHERMOST REACHES OF THE PENINSULA AND PUT DOWN REBELLIONS IN THE SOUTHWEST COAST, IN LORNATIUM.

IT WAS DURING THE LORNATIUM EXPEDITION THAT SERAPO REX BEGAN TO SHOW HIS FIRST SIGNS OF MADNESS. HE REPRESSED THE REBELLION WITH SUCH BRUTALITY THAT THE PEOPLE OF THE SURROUNDING CITIES COMPLAINED TO THE EMPEROR. THE EMPEROR ORDERED THAT SERAPO REX WITHDRAW BUT SERAPO REX REFUSED, AND EVENTUALLY STOPPED RESPONDING TO THE EMPEROR'S PETITIONS.

SERAPO REX THEN DID THE INEXPLICABLE. HE BUILT A NAVY FROM FISHERMEN'S VESSELS AND BOATS AROUND THE SOUTHWEST COAST, AND, FITTING THE MEN OF THE SIXTH ANTHANIAN ON THOSE NON-MILITARY CRAFTS, UNDERTOOK AN EXPEDITION TO THE ISLE OF SERPENTS.

FOR REASONS ONLY SERAPO REX CAN EXPLAIN, HE INVADED THE ISLE OF SERPENTS, THEN A TRIBUTARY KINGDOM OF THE EMPIRE. HE UNDERTOOK A LARGE-SCALE GENOCIDE OF THE POPULATION AND EXTERMINATED THEM COMPLETELY. THERE WERE NO SURVIVORS, AND THE ISLE OF SERPENTS REMAINS UNPOPULATED TO THIS DAY.

THE OUTRAGE IN IMPERIAL CITY WAS SWIFT AND SEVERE. THE SIXTH ANTHANIAN WAS CONSIDERED ACCURSED BY THIS HORRIFIC ACT, AND WAS

SWIFTLY DISBANDED BY A DECREE OF THE IMPERIAL COUNCIL (SEE LEGIS 4422, THE ABOMINABLE ACTS). SERAPO REX FOR HIS ATROCITY WAS EXECUTED IN IMPERIAL SQUARE AND HIS BODY THROWN WITHOUT FUNERARY RITES INTO THE SOUTH RIVER.

A chill passed up Spyke's spine, reading the ineffable words, not because of the atrocities. Atrocities were innumerable throughout Varda's history.

Why was someone almost a thousand years later, in a city far removed, speaking of this legion today?

He looked outside his window. He saw the Bull constellation rising in the moonless sky.

Chapter Twelve:
The Night Market

Wheat, spelt, emmer.

But it was night.

Reev's fear, the accusation he had heard once before, would prevent him from returning to the royal palace, tonight, perhaps forever. He would not tolerate such a lie. He would hear the truth.

As he staggered, wounded by words, away from the Sibyl's house, in the dark of night, he saw that there was not only darkness in Danarion. There was light up ahead.

There was light down the street, to his right, and a pounding so rhythmic it could only be drums. Reev, swept away by the light and driven on by fear, had no resistance. Any distraction from his fears was good to his mind.

Anything… anything at all…

~

The lights were paper lanterns. The drums were drums indeed. In dark of night, a market had been set up on either side of the street.

There were hundreds of elves in the street, going from one stall to the next, at one stall strips of raw elk lathed in brown sauce, at another stall dumplings steaming on coals.

There was a gold statue of Solarias in the center of the night market, its eyes of diamonds and its bodies studded with ruby and lapis lazuli and emerald.

"Welcome!" a woman cried to Reev. "Welcome, and *tó Solarias!*"

Reev passed by the stalls, at one a woman selling paper prints, at the other a man selling an assortment of rings and gemstones. Another woman stood in the cold, behind her a vat of hot spiced wine, in front of her a line that stretched well down the street.

Reev continued down the way, past the bustling bodies, as music echoed — the harp and the clavier and the viol — and in the midst of a small square a group of elves dancing and twirling streamers.

Past more stalls he walked, a woman selling glass eyes, a man selling toys fashioned from driftwood, another spicy dumplings, a woman sweet dumplings… there was honeyed candy and sugar candy, fried slugs covered in salt — *how cruel!* — elk pies and fish fritters, octopus breaded and fried, and another stand of spiced wine — and another long line.

"Wheat!" Reev began to cry, in a daze from the spectacle, "Spelt! Emmer!"

There were books for sale at one corner, and more art prints that seemed to tell a story along the breadth of the pages. "The latest leaf from esteemed author Banenvi!" a woman cried.

"Poems of Annenwé!" said another elf standing beside a pile of tomes. "Her best, collected in one volume."

"Wheat!" Reev cried, and this time he was shouting, above the noise, above the spectacle. "Wheat! Spelt! Emmer!"

There was an artist selling portraits for a copper apiece, and foods wholesome and bizarre. There were more statues of Solarias and more music playing, and more dancing in the street. But Reev didn't care about the night market.

He stood in the street, and this time he screamed: "Wheat! Spelt! Emmer!"

A woman was in front of him in a pink gown, her blonde hair flowing down her back. "What bothers you, Sage, on Solarias's night? Shan't you enjoy the festivities?"

"Wheat, spelt… emmer," Reev's voice was softer now.

The elven woman smiled. "That is what you require, human?

Anything can be found in the market of St. Solarias. The market is at every week's end, from dusk until dawn, the whole month of Dorion.

"Wheat… spelt… emmer…" Reev was almost whispering, now.

"Spelt is a kind of wheat. Emmer is a kind of wheat. What type of wheat do you wish on top of it, human?" said the elven woman.

The terror of the accusation had not lessened. "Wheat," Reev said. "Spelt…. Emmer."

~

The woman led him down the street, past a woman who was selling prayer books and a man who had raw oysters on offer, past twin girls selling fruit juice by the cup. The woman led him down another street where the market continued, to a place where the paper lanterns were not so luminous, in the dark, in the shade. And there he saw it — a man selling sheaves of spelt, and to his right, a woman selling emmer.

"Wheat! Spelt! Emmer!" Reev had become a drone, a monk chanting plainchant underneath the vault of the sky.

"One silver for a bushel," said the woman selling emmer. "Two silver for three."

"I only need a little bit," Reev breathed.

But the woman who guided him had spoken truth. Emmer was a kind of wheat, and spelt was a kind of wheat, so what other kind of wheat would she want?

It was then, in the dark, in the shadows, he noticed a tall form standing across the way. He was lanky and lean, and his arms seemed far too long for his body. In the moonlight — could it be? — his hair was the color of rainbows, and his ears, pointed like an elf's, were larger and protruded far longer than any Reev had seen. He was standing at a stall of his own, and he himself was selling what looked like wheat, of differing colors — black and gold and white, yellow and reddish-ochre.

"Wheat," Reev said, "spelt. Emmer." He had almost whispered it.

"One silver for a bushel," said the woman selling emmer, cuttingly. "Two for three."

And Reev realized he had not brought his coinpurse, and what's more, his coinpurse contained no elvish currency. "I have no money," Reev said.

The woman selling emmer glared.

"I have no money," Reev said, "but *sí eldari*. I am the Sage."

"*Thó eldari*," the woman selling emmer said, "but I have to eat."

"*Sí eldari*," Reev said, "and I must see the Sibyl. I must hear her truth."

The lanky elf from across the way had crossed the distance between them, and was carrying in his hand a sheaf of pink wheat. "We shall not let the Sage suffer on the day of Solarias." He flipped the woman selling emmer a silver coin, and flipped the man selling spelt two. "He shall have what he requires."

"Mikal," said the woman selling emmer, "he says he wishes to see the Sibyl, but he is not wearing a *laeras*, and he has not doused himself in a *kival*. The *kivals* are closed, for it is half past midnight, and no *laeras*-sellers can be found in common markets."

"We shall try the Sibyl's mercy, Haré."

"Godspeed," the woman selling emmer, Haré, said.

~

As Mikal led Reev through the dark streets, having given him the bundle of spelt, emmer, and pink wheat, Reev noted he was taller than any elf he had seen before, and that his hair indeed was colored rainbow. He walked with a swift gait Reev could hardly keep up with at a jog, and at his side were twin sabers that looked like they could split rocks.

"I shall make certain your request is granted, Sage," said Mikal.

The lights of the Sibyl's house were up ahead.

"Wheat! Spelt! Emmer!" the green-eyed Kydé bellowed. Her cerulean gown was rich as the sea in the light of torches and lanterns, in the yard of the Sibyl's house. "The Sage is no longer unaccompanied. The *selen'veni* is with him.

"The Sage is not dressed in a *laeras*. He is ritually impure and unwashed. He has not made a trip to the *kival* or made an offering."

"But he has brought wheat, and spelt, and emmer," said Mikal.

He dropped the multi-colored sheaves before Kydé's shoes.

"The hour is late," said Kydé, "but her eminence Callisti rises by night. At morn she prophesies by groans and wails which the *Loctari* must interpret. At night she speaks herself. How did you know, Sage?"

"I knew nothing of it," Reev said.

"Fortune smiles on you," said Kydé, and for the first time Reev saw, she looked happy.

Chapter Thirteen: The Words of the Sibyl

"He is the Sage," said Nenré under the light of the torches. Fortunato had followed her out onto the balcony.

"He is the Sage," Nenré continued, "I know it. I know it in my heart."

What doubts Fortunato had were planted by the whispering of the elves and their cutting looks. He had seen Reev transformed. He had seen him burn the Servants of Seymus to dust.

"I know something else," said Nenré. She touched Fortunato's left hand, where she had tied the hafri. "I know we cannot be apart any longer."

"How do you mean?" Fortunato said.

And then he saw, in the light of the torches, on this chilly winter's day, something in Nenré's eyes he had not seen before. It was something he did not think was possible in the eyes of an elven princess. It was burning lust.

"Your brother Avernathi said the penalty for love between a man and an elf is death," said Fortunato.

"So you don't love me," said Nenré.

"No, I — "

"There are places in the palace that no one goes to," said Nenré, "places where we shall never be discovered. I will lead you there. I cannot be apart from you no longer."

"I — " Fortunato started, but Nenré took him by the hand, and when she pulled him, he did not resist. He realized he wanted this, too, wrong though it was in the eyes of the law.

He followed her, and his appetites carried him forward. The son of Petro of Ríva would have the elvenking's daughter.

~

The Sibyl's house was simple and plain. To Reev's mind, the best word he could think of was "homey."

The walls were painted in warm rose colors. There were couches and beds, and tables in the parlor. It was the house he imagined a grandmother would live in, not a seer and a truth-teller.

Kydé led him through an open door. Mikal was still in the courtyard, as far as he knew.

And in the room, simple yet cozy, lying on a bed, was a woman. At the foot of a bed, an elven man was sleeping on a cot. Was it the *Loctari*, the speaker?

The woman was wearing a blindfold. Her hair was a brilliant blonde. She was wearing a tunic, dyed green, and she did not seem to Reev's mind a prophetess, nor did her bedroom seem to be any different from a simple house.

"He is here," said the Sibyl, "I see him. I know him. The one promised to us has arrived. But two were promised."

Reev shuddered inwardly.

"One to attack us and one to defeat the serpent's children. One, a serpent — the other... to crush him underfoot."

"Who is he, Callisti?" said Kydé.

"His name is Reev Nax," said Callisti. "His father is Simeon, the son of Kal and Trita. His mother is Nimue, the daughter of Halloran and Helga."

"Who is he, Callisti?" said Kydé.

"He is Reev Nax," said Callisti, "and a wall of smoke and ruin stands between him and the completion of his quest. He will not leave by the River's Gate until he defeats it."

"What hunts me?" Reev said.

He thought of that dark shape, of those horns, of those eyes, and he shuddered again.

"A wall of smoke and ruin," said Callisti.

She sat up suddenly, twisting like a phantom. She turned, still blindfolded.

"He is the one promised," said Callisti. "There is no doubt. But *two* were promised."

"Who am I?" Reev said at last.

And Callisti rose to her feet. "There is only one way to know," she answered.

~

Love or lust, Fortunato did not know, but when the deed was finished, and they were both overcome, it was then the fear set in, the fear of being discovered.

Nenré, unclothed, grasped the hafri about Fortunato's wrist. She began to untie it.

"What is this?" said Fortunato.

"When the deed is done," said Nenré, "the hafri is thrown into the fire. It is unlucky for you still to wear it."

But wouldn't it draw suspicion?

The closet where they hid, hid all prying eyes.

But fear now filled Fortunato, fear and regret.

Chapter Fourteen:
The Way of the Staff

"You promised us."

The voice that spoke, Wrinn knew.

The voice was old, it was ancient, but it was past midnight.

It was past midnight, but Wrinn was possessed of a strange energy.

He recalled the promise he had indeed made, and though the trek would be long, he remembered the promise he had made to the trees of Daron Hen… that he would enter in.

"Come to us! The hour is here! The son of darkness is far away and you are safe in our embrace."

Wrinn stood up. The feasting hall had not yet emptied, though it was late. Fortunato had left an hour ago. Nenré and Gastreel were nowhere to be seen.

The forest of Daron Hen was far. Yet Wrinn was not tired. It was strange… an energy filled him. A strange desire filled him, too.

"You promised us," the trees said from afar.

Wasn't his word his bond?

~

Outside the palace, Wrinn walked, using his quarterstaff as a walking stick. He ventured out through the streets under the starlight and the moonlight. It was Dorion, or rather Anthanos, and the elves complained of the cold, but they did not know what cold truly was. They had never been to Gallia. Wrinn could walk outside in his thick tunic, with only a little discomfort.

"Come to us," the trees, from where he stood now at the edge of the city, were growing louder and louder, more numerous.

He walked through the misting rain, on this day, what was it the third, or fourth, of Dorion? He walked, and he hurried, beyond the borderlines of the city.

The voices of the trees were growing, and so was their anguish, and their desire for him. He had pushed on, over hills, past spruces and hemlocks, and it had to be the witching hour.

The forest was before him, down a hill, stretching into the interminable sky, ancient, old.

Not evil. So the trees had promised him.

And he had made a promise.

He walked ahead, still not tired, still unfazed, down the hill, committing the very act that Ivan Xandrast had warned against.

He pushed past the first of the trees, beyond the first of the eaves. There was a flash of light, and he was struck, and he went tumbling to the ground.

In a daze he looked up, seeing a figure clothed in white. An elf stood there with a thick yellow mane. In his hands was a quarterstaff, at his side a knife. His robes were long and flowing.

The trees had deceived Wrinn.

"Wrinn," the trees uttered, *"your teacher."*

Wrinn looked up at the elven figure. "Who are you?"

"My name is not yours to know," said the elf with the golden mane. "I am the Way… the Way of the Staff. I am *Dó Kentas.*"

Chapter Fifteen:
It Is He

The blind guide Callisti led Reev alone, down a road that led from the city, countless miles through the forest. The road began to bend, and they were at the coast.

It was apparent to Reev's eyes that the sun was in the process of rising, that the dawn was imminent. Light was growing in the firmament, as Callisti's purposeful walk began to slow. As the light grew, the air warmed, and smelled of pollen.

"At the World Tree, which only the Sage is permitted to see," said Callisti. "The World Tree spreads springtime about its branches."

The sun began to rise, gold and red.

Before a vast plain was a platform on which an ancient dull starstone still glowed. In view of that platform was a tree, what appeared to Reev's eyes to be a titanic elm, its leaves as red as flame — brilliant in the sun — its bark white like snow. Dandelions and lilies in bloom spread beyond it, and it was springtime indeed, in the dead of winter.

"What do you see, Reev Nax?" said Callisti.

"A tree," said Reev.

There were white flowers growing in its branches.

"A tree," Reev said, "and it is flowering."

"The World Tree is flowering," said Callisti, "and you are the Sage, the Prince of the Dawn, the one promised. The tree shall bear its fruit, and you shall crush the serpent's children underneath your feet."

Reev looked down at his feet. How good it would be, he thought, to crush Seymus underfoot.

He was the Prince of the Dawn. No doubt remained.

~

"In dark of night he arriveth, and he arriveth with the dawn!
He cometh with the dawn, the prince, and the world shall be the gods'
footstool
Under his feet shall he tread Seymus, and he shall bring to ruin Seymus's
seed
Lo! Look! He is coming! Behold, he shall crush Seymus under his feet."

—The Song of Danitari

~

Halfway to Danarion, an Elvish horse approached Callisti, and she swept herself onto its saddle, mounting it. Reev joined her a moment and a breath behind, and they rode together as one unit, on the Elvish horse, as dawn turned to morning and the birds of paradise began to sing.

Not long after the horse began to gallop, messengers were sent ahead, and those messengers began to blow trumpets. The gates were open, and the city was alive with activity. Small crowds had gathered along the street, in view of the palace and the towers of Danarion. Reev had a feeling he had started something which could now not be undone, a process unfolding which had long ago been told, which now could not be reversed. And the faces of the elven crowds were ones of great joy.

Callisti was jubilant, and the trumpet sounds seemed to announce the arrival of boundless hope and victory.

Astride the Elvish horse, they slowed to a trot as they clopped along the cobblestones. Reev had had a sleepless night but was possessed of a strange energy. A second wind, a second breath, and he was buzzing about energetically. He felt he could fight all day, and into the night.

In the courtyard of the palace, a party had greeted them.

The faces of the king's court were no longer stoic, but radiant with joy. The King of the Elves was smiling like Reev had never seen him smile. A bright, white-toothed smile was on Nenré's face. Lord Calion was brightly smiling, and their happiness had spread to Fortunato, Spyke, and Gastreel.

But Wrinn… where was Wrinn?

"The Sage arrives on a cock-horse, accompanied by the Sibyl," said the elvenking. "Now, he who sits on the Throne of Solendir shall bring from the far towers and donjon-keeps the prophecies that the humans called lost, but never were. He shall call a council of all the elven tribes and of the elven treaty-allies. The end shall come, then, the end… and a beginning."

Messengers were sent that day, to the Umen of the rainy western forests, to the Nurnen of the gray hills, to the Lonen of the furthermost east, and even to the *druen*, whom humans called vampires, inviting them to the "Council of the Last Time."

From that day on, Reev no longer slept in the king's apartments, his identity no longer in doubt, sleeping instead in a chamber in the Royal Palace that had been prepared, for millennia, for the Sage.

Chapter Sixteen: Where Narenvi Walked

In the forest of Daron Hen, there were wonders that Wrinn had never thought possible.

The misting rain was constant, and sometimes swelled to droplets, and often rain dropped in streams from the boughs of the giant spruces and hemlocks. There was moss on the ground, and bright green moss hanging in curtains from the trees. The brilliant green moss was of a richer and brighter hue than emerald. Moss was all about them, and life, pulsing life.

The one who presumed to call himself Wrinn's teacher had relented in the past day and admitted his name was not actually *dó kentas*, the Way of the Staff, but instead Iradahon. The trees' ceaseless chanting had quieted to a constant low moan, but now Wrinn was in the midst of them, and totally under their control.

Iradahon had in his possession a tent which he had erected near the streams of a gushing river, and a fishing pole from which he procured the days' lunches and dinners. But Wrinn knew he could use his powers of tree-speaking, if he wished, and locate all the forests' bounty. He would not go hungry, even if he was lost.

"Wrinn," said Iradahon as they walked through the rainy dampness, "you have so much to learn. But there is a seed of a *dó kentari* in you. The elven warriors have lost their adherence to the Way, and forgotten the elves' most ancient martial art. The followers of Solarias do not bear swords and axes and works of iron, but instead sticks and poles, rods and staves.

"You, however, *dra'datsi*, have somehow seen this despite being far from Danarion's light. You seem to know, or perhaps the gods told you, that the elf's weapon is not a sword, but a stick."

"It was only an accident I developed this fighting style," said

Wrinn, "like I told you… I was a pit fighter in the human kingdoms. I fought for blood sport. Stick-fighting is better in such a situation, for obvious reasons."

"What the bloodthirsty crowds intended for their sick pleasure, the gods and honor determined something else," said Iradahon amid the dripping rain and thick cold damp.

His devotion to something so extraneous seemed bothersome to Wrinn. He viewed the fighting style of the quarterstaff in a similar way to religion. Yet Wrinn could have departed from this man, who called himself his teacher, and he had not. For he thought Iradahon, mad though he was, was of a greater skill than Wrinn, and had much to teach.

If Wrinn and Reev fought Seymus together, his skill with the quarterstaff would have to be second to none.

"Come! Let's go! We run!" said Iradahon. He took off at a jog.

~

In the Forest of Daron Hen there were moss-covered trees, and there were moss-covered trees that had died and fallen on the ground. Navigating them was treacherous work. The stinging rain had bothered Wrinn at first, but he remembered it was deep winter, and he was glad not to have to deal with the drifts of snow piling up to the Dragonpaw's doors. His tunic was dripping wet, he was cold — shivering, even — but the bitter cold arctic blasts, the frozen landscape, was something he would not have to deal with in this blessed place.

"Wrinn! *Avast!*"

Wrinn whipped around, and Iradahon was upon him, knocking him to the wet moss-covered ground in the span of a moment so that his body and bones cried out in agony. Iradahon had braced his quarterstaff against Wrinn's neck, and if Iradahon were not his teacher, he would be as good as dead.

"See?" said Iradahon. "A *dó kentari* must be aware of himself at all times. He must have eyes in his front, and eyes to his back. He must have his ears perked up and listening. For the servants of Narenvi are everywhere. They walk about in mortal form, and they whisper in your ear."

Wrinn shuddered.

The trees seemed to cry out in pain. *"Narenvi,"* he heard a wise old spruce call out to him, *"he has walked in these woods before."*

"Narenvi?" Wrinn said. "Who is Narenvi?"

"He is the staff-master's enemy," said Iradahon. "The one the staff-masters were taught to fight against."

"Is he a man? An elf? A woman?" Wrinn said.

Iradahon smiled. "Let us continue, Wrinn. Eyes ahead, eyes behind, listening for any threats. *Dó Kentas* will serve you well."

~

After Iradhon had said the word Narenvi, the trees seemed to be whispering among themselves, yet not speaking to Wrinn. As Wrinn and Iradahon did battle in view of a hall of mosses, striking and parrying, ducking over downed mossy trees and sprinting beside gushing springs, the sense Wrinn felt from the trees had changed from love and devotion to enmity.

Wrinn was growing tired, desperate for water and rest. His arms were covered in bruises and welts from Iradahon's many successful strikes.

"I thought I was a good fighter," said Wrinn, "now, I see it is not so."

"Skill is relative," said Iradahon. "You could lay low the rokahn of the mountain halls. But you could not savage Narenvi."

"Perhaps," Wrinn said, "you should not say his name."

Exhausted and bruised, they walked through the mud and the rain, underneath the brilliant green moss hanging from the trees above. Wrinn had not seen the sun in days. The trees were too tall, and what little he could see of the sky was a steely gray. He had a thought that the sun did not often shine in the Forest of Daron Hen, and that when it did, it was cause for celebration.

At last, they reached Iradahon's tent, perched by the waters of a gushing stream. Iradahon handed Wrinn an oiled cloak to warm up, and Wrinn walked over to the twisted roots of a tree and sat down. As the throbbing of his bruised biceps and legs began to fade in importance to him, his deep ravenous hunger became apparent.

He had tired of the constant feasting in the king's hall, but now there was little food to go around. Everything Wrinn ate, he had to earn from the forest itself. It was a most unfortunate proposition.

Wrinn shivered as he watched Iradhon fish in the river's stream, at first laying his line in the waters near the tent but eventually disappearing from view.

It was not as cold as Gallia, but it was damp, and Wrinn's shivering was constant. He wondered if the rain actually was getting to him, after all. Perhaps, getting some exercise would warm him up. Perhaps, if he went for a long walk and got his muscles moving, the effects of the damp and the rain would lessen, and he'd be able to eat in peace.

~

Covered in the shawl, he passed through the moss-covered woods, spying an elk standing far-off amid the fluorescent green vegetation. The elk regarded him in alarm, then bounded off as Wrinn walked on.

The chattering of the trees was growing, the noise of their conversation growing in Wrinn's mind, as he himself was beginning to succumb to the elements. But something else he thought — he was being followed.

Eyes in front, eyes behind.

Wrinn grasped the center of his quarterstaff and found his center. He whipped around in the opposite direction and saw nothing but the shifting shadows of the afternoon light.

"What do you search for, Son of the Forest? Do you know what hunts you?"

A million trees were talking, ten million at once.

"What hunts me?" Wrinn said aloud. His voice echoed in the forest.

"Narenvi," said the voice of a wizened old hemlock.

"Danger comes to us, Wrinn," other trees added, a thousand, ten thousand at once. *"In the far north of here, where the slopes begin to rise… the darkness is at work, and the one promised to you is in danger."*

"What do you mean, darkness?" said Wrinn.

"Do you know who has walked in these woods before you, Son of the Forest? If you did, you would not tread so lightly. If you knew, you would not have come." The voices were a million, ten million, a hundred million at once.

In the north, they said… the one promised to him was in danger. Reev they meant, surely, Reev.

~

When Wrinn returned to camp, Iradahon had in a basket three wriggling salmon.

"I think we've exhausted this river," said Iradahon. "We'll go hungry soon. We must move…"

"North," Wrinn said, insistent, thinking of the voices of the trees and how they shuddered at the word *Narenvi.* "North… let's go north."

Chapter Seventeen: Bull-Cutter

The days since the Sibyl's pronouncement had been joy for the elves, and days of preparation, but for Gastreel, they had been marred by his physical pains and ailments. The Chief Healer of the elves, the *Amanddori,* had declared his wounds incurable, and had determined that when Reev, the Sage, departed from the Elf Lands, Gastreel would not be joining him.

As he sat in the Healing House, looking outside, seeing rain, turning toward sleet, tilting toward snow, he felt no bitterness. He had expended his life's energy, his bodily health and all he had, to invigorate the Gate of Tedron, and transport them all these thousands of miles in the blink an eye, from grave danger to safety.

The elven seers and sooth-speakers had said that Danarion would never fall to Shadow. And though in Varda abroad the darkness was on the increase, and wars and tumults there were innumerable, here the steady peace remained.

Yet even here there were signs, even here there were matters that troubled Gastreel. In the City of Light, everyone knew that Gastreel's work had not just brought the Sage to their doorstep. As they traversed, in the blink of an eye, the mountains and the steppe, unwitting dark passengers had followed them here. The Servants of Seymus that dogged Reev were at work in the Elf Lands. They would not stop until they had claimed Reev. They would not cease their work until the Shadow had fallen over all Varda, and the City of Light fall, and the power of Seymus usurp the power of the gods.

But for now, the elves' strength remained, the walls of the city of Danarion proved secure. For now, the Shadow that engulfed the whole world had failed to extinguish the candle that was Lamdar.

The Council of the Last Time had been summoned. It was a

wonder that Gastreel Osiris would witness it. Here it was, the fulfillment of the elves' and mankind's hopes, the Sage at last arrived to do what was promised, to crush underfoot Seymus and all who followed him. Here it was, and how good it was that Gastreel was born at this time. How good it was that Gastreel was born at all.

A door opened. The Chief Healer stood there. Yesterday at tea, Gastreel had learned his name was Fenari.

"Hello, Fenari," Gastreel said.

"Hello, Gastreel," Fenari said. "How are your breathing exercises going?"

"Breathing," Gastreel said, "is getting easier. Walking here… well, it is still difficult, but getting better."

"Not daily shall you come here," said Fenari, "not any more. You shall remain at the palace, and I will come to you. The king wishes to keep you apprised of his every action, and in the company of the Sage. He believes your knowledge and foresight shall avail us all at the Council of the Last Time."

Gastreel knew bits and pieces of what was intended. The representatives of the elven tribes would come — if not the kings themselves, someone to speak on their behalf. So too would come the elves' treaty allies from a far country, humans who had formed an ancient bond of blood and were considered the elves' equals — a wonder, if possible.

Through the shadows beyond the door, Gastreel could see shapes approaching, then footsteps. The Chief Healer was not alone.

Through the light of the window Gastreel could make out the glint of metal.

"I know these journeys back and forth are troubling you," Fenari said, "but no more. The King's Guard shall escort you to the palace, and all our meeting from hence forth will be there."

"I thank you," said Gastreel.

~

The King's Guard was splendidly garbed, handsome elves richly arrayed in full plate and blue capes. Their chief was a man of black hair and green eyes, tall and fair faced. He greeted Gastreel outside the Healing House, amid the biting sleet, with a "Hail!"

"Hail!" Gastreel said in answer.

"I am the captain of the King's Guard, Keras son of Kulas, of the House of Ridias," he said.

"And I am Gastreel, of no noble birth," Gastreel answered.

"You are, however, the wizard who accompanied the Sage," said Captain Keras, "and so that makes you noble in the elven view — royal, even. It was brought to the king's attention that you were making these journeys unaccompanied, which is against our laws and regulations. Every member of the king's court is to have an escort, though you were in no danger in these streets."

"No," said Gastreel, "I wasn't. But I shall be glad to have your company, Keras son of Kulas, of the House of Ridias."

~

As they wandered down a forested road in the center of the city, the gleam of something more than iron sparkled in Gastreel's eye. The sheath that bound Captain Keras's sword was transparent, made from the skin of some animal unknown in human lands. His sword was plain to be seen, proudly displayed for any passersby. The metal was white like a diamond, with a keen edge, and blue square patterns in a sequence on the surface. Gastreel felt drawn to it for a reason he did not know, and though he knew it was rude to inquire about an elven warrior's sword, he could not resist speaking. "Keras," Gastreel said, "what weapon do you bear?"

Keras turned amid the trees and the smile was as bright as any

Gastreel had seen before. He grasped the hilt of the sword and swept it from the transparent sheath.

"Helvenhari," Keras said.

"That means 'Bull-Cutter,' " Gastreel said.

"A strange name," Keras said, "and the names of the *estirion* blades have oft changed with new owners. When Danthelon Lunitar, the Wonder-Smith, forged them, he called after them by their true names when they emerged from the forge. When the Sage arrived with Pelladrimas, 'Flame of Fire,' in his possession, he called it Doomblade. But 'Bull-Cutter' has retained its name, and it has always been in the possession of the Captain of the King's Guard."

"Helvenhari," Gastreel said. "Well do you use it. Gods be with you, Keras son of Kulas, of the House of Ridias."

Chapter Eighteen: The Request

When Reev arrived at the palace, and the Sibyl proclaimed he indeed was the Prince of the Dawn, the elves had reacted in great joy. The kings of the elven tribes were being summoned to a great council, and perhaps at that great council Reev would learn the answer — he was to defeat the Dark One, an immaterial being… but how?

Outside the windows of his private chamber, through the frosty glass, he could see the cold rain and feel the harsh wind in his mind, though inside the palace it was warm. He was filled with hopeful expectation, but also with dread, that this task was placed upon him.

Wrinn had disappeared, and Fortunato had voiced his concern, but Reev heard a quiet voice in his heart telling him his friend was in good health and in good spirits, that he had been taken away from the Sage's company to become a better *adari,* a better helper.

In Danarion, the street lamps were now crowned with holly and mistletoe. Yule was approaching, but all anyone talked about in the City of Light was the approach of the Council of the Last Time, the time of decision for Seymus's final defeat and the long-awaited hope of every man and elf, the return of the gods.

There was a rustling behind him — footsteps — and the door creaked. Reev turned around and looked to the door, through to the bright light of the hallway, and saw a figure standing in the light.

It was Yanenré's father the elvenking, wearing his rich silk robe and his starry crown. "Sage," he said, "come walk with me."

~

Reev walked with the elvenking into the hallway, down a series of steps. The elvenking smelled of rich oils and aromatic scents.

"Sage," he said, "how good it is to say, with absolute certainty. How good it is to know that the Enemy's defeat is nigh."

The elvenking was clearly leading Reev somewhere, but he did not know where.

As he walked, Fortunato's concerns bubbled up in his heart — *Wrinn, missing* — and he questioned the comforting voice he had heard, that Wrinn was being prepared for the task assigned to him. Of what worth was a voice in one's heart?. One's heart was bound to be wrong.

"At the Council of the Last Time," said the elvenking, "the Sage takes the seat of the king. I shall show you the council chambers where we are to meet, the council where the elders and all the kings of the Light's firstborn are to make our best-laid plans."

The palace was a labyrinth of staircases, rooms and chambers, some of which to Reev seemed hardly used. There were kitchens and servants' quarters in every wing in the palace, in addition to great closets — some empty — and a never-ending network of hallways. It would be easy to get lost, he supposed, in the king's house, in the elven seat of royal power.

Yet the elvenking was a good guide, the best guide in fact. Reev knew elves lived much longer than humans, and he wondered if the elvenking had lived in this opulence for two hundred years, or for longer than that.

There was a dark doorway up ahead of them, on either door the engraved symbol of a fruiting tree. "Sage," said the elvenking, "enter first."

Reev hesitated only a moment before obliging. He laid his hands on the knobs and tugged them open. They fell open by themselves, baring the vastness of a great chamber, air that was musty, and stone carving so wondrous that Reev thought it impossible.

Beyond the doors were seats, and up above was a glass dome, baring the light of the cloudy sky. The greatest seat was higher than the rest, facing the door, with another high seat beside.

"Who will sit next to me?" Reev said.

"Why," the elvenking said, "whoever you choose."

"I know who I would choose," Reev said, "but I don't know where he's gone off to."

"Who do you speak of?" the elvenking said.

"The night I fled to the Sibyl," Reev said, "my friend also disappeared. His name is Wrinn. He is dear to me. It's not like him to disappear."

"Do not worry for Wrinn," the elvenking said. "Worry for your task, here, in the Elder Chamber."

But something could have happened to him. The agents of darkness could have set upon the City of Light. Perhaps, a Servant of Seymus snuck in through the gate and spirited his friend away. One's imagination was liable to run wild in the absence of knowledge.

Yet in some sense, the elvenking was telling the truth. What was Reev's purpose? To tread Seymus and his followers underfoot. Whether Wrinn lived or died, the completion of Reev's task would benefit him.

Yet Reev worried. He wanted to know for certain. He wanted to know Wrinn was all right. It was not like Wrinn to be unwell. He was brash and he was bold, but he was capable.

"Sage," said the elvenking, "look about you. Come to this room each morning and pray. Clear your mind. Your resolve must be total, your doubts few. For the enemy you fight will stop at nothing beside the ruin of Varda and the slavery of mortalkind."

Reev tried to put aside his concerns about Wrinn for a moment. He stepped into the light of the dome.

He did not like sitting higher above everyone else. He did not like the idea of feeling superior to the rest, when he himself felt so lowly .Yet he would comply with every regulation and law of the College of Priests. He would do as he was asked. He would crush underfoot Seymus and his followers. There was no doubt in his heart.

But was there doubt? How could he defeat a being, immaterial? What tools would have to be at his purview? And where would have to go, and what would he have to suffer, to do what the elves expected of him?

And Wrinn… Wrinn, he still thought of, above all. Where was Wrinn?

~

The dinner that night was light, chicken skewers and mashed tubers generously seasoned with salt. As Yule was approaching, dessert was Yule bread with piping-hot Yule wine.

Though the elves' joy had not lessened, and Gastreel — it seemed — was now staying in the palace morning, noon, and night, the worry in Reev was growing, for his friend who had disappeared.

At night, before bed, he prayed for Wrinn, and while he slept, he was overcome with a dream.

The Lady of Danyen stood before him in a heavenly orchard, her hair a burnt gold, her bright green eyes brilliant like the sun. Her eyes were kind, and the sun above her was kind as well, kinder than the sun in Varda.

A wreath graced her brown hair, and she wore a shift as white as snow, bright and clean.

"*Velati Sonoren*," she said to Reev. "Do you wish to know what has befallen your friends?"

"Wrinn," Reev said to the Lady of Danyen, and was sad at the thought he would have to leave this dream, to leave this place.

"I shall tell you," said the Lady of Danyen, "if you request it."

"Tell me," Reev said.

"I shall tell you, then," said the Lady of Danyen. "I shall tell you, *Velati Sonoren*, what has happened to *Adari*, but you will see things you do not wish to see, and know things you do not wish to know."

"*Tell me…*" Reev breathed as the dream faded. He longed for the dream, he longed for that place, that place of perfect peace.

Chapter Nineteen:
Blue Eyes, Brown Hair

In the city and in villages abroad, traditional Yule bonfires were lit, celebrating the Light's defeat of the darkness.

Fortunato stood before a bonfire outside Perenddon, surrounded by evergreens that grew even within city walls and deciduous trees that had shed their leaves, whose branches were licked by ice. Nenré was beside him, laughing beside the roaring flame, with a cup of red Yule wine in her hand.

To him she had become a creature of basest passion, and it was Fortunato who was having to push her away. He had lost count of the times they had made love, in closets and outside the city walls, in forgotten rooms of the palace that seemed to be inching ever closer to the royal bedroom.

It was against the law. Fortunato's guilt at first had been great, and to that was added fear, fear of what would happen to her if it were ever discovered, and fear of other things as well.

The elves before the Yule bonfire were laughing and singing. A few were dancing before the crackling brightness. "Fortunato," Nenré said and turned to him.

Fortunato shuddered at what she would do, if she would leap upon to him and make love to him in the open air, with guards and the other elves looking on. Instead she set her wine on the ground, and took Fortunato's left hand. She untied the white cord that was around Fortunato's wrist, and before he could protest, tore it off him and tossed it into the burning flame.

"Wha — Why? What have you done?" Fortunato said. "Now people will suspect…"

"But it is bad luck to keep it on, after the deed is done," said Nenré.

"I…" Fortunato was beside himself. "I would have taken my chances…"

~

Nenré began to walk, away from the Yule fire, and Fortunato followed her. He wondered what locale she had in mind. Fortunato's very body ached, and he realized that the elven princess walking beside him had become a creature he had not expected, more forward and filled with passion than Edith at Aerie Hold.

Perhaps, that is a stretch…

But all this love could have consequences, and Nenré seemed to be acting only with the carnal in mind.

He realized they were heading south of the city, toward the gate and the borderlines.

It was night in the forests outside Danarion. In places there were patches of snow. About all, there was a pattering rain. Occasionally the clouds would shift position and lay bare a crescent moon, glowing through a foggy veil.

The snow was crunching on Fortunato's boots, and though his body protested, he was not immune to basest passions, to the passions that had consumed them both. He was not immune to her red hair, her soft skin, her brilliant eyes of sapphire, and the parts of her that others did not see.

They were treading through the winter wood, in the rain. It was a metaphorical bridge that Nenré had not crossed before. But Fortunato supposed there was no chance of discovery here. In the snow, in the mud and the rain, like two pigs in the wild… would it be them, Fortunato and Nenré? Was there no grimy low they would not stoop to?

She stopped in a clearing. The moonlight shone on her red hair.

In view of the moon and stars, it seemed to paint the clearest portrait of what they were doing, violating the king's law, the law passed down through centuries.

As Fortunato stepped into the clearing, there was a loud bark.

A dark shape burst through the trees, a wagging tale, two bright red eyes and a body more massive than them both.

Tyra Jade leapt upon Nenré and licked her lips, and Nenré giggled in turn, batting the black wolf away.

"Tyra!" Fortunato said. "Does she love you more than me, now, Nenré?"

Nenré's giggling reached an apogee.

Fortunato's two loves were here.

No, there is another… greater than them both. But Fortunato dared not tell Nenré that.

"Ah, Fortunato, how good it is that you and the Sage are here at last," Nenré said. "In the forests of Alonar, you confessed your love to me. We departed in the summer sun, but there was trouble in our wake. The Shadow began to fall… the Sage, we left behind. And the anxieties, here, on the other side of the world, was almost enough to bring shadow to the land of light."

"But it was not so," said Fortunato. He drew near to her, and grasped her wrists, left and right. "It was not so. The Sage was brought, safe and happy, to the land of light. And for here, for nor now, he is safe."

There was a pause, and Tyra Jade backed off.

"Shall we make love here?" Fortunato said. "Here, in the mud and the rain?"

There was a twinkle in Tyra Jade's eye.

Fortunato's lips moved to Nenré's, and they met in a lustful embrace.

Chapter Twenty: True Seeing

Reev stirred awake, sad that the dream had left him, sad he was no longer in the heavenly orchard where there were no cares and only eternal joys.

It was the middle of the night, and he was sleeping in the bed prepared for him, in the room prepared for him. Memories of what that happy dream had entailed swirled about him, a meeting with Amané the Lady of Danyen in the heavenly orchard.

I will show you things you do not wish to see, she had said. There was a flash, a bit of brightness, and Reev looked down from his window.

A woman was on the grounds of the palace, many fathoms below. She wore a white gown and a white veil, and her body seemed to glow, giving light to that bright white clothing like the sun. It was not an apparition Reev was seeing, he was certain. It was a woman down there, and as his eyes fixed on her, he could see she was carrying something, a lantern.

Reev asked the gods for quickness, and lightness of feet, and gave chase.

~

Reev rushed outside, into the misting rain. He looked about, seeing the inky darkness of the winter night broken up by streetlamps. Then — far away — he saw the woman again, now walking down the street and bearing her lantern.

Her white shining raiment was like a beacon to his eyes, and he followed that beacon, rushing after her and her graceful steps.

Though she walked at an easy gait, she had a long head start, and so Reev was almost sprinting by the time she exited out the

North Gate. He was in his smallclothes, dressed for bed, but no one in the city had seemed to notice, nor had any guards stopped to question him.

She was treading through the forest, spreading the light of her lantern wherever she stepped. She spread light from her clothing and light from her lantern, and in view of that light Reev's fears were eased, and his trembling ceased.

He slowed down, following her from a distance, wondering if he was dreaming, but the bite of the winter wind was harsh, and the sting of the droplets of rain were fresh and sharp.

At last, they rounded a hill, and Reev saw down below them a vast forest stretching into the interminable distance, as far as the eye could see, a dark behemoth, a black horizon that terrified him and stole his breath. He shuddered, and wondered what feet had trod in those woods before.

The woman of light was treading through the eaves, disappearing through the brush, and Reev swallowed his panic. He ran in, and no sooner had he burst through the moss-covered eaves, into the deep darkness of the woods, that the woman spun around and confronted him.

~

The woman stood before the stagnant waters of a pool. About her, Reev thought, was snow, but on further glance, they were white leaves fallen from a tree above-head, adding furor to her majesty.

Majesty — he would not quite call it that. For her eyes were hollow and sunken, and her skin stretched tight to thin bones. Her wrists were emaciated, and what hair she had hung to her in wiry strands.

Reev screamed, said, "Who are you?"

And the woman answered, "Amané, what you call the Lady of Danyen."

"No," Reev said, "the Lady of Danyen is fair and beautiful, her hair of gold, her eyes of emerald. She is the fairest elf of all…"

"So she was, in her youth," said the woman who claimed to be Amané. "But when she found the gods' golden apples, and consumed them, and added years to her life, they did not change her body. She aged, though she lived, and so she was at this state, in death."

"I saw her with my own eyes," Reev said, "Hair of burnt gold, eyes like fiery emeralds. The fairest elf of all."

"I was a sorceress of light," said the woman, "and I could control what others saw. By illusion I appeared to you. And by the time you arrived at my home, the fruit was rotted and bitter to the taste."

"I saw the apples… they were pure," said Reev.

"So too was that an illusion," said Amané. "So too, was that my craft.

"Do you love me, still, Reev, despite my state?"

"Of course I do…"

"Then I give you the advice you seek," she answered. "Wrinn is now far into these woods, the woods of Daron Hen. He goes in the company of one who hides a secret, but one of a good heart and good faith. He goes to inestimable danger, and whether he shall live or die, or return to you, I cannot say. But the gods guide his every step, and if they allow, he will be with you when you enter the Dark Land."

"The Dark Land?" Reev said.

"Remember this, in the coming trials," said Amané. "A last word, one you will do well in remembering.

"Your greatest ally will surprise you. For there is none so lost as cannot be found, no darkness so deep the light cannot touch. There is none fallen that the gods cannot restore. And perhaps in the spirit of one laid low, you can find the torch to light your path.

"Begone from me, and remember. I have passed the test. In Danda I shall now rest."

~

Days passed, and weeks. The air's chill grew colder, enveloping all, but to Reev's mind it was never a crisis, never anything that couldn't be solved with thick woolens and a thick winter cloak. Unlike Gallia, where the icy winter wind cut the neck like a knife and the endless snows made travel impossible, here winter was not much more than an excuse to stay indoors by the fire in the company of others, to sleep perhaps a bit better in the palace's cool damps, to give an excuse, on colder days, to do nothing at all.

The month of Dorion passed into the month of Dandathon, and it was Candlebright by human reckoning. Sometime in the days leading up to Yule, a thick snow began to fall from the heavens, white flakes in the winter sun, but this too Reev had no fear of. The air was cold, but never unfathomably fierce like in Gallia, and even standing in the snow it was not much more than something to take pleasure in — the way the white tufts lay upon the roofs of Danarion's houses, the way it made the fire inside more delightful, and the smell of roasting chestnuts the more wondrous. In ponds outside Danarion proper, elven children took to ice skating, and others went on excursions, as the king's servants hung from every lamppost holly and mistletoe, and proclaimed in loud voices the Light's defeat of the darkness long ago.

Some in the palace had taken to caroling; others spent their days fashioning their gifts. Food there was aplenty, and Yule wine, as the season of Yule coincided with the planning of the Council of the Last Time, and Reev counted down the hours to that happiest of days. The light and the feeling in the air, the joy of Yule, was enough to banish all thought of the coming struggle he would have to face, and all the troubles that were to come.

It was Yule eve, and the court of the elvenking was gathered in the great hall. A Yule tree had long been erected near the hearth, festooned with glittering ornaments and candles. The elvenking had taken his seat, and Nenré and Fortunato were chatting on the corner, on this happiest of days.

"Prithee, members of the court," the elvenking said, "tell of the person who has helped you most since last Yule. Take a drink in their honor, and utter a prayer for their beneficence."

"To Gastreel!" hollered Fortunato. "Who brought us here, who by the punishment of his body took us through the Gate of Tedron, to safety."

"Hail, Gastreel!" said the elvenking, and the members of the court took a drink of wine in unison, Reev with them.

"To the Sage!" cried Annenwé, the youngest member of the royal family and the famed poet, a little child with her blonde hair tied up in pigtails. "For he has brought I, and my people, hope."

"Hail, Reev!" said the elvenking, and this time Reev did not follow the elves in their drinking.

"And what of the Sage?" said the elvenking. "Who does he regard with most favor, in the year since last Yule?"

They had asked a good question, and Reev thought it deserved a good response. He searched his heart, and thought of Gastreel, his body ruined by his transportation of them here. But in the end, he settled on one who had ended the deepest crisis of his heart, the deepest crisis he remembered.

"The Sibyl asked before she told me the truth," said Reev, "an offering of wheat and spelt and emmer. I had no money to pay. But someone paid in my stead. His name was Mikal, and his hair was like a rainbow. They called him *Selen'veni*."

"*Selen'veni*," said the elvenking, "Half-Fey. There is only one as fits that description in the City of Light. He lives in Aqardon, near the River's Gate. I did not know this about him, that he ushered in our hope. Surely, he deserves a place of honor, this Yule night. Let us go fetch him."

~

Reev walked with the King's Guard, with the elvenking and Annenwé, down the lamplit streets. The Yule Eve was utterly quiet, and business was forbidden. The elves of the City of Light, like humans, gave gifts on this holiday and reflected on the Light's defeat of the darkness.

The snow crunched against Reev's shoes, but even the crunch of the snow seemed less harsh than in Gallia, and the air though cold was not threatening to one's life. What a blessed place this was, what happiness it entailed. And Reev was glad to be here as long as he could.

Through the darkened streets they passed, until they came to the glittering waters of the Watercourse. There was a house on the edge of the Watercourse, silent and serene, but there were candles in the windows and a Yule wreath on the door. Reev walked up to it — "Is this the one?" he said, and the elvenking nodded — and he knocked firmly until there was an answer. The door opened a crack, and a familiar face greeted him.

Mikal was there, dressed in a winter tunic, tall and lanky, with long arms and long legs that seemed disproportionate for his body, hair every color of the rainbow. He smiled at the sight of Reev, and said, "Sage, how good it is to see you on this Yule eve."

"We thought in the court," said Reev, "it would not have been as good a Yule eve as it could have been, were it not for your company?"

"Pardon, Sage," said Mikal, "and pardon Your Majesty the King, my mother is sick and she is old, and I cannot leave her for long. May she come with me on this Yule eve?"

~

Mikal and his mother entered the great hall as outside the snows began to fall again. His mother was a slight woman, her back almost hunched, and Mikal's rainbow hair and long arms had certainly not come from her. Her hair was a dull gray, though her eyes were bright and warm. She walked with a cane, and as soon as she entered, she was treated with much kindness.

The king's orchestra began to play a Yule song. More wine was poured, and glasses were placed into Mikal's and his mother's hands.

The night continued on, happy and warm, as the snow continued to fall. At some point in the night, Reev found himself alone on the balcony with Mikal's mother. Her trembling, wrinkled hands were clutching her wine cup, which she had almost finished. The cold brisk air was all about them, and white flakes were dropping from the heavens.

"Your son's hair is the color of a rainbow," said Reev, "and his arms and legs are long. He is lanky and quick on his feet. That surely didn't come from you…"

Mikal's mother smiled, and she stared out into the white expanse below the palace. Her eyes seemed to glaze over, and it seemed she was no longer in the royal palace on Yule eve.

"Oh, so many years ago," said Mikal's mother, "so many turns of the seasons. I was a young doe, happy and carefree, a girl of the Southern Reaches. I had not married, and worried that I never would. One Midsummer's Eve, I entered the summer woods with a heavy heart, intending to take a shortcut to my grandmother's house. But I became lost. I wandered that midsummer night through the woods, trying to find my path back, when I saw the lights of a great city.

"But when I entered the gates of the city, there were people with shining faces, and hair of sapphire and emerald and azure. I thought I had entered heaven, but then I realized I had stepped through a mushroom ring in that midsummer wood and entered *Avenda*, the Enchanting, the Land of the Fey.

"I spent years there, and married a Puck in a summer glade. For months we were wed, but then he left me, as Pucks do. I followed after him, trying to set things right, trying to find him amid a great expanse. I stepped through another mushroom ring. I was back in that midsummer wood, and no time had passed in this world, though to me it had seemed seventy years.

"No time had passed in this world, but I was pregnant with Mikal…"

Chapter Twenty-One:
A Name Remembered

In the forest of Daron Hen, it was dark, and the rain had turned to snow. The snow had not accumulated, and had mostly melted into the trickling pools and streams, amid the avenues of mosses and halls of lichens, draped from the branches of trees both living and dead.

The constant dampness, the wet precipitation that had now not ceased for many weeks, was beginning to wear on Wrinn, and he wondered if he liked the arctic winds and drifting snow of Gallia better after all. Of course, back in Galiope, he was never far from a fire, never far from the shelter of a house or an inn, so the elements were more bearable.

Between daily lessons and nightly mock battles, Iradahon was steadily leading Wrinn north, as the trees had suggested to him. They were getting further and further from Danarion, and Wrinn worried that Reev would be beside himself, that Reev and others would think he was dead.

But he was not dead, for now, amid these ancient trees, these mosses and these bright yellow slugs. Amid such verdant life, there was plenty to eat in the streams and rivers, and if Iradahon had brought a bow, there would be plenty of elk and deer to hunt down and boil into a stew.

Yet Iradahon had warned him, and Wrinn had gathered, that these woods were not empty, that an enemy named Narenvi had been here once before. Amid these ancient spruces and hemlocks, both living upright and rotted on the forest floor, there was danger Wrinn sensed from the talk of the trees, and danger Wrinn sensed from the pattering of his own heart.

At last Iradahon stopped his walking, and began to erect the tents.

"Perhaps, the thought will trouble you, Wrinn," said Iradahon, "that it is Yule eve."

Yule eve… the thought did make Wrinn sad, the thought of the royal palace festooned in holly and ivy, of the celebration, of the giving of gifts in warmth and joy, comfort and peace.

But Wrinn supposed, if he were to be *adari*, the Sage's helper, he would have to make sacrifices. He would have to learn at the feet of Iradahon and more.

For Reev's sake, he would have to forgo Yule, this year of 1153 and all it entailed. Perhaps, he could celebrate a Yule in peace after Seymus's final defeat. How good it would be to celebrate Yule then, with the forces of Shadow and evil forever extinguished. There had never been a Yule as good as that. Or had there been?

Iradahon began to erect the tents. Amid the wet snow, now shifting toward sleet, tilting toward rain, Wrinn began to back away.

He heard a voice, "*Wrinn,*" a wise old hemlock said, "*Narenvi is here…*"

Wrinn drew his staff and looked about. Then he shut his eyes and listened with his own two ears.

As an elf, his ears were attuned to the slightest discrepancies. Reev had wondered at his ability to detect sounds he himself had not heard. It was a blessing of being an elf, among other blessings, and he intended to use it, for as the trees said, Narenvi was here. He did not have to take their word for it. He felt it in his heart.

Beyond the sound of Iradahon toiling with the tents, and the constant patter of icy rain, there was the sound of a gushing river, rapids, and something else — something he could not tell — rising above the noise.

"Narenvi is here," Wrinn said under his breath, and followed the source of the gushing river.

~

Through the dense foliage, which he had to push through, through thorny vines that tore his already-marred trousers and tunic, he found himself on a rocky outcrop overlooking a bit of high ground.

There was indeed a gushing river, fresh clear water so that Wrinn could see the pebbles underneath. There was a set of rapids in the distance as the water made a steep incline.

And Wrinn, to his trembling heart, realized the trees were right, that he was not alone.

Three figures stood by the waters of the gushing river, two of them holding torches to light the night. Their faces were unmistakably not human nor elven. One was purple, another muddy brown, another spotted brown and green. The two carrying torches had horns. They were rokahn, Wrinn realized with a shudder, and Wrinn had a thought that rokahn did not belong in this place. To his mind the forest of Daron Hen was sacred, and for rokahn to tread their feet within seemed the darkest sacrilege.

Wrinn did not move, did not bend or twist his way through the brush. He remained completely still, and tried to breathe quietly.

The three rokahn were speaking in their guttural tongue. They had not noticed Wrinn, the Son of the Forest. They did not know that the Son of the Forest was watching them.

Then there was more motion — more torches, more rokahn. These rokahn wore armor. He heard a word — *Lothan* — and found the word familiar to his ears, though he couldn't place it. Where had he heard the word before? It was on the tip of his tongue.

Behind the armored rokahn, bearing torches, were many elves, some bound with iron collars and others in manacles, all utterly subdued. And at the sight of that, and the thought that such a fate could be his, fear overcame him. He darted away through the brush.

"Ah, Son of the Forest," said the trees, a hundred, a thousand, a

million as one, *"you could have learned something."*

~

Wrinn was trembling by the time he got to Iradahon's tent.

The tents had been erected, and Iradahon was waiting for him.

Iradahon, it seemed, could detect his fear. "Student," he said, "what is wrong?"

"There are rokahn in these woods," said Wrinn.

Iradahon's eyes hardened with disbelief. "Impossible," he said.

"I saw them with my own two eyes," Wrinn said, "about a dozen, maybe more. They had many elves as captives."

"There are rokahn far south of the forest, in the Dragonteeth. There are rokahn north of Daron Hen. But they have dared not tread on such sacred ground before, where judgment was pronounced on Narenvi."

"Who is Narenvi?" Wrinn said.

The look Iradahon gave Wrinn made him think he would never tell.

Chapter Twenty-Two: Red Rooms

Within a week the snow had melted, and the air had considerably warmed. The snow had given way to rain and occasional days of sunshine.

Yet despite the kinder weather, despite the sun finally making itself known, new worries had assailed Reev's heart. His anxieties had turned from Wrinn to Ivan Xandrast, who had turned to works of darkest darkness, if his visions had been true.

The air though warming was still chilly, Reev thought, the nights though shortening were still much longer than the day. As he stared outside the windows of his bedroom, he thought of the messengers sent out to announce the Council of the Last Time, and the difficult path they would have to take in the mud and the rain. He uttered a prayer, silently, that their horses would swiftly bear them and not tire or die. He prayed everything would occur as he hoped, as had been prophesied.

"Reev Nax." The voice that stirred him was one that commanded instant respect and reverent awe wherever it was heard, a voice more honored than the elvenking. Reev turned and saw him, Lord Calion with his hair so fair it was almost white, an elf-lord and — Reev thought — something much more. Much more power did he have than his silver tongue and his noble title. "It is bleak in midwinter, but midwinter in Lamdar does not last long. Still, it can weigh on one's spirits. It is my custom to invite members of the court to my estate when the long nights have stretched for many weeks. It is my custom to invite distinguished guests, during these darkness-filled days, to my house by the sea."

~

The journey to Lord Calion's house, it was said, would take a day by horse. It had grown difficult, to Reev's mind, to operate without Cobalt, and his heart pained at the thought of what had happened to him, his prized Elvish horse.

He did not easily accept a new master. If the Imperials tried to break him with whips and rods, he would die before accepting an unsuitable rider. The thought of him dead, stricken down and left to rot, was too much for him to bear.

The fears he had swirling, the anxieties for Ivan Xandrast and Wrinn and Cobalt, would not easily be quelled wandering the palace, as they made preparations for the Council of the Last Time. Perhaps, a journey would ease his pain.

And so he left, the following day, riding two-a-saddle behind the Captain of the King's Guard, Keras, part of a train that included the crown prince Vélerion, Mikal, and Nenré.

The skies above-head were gray, and the rain that fell came down in misting droplets. It was cold, but the ground was clear of snow as Reev pressed down the way, as a wind seemed to blow, cold and somehow familiar to his mind.

The wind — its taste, its feel — brought him back to a place he remembered only vaguely, a place he wasn't sure he liked. The taste of the wind, its feel against his skin, troubled him, and when he had traveled a little while, and began to hear the rushing of the waves, that haunting feeling made him rue the moment he had agreed to come.

He could see the moonlight glittering in the waters of the sea, and smell the salt air of the ocean. He could hear the rush of the tide, as the gait of the horse slowed, and through a veil of fog appeared a fence, and beyond it, the lights of a house.

~

They were in the yard of the house, dismounting from their horses, and under the moonlight one was approaching. His hair was lustrous and white in the starlight, and he had on a white robe of silk that covered his feet. It was Lord Calion, and in the light of moon and stars, on this midwinter night, he appeared to Reev's eyes to be not a mortal at all but something much more, a creature of terror and terrifying glory, made more glorious and terrifying by the rings on his hands which seemed to wax or wane in size with Reev's attention or inattention.

"Sage! Greetings!" said Calion, standing in the yard, amid that wind that had troubled Reev and now, in sight of Calion, was beginning to terrify him.

"Vélerion, hail! Your brother is here… Yanenré… a pleasure, Your Grace. Mikal — an honor, *Selen'veni.*"

And Reev realized, in that moment, that he was the only human among these gathered, that he would have to spend a night and perhaps more as the only human in the house.

~

He ventured through the doors of Lord Calion's house, beyond a vestibule in which were marble busts of elves and potted plants, through another doorway, and he was a room that overlooked the sea.

Beyond the window were rocks and rocky ground descending toward the stormy seas, beneath a dark and stormy sky. The waves were raging, stirred up by that wind that had so troubled Reev.

Vélerion's brother, Avernathi, was standing before the window, gazing at the waves, his silver hair sparkling in the light of starstones and torches, and he was holding a cup of wine in his hands. "The Sage comes," he said softly. "The wind responds, and kicks up the waves of the Great Sea."

"Greetings, Avernathi," Reev said. He would not be

intimidated.

The elves were entering behind him, through the vestibule. He could hear them stomping the rain off their boots.

"Good tidings, Sage, for me and mine," Avernathi said. In all this time, he had not looked back from the window and the raging sea. "I have become the senior candidate to become a member of the College of Priests. I may preside over your council."

But was that good for Reev, in all?

"Hail, Reev!" The door had opened. Yanenré was standing there, in the light. "I am sorry you are alone among our kindred. Fortunato would not come."

Would not — did he know better? The raging of the waves, the memory of the troubled wind, was stirring in him angst and fear. He was utterly alone, in a place he did not belong, and though he knew who he was, the Prince of the Dawn, a nameless terror seemed to be all about and beyond this house.

~

They played cards, first, the elves and the lone human, cards written in a style of Elvish that was difficult to perceive, in a language Reev did not know every word of.

Sargé was the card he chose out of the pile, "Lion," and the elves presumed he was supposed to know what he was to do with it.

Yet he laid it down on the table, and there was consternation on Calion's, and Avernathi's, and Nenré's face.

"You have won," she said.

"I have won?" Reev said.

Next they went back to the room overlooking the sea, and a servant garbed in a green hooded robe strummed a viol as they listened. Another servant in a blue hooded robe brought out a platter of wine cups, a servant in a yellow a tray of shrimp and river fish.

The elves began to sing, in a dialect of Elvish Reev had not heard, glimpses of words he knew, *helvé* — cow, *hon* — love, *hiral* – courage. And it seemed, to Reev's ears, they were singing the tragic tale of a man and his wife. But then he heard the word *selad* — wives.

The singing ceased. The viol ended its playing. And before Reev asked any questions Lord Calion was explaining. "At the dawn of the Age of Humankind," said Lord Calion, "the elves received a revelation of the gods, that an elf was permitted only one wife. And so Danthemari chose the wife he loved best, and sent the rest away."

"A tragic tale," said Nenré. "A tragic ending."

~

After the song, the elves gathered by the fire and began to tell stories and speak of great things. Vélerion boasted about partaking in wars in the mountains, of hewing down countless rokahn in view of his soldiers. He boasted of a soothspeaker telling him he had a great destiny, but that he would be thwarted.

Lord Calion regaled the days of his youth, spent in the Southern Reaches, how he would collect seashells by the shore and sell them in marketplaces. Yet when Reev asked about the rings he wore on his fingers, he would tell Reev nothing at all.

Yanenré told the crowd gathered that as the daughter of the elvenking, she had been granted every desire she wished. But she had a sense deep down that she had longed for something more, something that she had now found.

"What have you found?" Reev said to her.

"Ah, Reev," she said, "if I told you, I would be done for."

Lord Calion stared into Reev's eyes. "The Sage is a blessed young man indeed," he said. "For I met him in the woods of Alonar, but one thing I did not know on our first meeting that he had come into the presence of the Lady of the Wood Amané, and saw with his own two eyes her face."

Not her true face, Reev thought, and he shuddered at the skeletal visage he had witnessed in the woods of Daron Hen.

"You saw her?" said Nenré. "You saw the Lady of Danyen?" Her eyes were touched with wonder.

"I met her, indeed," Reev said. "And I saw the apples of her orchard."

Well, not quite. Reev wished that Amané had not told him the truth. The trees themselves, like her beautiful face, had been an illusion cast by her magic. The fruit by the time Reev met her, thousands of years after her birth, had grown rotten and spoiled. The life the fruit gave her had been waning. She had been at death's door. Yet she had rescued Reev and Gastreel from rokahn. She had still had a little of her ancient power.

"Amané," said Lord Calion softly. "Amané Innué, they called her. Amané the Blessed, they said, for wherever she walked, the gods walked with her."

I still see her sometimes, Reev almost said, but he stopped himself. His heart trembled at these greats before him.

Not like mortals they seemed to him, these long-lived elves possessed of such great wisdom and power. Not like mortals, they seemed, but like gods, yet somehow falling short. And to be like a god, yet falling short, was terror unfathomable.

~

To a red room they drew, on the house's highest story, and to Reev's alarm they drew from cases and wooden chests a series of leather masks. It was there they began to utter words of a tongue Reev had not heard before.

In the brightness of the red room, on this cold midwinter day, he felt a dark finger of smoke and ruin raking at his chest. His chest shuddered. His body heaved. The elves were speaking, and he thought he understood the words.

He heard a child cry in the snow. He dropped to his knees, and then face-first to the ground. His eyes welled with tears, as he was overcome with a vision. He cried out, "Bala!"

Chapter Twenty-Three: An Army Born

"Balor!" Yaga cried. "How do you fare in the snow?"

The three hags, Bala's teachers, were behind him amid the raging storm. They would not stop calling him Balor. He had asked them politely, and used the nicest tone he could muster. He had said "pretty please," but the hags continued to call him by a name that was not his.

Bala, Bala, that was his name. That was what everyone called him. But when the hags had found him in the woods, they told him his name had been Balor all along, from birth.

For weeks, they had been walking through the snowy landscape, headed due north, to what the hags had called his "destiny."

The hags were possessed of great strength and skill, and each night they had managed to fashion a fire, and each night they had managed to find food enough for Bala, whether a mink or a badger or a squirrel — a squirrel, "baby food" they had called it — and each hour at dawn they would take the time to teach him magic, before they resumed their journey.

Northward, northward, they had traveled, and Bala had lost track of time. It had to be well past Yule, and where they intended to take him he had no idea, for they refused to tell him anything but that they were leading him to his fate as hags do.

His fate… they had said it before, and the word "destiny" to Bala's mind had a bit of a happier sound. His fate… yet the hags said his fate would not be terrible, that in fact, it would be good.

"Balor!" said Yaga, the tallest of the three hags. "I said, how do you fare in the snow?"

"Well," Bala said. The hags had bundled him up in bearskins

and deerskins, and the snowshoes they had given him allowed him to just barely grace the top of the snow without fuss. The hags, however, were built of lighter stuff than he, and seemed to touch just barely the edge of the snow even bare-footed.

They ventured on. The snow, building to drifts, was like a white desert. In places there were sheets of ice. But up ahead — through the howling wind, through the blinding white — Bala saw a dark color.

"What's that?" Bala said.

"Your home," Yaga answered.

Had they turned around, at some point in the journey, and come back to Galiope and Miss Glenda's inn? But no, there was never so much snow in Gallia, and the wind was not this deadly. In Gallia there were trees, and there were houses with lights in the window. In Gallia there was warmth, and there was love.

At the thought of the love he had left behind, tears began to form in Bala's eyes. He had left so very much behind. Part of him wanted to go back, but would he ever become a wizard if he did?

~

As the storm built, so did their pace. The dark color were the boughs of trees abutting a frozen river. Beyond the river, frozen solid, which Bala could walk upon, was a forest of black pine trees.

"A forest," said Bala.

"We have reached the Black River," said Yaga, "beyond which we can go no further. You have grown up before us as a mighty young mage. Cross the river and find your fate."

A bit of panic rose in Bala, and he turned around, and saw the snow swirling about them. There was blinding white, thick white flakes, a storm for a while, and when the storm ceased, and the snow stopped falling, they were gone.

Panic arose in Bala, but then that panic was overcome by

strength. They had led him to his fate, they had said. But they had said his fate would not be terrible, it would be good.

Bala took his first steps over the frozen river and entered the pine forest. In his hand was the wand that the hags had given him, in which he had imbued his magical essence.

His snowshoes slid on the ice, but he steadied himself on the snow. He continued his walk, treading down the snowy path, and then, to his wonder and alarm, he saw sticks upright above the snow, wooden sticks — marking a road.

No sooner had he seen the sticks, than a storm of a new kind overwhelmed him. There were trumpets — there was the gleam of steel. There were horses, and riders in shining armor, crimson capes and shining helms.

"Intruder!" said the man in armor riding before him. "None are permitted to cross the Black River. Only in the harbor of Druenel-Hai are foreigners allowed to enter the kingdom of the Vampire Lords."

Behind the man in armor were others, about a dozen in number, wearing steel full-plate and carrying falchions in their hands.

It had been terrible timing to enter the road at this time, but timing — it seemed — of the hags' design.

"The sentence for unlawful entry is death," the man said, "man, woman, or child."

The man drew his falchion, and ran at Bala at a gallop.

Bala's reaction was all instinct, drawing up his wand and allowing the magic that the hags had so expertly taught him to flow through his blood, his veins, his mind, his soul.

He fired his wand, and a beam of coruscating purple energy blasted in a line from the tip into the man's chest. The man in an instant withered and shriveled within his armor, like a piece of meat cooking in a metal pot. He slumped dead from his horse, as the other men — the other vampires — behind him, cried out, "The babe is a necromancer!"

Bala fired more beams, and then a blast. He fired more blasts from within himself, and then a storm. In the blink of an eye, the vampires in armor had fallen dead from their horses. Their bodies were withered within the iron shells, fallen from their horses, and the horses fled away. Their white faces were frozen in a look of terror and agony.

And then he remembered something, something from Yaga's lessons, how a necromancer was the deadliest mage of all. For once he had stricken down his foes, he would gain in power.

He gained power, for in the end, the dead were his servants.

Bala dropped his wand. He knew it would be a hinderance for the great strength he would have to summon. He raised his hands and called upon the magic well in him and about him, focusing on the dozen bodies lying in the snow. He saw them by a dark vision, bodies whose souls had escaped, whether to the happy realm of the gods or to perdition. He focused and sent magic into those vessels, giving those bodies animation, a false semblance of life. And he watched the bodies, shrunken and shriveled, rise up in armor, and bear their falchions.

"Master," one of Bala's undead servants said. "Where shall we go?"

Chapter Twenty-Four: The Investigation

In the weeks since the elves' proclamation, Spyke had tried to take stock of all that had happened to him, how he — a member of the Imperial military long ago — had gone to war against his own country. He had ventured to the city of Galiope to participate in the Pan-Vardic Games. He had met Fortunato. He had decided to fight not for his own country or people, but for something higher, for the Prince of the Dawn, and it seemed he had made the right choice.

Yet the palace now was not a site of endless feasting, but of endless preparation. And he knew something he had told no one else, the elven girl dreaming dreams in her parent's house, words of prescience no one else knew, the Sixth Anthanian.

And now Spyke knew more about the Sixth Anthanian than just about anybody. As he sat in his room in the royal apartments with a cup of spiced wine, he eyed the window, wondering if he might see the doomed Sixth Anthanian Legion's banners outside. And he thought of how the elven girl had been throwing herself into the fire, in a terrible state, as her mother had ranted words she had thought nonsensical… *The Sixth Anthanian.* But they were not nonsensical. They were far from nonsensical.

Now, those words haunted Spyke, and their meaning to him still was not clear. But he would endure, and he would guard the Sage, and he would be at the Sage's beck and call. All things duty required of him, he would do, as he had in the emperor's service, and now he would, in the service of something much higher.

Spyke would like to know more about the Sixth Anthanian, but the elven libraries had no knowledge related to it. The Sixth Anthanian had not been in existence for almost nine hundred years. They were a footnote in history, at least until now.

There was a knock on the door. Spyke set his spiced wine on the window sill and adjusted his tunic. Despite the relaxed nature of the elven capital, he liked to look presentable, as an ambassador of the empire and the human realms as a whole.

He opened the door and saw the steward of the palace standing there, in his hands a letter. Spyke could see its Imperial seal.

"Spyke," the steward said, "forgive me for my grumbling. A sailor arrived at port. The ship had sails of red and gold. An Imperial craft, I believe. I daresay, what evil have you brought to us?

"And yet, it has not been the Empire that brought ruin to the Elf Lands. It was another human kingdom. Nonetheless, they handed me this letter and demanded I deliver it to you at once."

Spyke had not brought them evil. If anything, he had brought danger to himself. The Empire had conquered much of the world, but the elves, whom they called the Elders, they had maintained a policy of leaving alone.

His fingers were sweating when he took the letter, and his palm was trembling when he took the seal. He had, after all, committed a bit of light treason, halfhearted as it had been.

Spyke read the letter in his quarters.

To Vitto Khandulis, not only a member of the reserves and a soldier of the rank of legionary, but a loyal soldier who has achieved the Expeditionary Mark.

The excursion to the Antipodes, and the dangerous conditions they had braved, had earned Spyke high praise and honor.

Do not be so humble in further

correspondence.

From the ward legate of the Metropolitan in Imperial City, greetings. Long live the emperor, and long live the Empire and her people.

It has come to our attention that you were a participant in the Pan-Vardic Games. As a soldier of high rank, who has achieved honors, we do not doubt your loyalty. However, a certain traitor named Fortunato of Riva, a man of the common classes, led armies against his own. Is he, perchance, in your company?

The panic rose in Spyke, and he tried his best to quiet it. He thought of how best he could protect his friend, and above all this mission they had both embarked on. Lies did not come easy to him, and lies to his superior were a crime that warranted death.

But lie he would, and he would tell him Fortunato was not among them, that he was here for a pilgrimage and nothing more.

Would the ward legate of the Metropolitan in Imperial City believe him? It would be difficult at so unfathomable a distance to discern truth from lies.

Yet the truth would eventually be revealed. The truth always was revealed, in the end.

Chapter Twenty-Five: Narenvi's Victim

As Wrinn and Iradahon pressed north, it dawned on Wrinn that they had ventured far from the civilized world. They had come to a place in the northern parts of the forest where no elves lived, where there was no sign of habitation, where trees and mosses and hanging lichens reigned supreme. And in such a place, there was nowhere to run for help, nowhere to go.

He uttered a prayer one morning, under his breath, as he passed by a moss-covered tree, that Reev the Sage would know his friend still was alive, and also that the palace was not in a panic because of him.

The forest hid dangers, and that sense of danger was only growing. Wrinn had witnessed rokahn, and with them elven captives, venturing not far from where they camped, weeks ago.

As Wrinn trained with Iradahon, then scoured for food, going ever northwards at a slow rate, he had kept his eye out for rokahn, but in the days since, there had been no sign. There had been terrors, there had been dangers, and his sleep had been troubled. All about him were the warnings of trees and of Iradahon, stating that one named Narenvi had stalked these woods, and was keen on Wrinn's death.

There was the sound of rushing water up ahead, and beyond a green mossy ground, and curtains of moss hanging from the boughs of a spruce, was a waterfall.

"Wrinn," said Iradahon, "you are my student, a student of *dó kentas*, a student of the Way of the Staff. Tell me, Wrinn, what does the *dó kentari* fight for?"

Wrinn strained to remember.

Iradahon turned, and his lion-like mane seemed to fluoresce in the rain-soaked light.

"Legitimate authority," Wrinn said, "starting with the elvenking."

"And what if there is a usurper?" said Iradahon. "What if a king arises who is not king according to the law? What if a tyrant seizes control of a human kingdom and brutalizes the people?"

"Then I would not resist," said Wrinn.

"Wrong," said Iradahon. "Only legitimate authority do you respect. Only legitimate authority do you fight for. If an impostor steals power, you wage war against him."

"Is the elvenking legitimate?" said Wrinn.

"The elvenking derives his power from the Sage's blessing," said Iradahon. "The elvenking is but a steward. The Sage may remove him or replace him at will."

But Wrinn knew Reev, and Wrinn thought that Reev would despise such a responsibility. Reev desired only to do his duty, what the gods demanded of him. He wanted no earthly power.

"So the Sage, then, is who I fight for," Wrinn said.

Iradahon nodded.

"*Adari*," said Wrinn. "I am his helper."

"And you are growing in strength," said Iradahon. "But you have a powerful enemy. And you were not my only student."

"What do you mean?" Wrinn said.

"Follow me," said Iradahon.

Iradahon led him up to the gushing waterfall, and passed through the icy waters. Wrinn followed a step behind. The water was frigid, yet exhilarating. And Wrinn had a thought, that Iradahon had passed through these waters before.

~

"Innuvi was the young man I had been training, whom I thought would carry on my legacy," Iradahon said.

Within the cave beyond the waterfall, it was utterly dark. But Iradahon began to shift in the darkness, and manipulate some object with his fingers.

Then there was light; a starstone in Iradahon's hands that had been covered by a pot.

"I did not want anyone to find this cave," said Iradahon, "except my next student."

Wrinn stepped back, and looked about the cave. There were drawings on the rock wall in chalk, a table, a bed.

But then he turned, and saw in the corner, underneath a pair of stalactites, the makings of a grave.

There was no body, nor skeleton, but a white shift that had been cut, spotted with blood. There was a long, curved knife of elven make. And there was, in crude writing, "Innuvi… remembered forever" in chalk near where the relics lay.

"I buried him outside the cave," said Iradahon. "But his clothing and his longknife I wish my student to have. Your quarterstaff is better than his, crafted of red yew from the forests of Doncalion. You shall not have his quarterstaff. It is buried with him, anyway, as is proper.

"We will wash the blood from his shift, and then I will mend it. Only pure and white will you wear. You will find the clothing perfect to leap and spring about, and make the attack, as is fitting for a *dó kentari*. When you return to the Sage, you will be unstoppable."

Wrinn paused and looked at Innuvi's relics, the one he had replaced. He could not help but notice the shift was torn, as if by a sword. "Who killed Innuvi?" Wrinn said.

Iradahon paused, and his visage became grim and dark. "*Narenvi.*"

Chapter Twenty-Six: In Tharvané

Reev had returned from the Lord Calion's house, and he had not recovered.

No, the memory of the troubled wind, the thought of the raging sea, the image of Lord Calion white-haired and terrible-eyed were burned into his mind. He could not forget the night at his house by the sea.

But in the land, in the city and in the forests, there were signs of hope. To Reev's mind, winter had only just begun, but the weather was warming, and during his walks outside the city's borderlines, there were the beginnings of buds on the trees. It was sunnier more often than it was cloudy, and though Danarion could not escape the long nights of the far north, in every other way spring had begun to make itself known. Winter was already gone; spring was already here. And not just the soothsayers and the books of prophecy declared Danarion a place of eternal hope, the weather and nature itself declared it. The Light of Danarion could not be extinguished. The hope of the gods would never fail. Winter was already gone, and spring was already here.

Yet though the gods showed Danarion's eternal hope in nature, not all was well in Lamdar.

Looking outside his bedroom window on the city below, he knew what troubles had already showed themselves. The Six Servants of Seymus had not been seen since autumn, and they would not cease in working evil. Where had they gone off to? And what had happened to Xan?

As the elvenking had asked, Reev had ventured each morning to the Elder Chamber to pray. He was to prepare for the Council of the Last Time, to gain direction for the battle ahead of him.

He did not know how that battle would take place, the battle for the final defeat of Seymus. He did not know how to defeat an immaterial enemy, nor how the gods would tread him under Reev's feet.

But it was his duty; he had been asked. And he had been diligent. He would be diligent today.

~

The Elder Chamber was lonely. It was in a part of the palace that was utterly silent. It was in a part of the palace that was not often used, and that was by design. The Elder Chamber had not been used before. It had been prepared for this time. It had been waiting for this time.

Reev threw open the double doors. He entered. And to his surprise, he was not alone.

Gastreel was kneeling before the seats in his green robe, praying. His black staff, which he said he took from the hands of another wizard, was in his hand. Reev had not seen such mobility in him for a long time, to kneel.

"Reev," said Gastreel. "How good it is to see your face."

"Gastreel," said Reev. "The same. You were praying…"

"Yes, praying," said Gastreel, "for the council approaches, and Wrinn has disappeared. I fear something has happened to him. And he, I thought, would help you. He, I thought, would be with you at the end."

"Don't worry," Reev said, "I know he is all right."

"You know?" Gastreel said. "Who told you?"

Would he also not tell Gastreel what he had witnessed, and who he had seen? Would he not tell Gastreel that the Lady of Danyen had been his guide, that after she had died, he had seen her in visions?

Perhaps, he would not tell. There was another threat, one that not only Reev but Gastreel should be worried over.

"Wrinn is alive," said Reev. "I know it in my heart."

"But something troubles you, Reev," said Gastreel, "I know you well."

"Xan," said Reev, "it's Xan."

"Xan has turned back to darkness," said Gastreel.

"I thought he had been healed," Reev said, "I thought he had been cured... I... I..."

In his spirit he felt that troubled wind, churning up the waters of the Great Sea. It was happening... it was happening again.

~

Where Reev stood in his vision, the winter had not quite ended. The grass was brown and withered, and there were no buds on the trees.

South of him were mountains covered in snow, and beyond the town was a jungle of withered brush and tangled growth, dead in winter.

He was in the town square, then, present yet unseen. Elves were gathered, elves in brown winter cowls and dull clothing.

In the vision he was standing in the crowd, and they were not seeing him. They were staring all ahead, and in the middle of the square was one he knew. It was Ivan Xandrast.

His hair was black and tangled, his eyes cunning and keen. Despite his disheveled appearance, the elves were taken by his dark charisma, and devouring his every word.

"Elves of Tharvané, for millennia you have been ill treated. The elvenking has treated you poorly and with derision. So too have the gods abandoned you, but it is not your fault.

"For you saw it in yourselves to give the gods gifts of what was precious in your mind, gifts of wheat and apples and not of gold. But the gods were haughty; the gods demanded something else.

And it is not your fault. None of it is your fault.

"I bring you good news, elves of Tharvané, for there is a god who hears you. There is a god who wishes to have your worship, and will not betray you. There is a god who will bring vengeance to the elvenking, and him you shall not turn away."

The crowds were enraptured by Xan's speech, overcome by his speaking. But horror was dawning in Reev, horror at what had overcome his old friend. For the words of Ivan Xandrast were not coming from Ivan Xandrast's soul, but were coming from another.

The elven crowds gathered in Tharvané were howling their approval.

"The gods have abandoned you," said Xan, "but it is not your fault. The gods have abandoned you, but there is another you may serve..."

Chapter Twenty-Seven: Good News

It was springtime already in the land of Lamdar. In the fields of Telemon, where Fortunato and Nenré had retreated and were now riding on horse, there were white flowers blooming in the grass.

Nenré and Fortunato had disappeared from the palace together, and she had cast aside all cares of suspicion, all cares of being discovered. And Fortunato wondered why she was so reckless, with her life hanging in the balance.

They had been riding for days, and camping amid the green fields, amid the flowers that were blooming under the sun. More and more sun they saw, and less clouds, as the short winter already gave way to spring, and in the fields, farmers had begun to plow their fields for the spring planting.

"How many winters, and how many springs, have the fields of Telemon seen?" Fortunato said.

"Lamdar is the elves' birthright," said Nenré, "the gods gave it to us. And the gods have given something to me, Fortunato."

"What do you mean?" Fortunato said, and he realized a lump had formed in his throat unbidden, as if he were preparing for some disaster he had expected all along.

"Soon, I will not be able to ride," said Nenré. "Soon, we will not be able to traverse the Fields of Telemon together, love."

"What are you saying?" said Fortunato.

"I shall wear clothes to hide my form," said Nenré. "I shall tell only my closest handmaids the truth. And in the end, I will beg my father's mercy."

What she was telling Fortunato was apparent, but Fortunato did not want to believe it.

"The elvenking stands supreme above the law," said Nenré,

"and the law he can bend or break according to his will. No law is made he cannot abolish. No statute is made he cannot alter.

"Fortunato, I am with child, and whose would it be but yours?"

"You have been taking Grayman's beard," Fortunato said.

She paused, and her blue eyes sparkled with tears. Her lip trembled.

"You have…"

"I told you so," said Nenré, "but it was not true. For it was my desire to bear the child of Fortunato of Ríva. It was my heart's desire."

"Now, we will both be killed," said Fortunato.

"No," said Nenré. "A father loves his daughter. A father would not harm his daughter. A father would not take his daughter's life."

But Fortunato was not sure, and now he was grieved. Fortunato was not certain, and now tears of his own were forming in his eyes, at Nenré's manipulation, at her deceit, at the tragedy that had befallen them both. It was what Nenré wanted, but it was not what he wanted. And how would a half-elven, half-human child fare in the court of the elvenking? With the world come to ruin, and trouble befalling Varda, was now such a time to bring a babe into the world, to nurse at his mother's breast?

"Fortunato," said Nenré, and her watering eyes produced a teardrop, falling down her face. "You seem disappointed."

"If I am disappointed," said Fortunato, "it is because you are bringing a child into the world at a time of such trouble."

"Perhaps," Nenré responded, "he will see the world made new."

~

Reev sat up from his vision, in the Elder Chamber. Gastreel was staring at him.

"The Sage comes to the City of Light," Gastreel said, "*avelairos avelairé, aumioros aumioré.* He shall see visions, and he shall have dreams. It was long foretold. More proof you are the one promised."

"But there were other prophecies," said Reev.

"Yes, there were other prophecies unknown to humans, which the humans arrogantly called lost. But they were not lost. They were preserved in writing. And they will be read at the Council of the Last Time.

"What an honor it is for me to be there. The kings of the elven tribes, or their representatives, will be there. The Dark Elves, ancient foes, were offered an invitation as was required. And so too, with much consternation, were the vampires offered a seat at the council promised. All elves, and their treaty allies, will be present at council. And we shall determine what is required of you, to cast Seymus into unquenchable flame."

But all Reev could think of, now, was Bala.

"Will the Vampire Lords truly come here?" said Reev.

And he felt the troubled wind again, in his heart. He swallowed a scream. He could hear again, the winds whipping up, the churning of the Great Sea.

Chapter Twenty-Eight: The Army Grows

Bala's twelve undead servants, he knew, would do whatever he commanded of them, but in conversation they were quite lacking. He asked them what their names were, and they only looked at him with dull, dead eyes and emitted a low groan. He asked them what they wanted most, and they would only stare at him with a glazed look, mouth agape.

But they followed him, the undead soldiers carrying falchions, and Bala found they were loyal warriors. As he walked down the snowy road, following the wooden markers, they did not complain or grumble, but stood watch over him, surrounding him.

Bala was growing hungry, and though he had walked for a few days, he had not run in to anyone else. He had about eaten all the road-bread that Granny Yaga and her sisters had given him. He would stop at the next town, and ask, pretty please, for a snack.

He had come to realize that this was where his Dada was from — his real Dada, Nocturne, whose blood flowed in his own veins. The vampires lived so far north it was winter all year long, and it made Bala glad he had lived in Galiope with Miss Glenda, where a warm fire was never far away and where he could wander outside in the summer air, comfortably, for months at a time.

But that was behind him, and now he was a necromancer like Gastreel had wanted to be, a mighty mage like he had dreamt of. He had transformed a small battalion of vampire warriors into undead thralls, and had found new friends, though they were friends of little wit or wisdom.

Through the boughs of the black pines, there was smoke arising in a dense mass. In his snowshoes Bala continued treading, imagining just what awaited him. Perhaps, a kindly homesteader would cook him a cherry pie. Perhaps, he'd have a bowl of milk, some sweetbread like Glenda used to make on high holy days. His little tummy grumbled as he imagined what was in store. He licked his lips, envisioning what was to come.

~

There were homes by the shore of a frozen river, built of stone. As soon as Bala appeared, the people began to scream. A vampire man grabbed a scythe from the side of his house and brandished it, then turned whiter — if that were possible — thought better of it and fled. Men, women, children — they fled from the doors of their homes at the sight of Bala and his undead host.

Bala realized something, then — they had left their foodstuffs behind.

~

From the larder of one house, he ate a goose that had been hanging on a line. From the larder of another, he drank a bowl of raw milk and some leftover fish fritters. In another he found a bit of honey candy, but the cherry pie was elusive. Yet he was full and satisfied.

A horn pealed, then a trumpet, then two.

Bala staggered out of one of the house's larders, then into the town square. He'd eaten so much sugar he could feel his heart racing. He was so full he wanted to lie down and sleep. But instead, there were figures appearing through the brush, some on horse and some on foot, all wearing bulky armor and bearing capes and cloaks of crimson.

They ran at him, they galloped at him, and without Bala's command his undead servants lurched into action. They met the horsemen head on and did battle amid growls and low groans. Bala went to their aid, as through the trees more appeared, more on horse and more on foot, a small army of about two hundred — he guessed, sent just to neutralize him.

Like Granny Yaga taught him he called up the magic well within himself and fired beams of necromantic energy — blasts of purple and balls formed of vampiric fire. One by one the horsemen and the men on foot sank to their death, and as they fell, Bala imbued them with animating force and they rose — shriveled and emaciated and turned to living horrors – to fight for their new master.

Within the span of minutes, the two hundred had either fallen or fled, and Bala's army of undead had swelled to one-hundred and forty-five.

One-hundred and forty-five undead, fighting in Bala's name. Or was Granny Yaga right, and was his name Balor after all?

He adjusted the wooden crown they had given him, and mourned the loss of his beloved top hat.

Chapter Twenty-Nine: An Ancient Curse

"Reev," Gastreel said. "Are you all right?"

"Yes," Reev answered, "I am fine. I admit, my visions are troubling me."

"What did the Sibyl say to you?" said Gastreel.

"She said that I was the Sage," Reev replied, "and that a wall of smoke and ruin stands between me and the completion of my quest."

"Smoke and ruin," said Gastreel, "will be defeated. This is my vow to you, young Reev."

~

Reev left the Elder Chamber without delay, waiting fearfully for the moment he'd hear the troubled wind in his mind, and witness in his mind's eye the churning of the Great Sea. But instead, as he ventured through the lonely halls, no visions assailed him, and nothing attacked him. But Gastreel's words reminded him, a wall of smoke and ruin stood between him and the completion of his quest. What could it mean? At the thought, he trembled.

That night the elves in the great hall feasted and ate, drinking wine and eating roast pheasant. The revelrous feasting of his arrival had given way to moderate portions of both drink and food.

He noted, Fortunato and Nenré were gone from their places, and Spyke had a troubled look on his face as he sipped his wine.

Annenwé, the youngest member of the royal family, stepped up on the small stage in the back of the room, up to a lectern lit by starstones.

"By the mountain of Sellendó, I thought and dreamt," she

began. "The dusk, the dawn. Long live Antheleon."

Her bright eyes turned to Reev, and then she slipped off nymph-like into the darkness.

There was light applause.

Dusk… dawn… There had been a Prince of the Dusk. There was the Prince of the Dawn. But what did that mean?

~

For the first time since he had come to Danarion, Reev had drunk more than he ought. He found himself staggering slightly as he stood up from his table, and he thought a walk through the garden would do him well.

He found himself in the cold brisk air, amid the smell of spring. Though the flowers in the fields were blooming, and though there were buds on the trees, the garden had not yet been restored to its glory. The branches of the bushes were bare but for buds, though they had still their characteristic silver color.

"*Eldari,*" the voice was one he knew, and Reev gasped amid the cool air, amid the dark of night. He turned and saw long hair the color of driftwood, a purple vest. He saw two keen silvery eyes and a countenance that had stricken terror in countless rokahn, if the stories Reev had heard were true.

Reev Nax had never been comfortable in the presence of the crown prince, Vélerion Iradahir, and he suspected he never would be as long as he lived.

"*Eldaren,*" said Vélerion. As he walked, he seemed to drift toward Reev rather than to walk, so graceful were his steps. At his side was his *estirion* sword, sheathed in black eelskin. "The name of the Script of Sages, which you destroyed, bears witness to the fact that there were two of you. The first Sage, Antheleon, was of us, an elf, and what followed the Prince of the Dusk was dusk. In dusk we lie, for these thousand years, but a bit of light has always remained.

Now cometh the dawn, the morning that shall never end. They who love the gods shall rejoice; they who hate them, cast down, *abolliu*."

Reev paused, gazing at Vélerion unsure just why he did not trust him. Reev had sensed, at all times, that Vélerion wanted something from Reev he could not bring himself to utter. But what was it, in all that Vélerion wanted? Whatever he wanted, Reev was not inclined to give him.

"Why shall a human bring the dawn," said Vélerion, "when we elves are the Light's firstborn? Why, when we were the ones first fashioned in the primeval forest, and given superior wisdom and intellect and magical aptitude? Why then should Seymus's defeat come from one so lowly… so lowly as you?"

The words, perhaps, were cutting, but Reev found he couldn't care. He did not care what Vélerion thought of him, only felt his sense of discomfort growing, the desire in Vélerion for something Reev could not give becoming more powerful.

"Humans are impetuous and rash," said Vélerion. "The elves, the opposite. Do not the gods love us best? Do not the gods love us, most of all? If not, why not?"

Vélerion was arguing with the wind.

"How good it would be, to take Nagaró and pierce the heart of Seymus," Vélerion said, and as he did, he drew his sword from its eelskin sheath. It shimmered in the light of far-off starstones, blackish-purple with celestial splotches of green and sapphire specks of blue.

"But Seymus will not be cut down with a sword," Reev said. "He will be trodden underfoot."

Vélerion snarled, and sheathed Nagaró. His eyes turned wrathful, and seemed almost murderous. He looked likely to wrest hold of Reev's throat, and squeeze, and not let go. "You think I don't know, *Eldari*, if that in the end is what you are? To the elves were given the prophecies. It was the elves that uttered those words. Why then shall the defeat of Seymus come by one unworthy, a human?"

"I am sorry it upsets you so," Reev said. "The gods' words will not be changed. It is what they want."

At Reev's declaration, the wrath in Vélerion's eyes seemed met with a wall of truth it could not penetrate. And Vélerion seemed to shrink inwardly, the fire in his eyes dull to colorless black. And he stalked off in the night.

In the cool of the night a wind was blowing. Yet that wind was not troubled. Reev could not hear, alone in the garden, the churning of the Great Sea. But he felt a vision falling on him anew.

~

He was standing unseen in the midst of the throne room of a great palace. In the certainty of dreaming he knew he was in the throne room of the castle of the Drazzandori, the King of the Vampires.

The Drazzandori was seated in his vision on a stone throne, garbed in a lurid red robe painted with skulls and crying faces. He had a head of long black hair, and on that hair was a gold crown, with emeralds and rubies cut into the shape of skulls. In his hand, ready to dispense royal justice, was an *estirion* sword, Lifedrinker, colored dark gray with a skull hilt.

The doors to the throne room opened, and in walked a Lamen elf garbed in gold and green, with hair of blond and eyes of blue, the messenger that the elvenking had sent.

The Drazzandori arose, hands at the ready to cut him down and drink his blood, but he stayed that hand, even as crimson-garbed guards stepped forth.

"Your Eminence," said the messenger, "I come to announce the Council of the Last Time, the time of measuring up and falling short, the time of sifting. Drazzandori, you were cursed long ago with the thirst of blood, for your conduct in the First Shadow War.

But you have a chance to right those wrongs, and wage war against the cause of your ills, the one you served in that dark era, all that time ago.

"However, because your crimes and conduct were so egregious in that time, long ago, if you deign to send an emissary and do not attend yourself, you will not be counted a participant, and your aid will not be accepted in the coming war. Nonetheless, you are invited, and in the summer of this year, on the twenty-fourth day of the month of Vlesti, the Council of the Last Time will begin, and if you yourself come, you will be welcome.

"So says the King of the Elves. So declares the Sage."

The Drazzandori stood up in a rage; he bared his fangs, and his canines, agitated, began to enlarge. And the crimson-garbed soldiers beside him rushed forth, and seized the brave Lamen messenger with their meaty fists.

Yet the Drazzandori froze, and did not assault him. The animalistic hunger in his dark eyes began to wane. He hesitated. His white lips turned pale. He said, "Cast him out of the palace. Do not harm him. Do not drink his blood."

~

Reev was back in the garden. Another wind blew. It was not troubled. Another sound he heard, a strange music. And another vision was upon him.

~

Another messenger was in the Drazzandori's throne room, a vampire with panic in his eyes. "Your Majesty!" he cried. "The necromancer has stricken down the thousands you have sent. His army has doubled… he is unstoppable."

Reev saw, then, from the corners of the room, a woman

approach with pale skin and dark hair, stunningly beautiful. Her beautiful was like that of a jungle cat, the beauty of a predator.

"Zarial," she said to the Drazzandori, "do you not see all these disasters as a whole? Do you not see the bigger picture? The gods at long last are sending their wrath on us. The Child of Varda's End has come.

"And shall we not do our best for our people? Shall we not throw ourselves at the gods' mercy? Shall you and I not risk all death and all the elements, to participate in the Council of the Last Time? Shall we not risk life and limb, and participate in the Council of the Last Time, and end our people's curse?'

Chapter Thirty:
To the North

The weather in the forest was warming, but the rain had not ceased. The rain falling on Wrinn's skin, misting droplets of unfathomable number, were constant, and stinging. Iradahon's training in the Forest of Daron Hen was almost turning to indoctrination to Wrinn's mind, his constant inveighing against Narenvi the forest's enemy, and against all who usurped legitimate power.

The trees' constant whispering, though, was turning to mad fear, to warnings for Wrinn to stop traveling so boldly. And Wrinn sensed, though they had come to a part of the world that since ancient times had been uninhabited, they were not alone.

Why were they not alone? It was the sense of the trees, it was the memory of the rokahn, though now they were hundreds of miles from where he had seen those rokahn. Why were they not alone? It was because of who had killed Iradahon's first apprentice, the apprentice whose loose white shift Wrinn wore. Narenvi had killed the one whose clothing Wrinn had taken, whose longknife was now at Wrinn's side.

"Who is Narenvi?" Wrinn said amid the giant spruces and hemlocks, the brilliant green moss, the constant rain which had bothered Wrinn but which now Wrinn had resigned himself to.

"Hush," said Iradahon, lion-maned Iradahon. "Do not say his name again. Do not say his name, ever."

"That is not his true name," said the voice of a wise old spruce.

"That is not the name he used," said the voice of a stand of hemlocks, a hundred, a thousand as one voice, *"when he walked in this forest, so long ago."*

Yet Wrinn would not press, and he would not ask his teacher

anymore. He would not try his teacher's patience, who had taught him the best of techniques with his quarterstaff, who had given him this shift and taught him to leap and to spring about, to strike and to cut and to batter, to vault from place to place, to escape to live another day. He was a *dó kentari*, practitioner of the Way of the Staff, and Wrinn would learn at his feet.

The brush was growing thick, and Wrinn had a sense it was spring. Yet Wrinn also felt, so far north, with the constant rain and occasional fog, that it would never get quite hot in the Forest of Daron Hen, even at the height of the summer.

And he uttered a prayer for Reev, surely worried for him, that Reev would know he was alive and at work, becoming better and better, a living weapon against Seymus and his servants in the mortal world, and that if the gods saw fit to return him to Reev alive, he would be a better *adari* than he had ever been before.

Iradahon froze in the forest's gloom. He turned, and for the first time since Wrinn met Iradahon, Wrinn saw fear in his eyes. He had turned a shade of white. He signaled with his hands and ducked under the brush. Wrinn followed, a moment later.

There was a snarl. As a shaft of light pierced through a cloud, illuminating the moss-draped branches of a spruce, a face appeared through the gloom.

Mottled and purple it was, with yellow eyes of a reptilian gleam, and two large horns emerging from a slimy face. A rokahn was standing just yards away, having heard something, having heard them. His eyes were straining, searching. At his side was a bulky sword. Even from where Wrinn hid, amid the brush and moss, he could smell a foul stench.

He was searching for something, smelling in the wind. Another soon appeared behind him, half his height and less than half his girth, scrawny, with veinous skin the color of blood and two nubby horns, a toltar. He held a small spear in his hand.

They began to grumble in their guttural language as they searched with their eyes. They took a step forward and Wrinn and Iradahon sank deeper into the brush.

More guttural utterances escaped their lips. Then they turned and disappeared into the forest's gloom.

Wrinn waited, then waited some more. When he had waited twice as long as he thought he ought, he began to stand up, but Iradahon placed a firm hand on his shoulder and sat him down. "*Stay still*," Iradahon whispered, so soft that Wrinn could barely hear.

When they had waited ten times as long as Wrinn thought they ought, Iradahon himself stood up and clawed his way free through the brush. Wrinn followed right behind him.

"You were right," Iradahon said. "Rokahn here, in the sacred wood. They have never been so bold before. They are searching for elves… I wonder what they meant, when they said to bring back any elf to the master."

"You can understand the rokahn tongue?" Wrinn said.

Iradahon's blue eyes fixed on Wrinn. "I can," he said, "for in my former days, I was a warrior in the southern marches, fighting for the king. I dishonored my hand by wielding a steel blade. One night I lost the steel blade, and a rokahn attacked me. A tree-branch saved my life, and then, my honor."

The religious devotion to a lifeless implement was something Wrinn thought he'd never understand.

Yet Iradahon seemed shaken, and he was silent amid the forest's gloom, as the constant rain was turning to a mist.

"What else did they say?" said Wrinn.

"They are hunting for elves," said Iradahon, "and why?"

"*North,*" said the voice of a wise old spruce.

"*North,*" cried the childlike voice of saplings just feet away.

"*North lies Narenvi,*" protested the voice of an ancient hemlock.

"They are coming from the north," said Wrinn, "shall we investigate?"

"Yes, yes," said Iradahon, "we shall investigate. You say they are coming from the north. You are a treespeaker. You are possessed of greater knowledge than I.

"And your training will soon be complete. You are of better character than Innuvi. Narenvi has no claim on you." Iradahon, in the cloudy light, had the look of a lion with his golden mane of hair. "Northwards we go, and we shall investigate. We will uncover whatever evil ails this forest."

"Then, will we tell the king?" Wrinn said.

Iradahon fixed his blue eyes on Wrinn, and something seemed to hover on his lips, ready to escape. But he was silent, and then began to make his way north. Northwards they would go, and they would investigate. When the truth was uncovered, Wrinn's training would be complete. He would go back to where he belonged, to the City of Light. For they were going far, to a place where the elvenking had no jurisdiction. They were going far, to the edge of the world, where no one could help them if they fell into distress.

Chapter Thirty-One: Sooth

"What shall we name our child?" said Nenré, far too loud for Fortunato's liking, as they walked together through the streets of Danarion.

The sun was shining, the weather was already warm, and the trees' green leaves had emerged, though it was only halfway through Primrane, or the month of Sindjé by elven reckoning.

For Fortunato's part, they were doing quite a lot he didn't like, and he thought Nenré was doing too little to hide the changes of her body. He didn't like openly walking in the daylight, alone together, or their journeys alone that Nenré insisted on. At first, he thought the elven court was tacitly accepting of their courtship. Over time, he realized that the thought that Nenré and Fortunato were courting was so unthinkable, such a grave crime, that it was considered impossible.

Yet Nenré was insistent, she would tell her father when she could no longer hide the development of her form. Her father loved her deeply and would not bring harm to her. Her father was not just the enforcer of the law; he was the law. There was no statute he could not overturn, nothing he could not overrule. His power over his people was supreme and unquestioned.

"What shall we name our child?" Fortunato said. "I hadn't thought about it. I'm only thinking of surviving."

"Surviving," Nenré huffed, in the sunlight, as they passed by a stand of rose bushes that were beginning to blossom. Her emotions had become a tempest in recent weeks, and little things said would upset her, words that Fortunato said unthinkingly would send her into a tailspin. To that was added a ravenous appetite, and though she had changed, no elves questioned it, so unthinkable was it that

Fortunato and Nenré were more than fellow fighters.

In the end, Nenré couldn't bring herself to even tell her handmaids. When would she have the courage to tell her father?

They would never wed, for it was against the law for an elf and a human to marry. And Fortunato's fear was growing amid he and Nenré's hot passions, and it was beginning to overwhelm the love he had for her. They were undertaking their secret rendezvous less and less, as it dawned more on more on Fortunato, and now on Nenré, the gravity of what they had done, and the gravity of what Nenré, whose blood was unblemished for generations stretching back to the creation of Varda, had engineered.

What shall we name our child? Fortunato scoffed silently. There were far greater things on his mind, now. Would he and Nenré, and the child growing inside her, even survive the Council of the Last Time?

He could do nothing, now. Nenré would give birth, or she would die. Fortunato could die with her. He had pursued her in the Forests of Alonar, and she had pursued him when he had arrived in this blessed land. Perhaps, their love had been inevitable. Perhaps, it would be tragic. But the deed was done, and it could not be reversed. Yanenré of the House of Iradahir had joined herself with the family of Petro of Ríva, as common as an Imperial family as you could find.

"Where are you taking us?" Fortunato said, as he realized he did not recognize the rabbit's warren of streets in this part of Luaddon.

Yanenré pressed ahead, apparently insulted by something Fortunato had said, again. And he would not bother to try to make things better. Tomorrow, she would act entirely differently, and something new he said she would take to heart, and despair.

They were at the gates of Pelladdon, which no elf could enter without a *laeras*, an offering and a ritual bath, and which no human elf-friend could enter without the same, and a ritual of purification. There, beside the gates of Pelladdon, was an elven woman by a table, beside her a jar full of coins.

"Sybé," said Nenré, "the best seer in all Danarion. The gods speak to her, and she tells the truth."

Fortunato wanted to flee, amazed that the elves thought such a crime was unthinkable, they said and did nothing when Fortunato and Nenré were constantly alone together.

He wanted to pull Nenré away as she sat down before the seer and dropped two silver coins in her jar.

"What do you wish to see, daughter of Danthemari?" said the seer.

"I wish to see," said Nenré, "if the gods allow, will a boy or a girl be born to me?"

"I see," said the seer, and a wind began to blow as her voice began her utterances, "war standards colored red and gold, amid a burning city. I see disaster that you have brought to the City of Light.

"I see untold thousands perishing. I see smoke. I see ruin.

"A male child grows inside you, daughter of Danthemari. A monster lies in wait, wishing to eat it as soon as it is born."

Nenré fell back from her seat and screamed, staggering backward. Fortunato caught her as she fainted, and held her up with a firm hand.

War standards… red and gold. The Empire had a policy of leaving the elves alone, out of respect for what they called the Elders. That wouldn't change, Fortunato had thought.

A male child… and a monster wishing it harm. What lengths would Nenré go to protect her child? She would sacrifice her life, itself.

Chapter Thirty-Two: Grim Tidings

Primrane, and in Galiope and Gallia at large, Reev knew they had a month of snow and harsh weather, as much as two if they were unlucky. But below Reev's private chamber, a drop of many fathoms, the garden was in full bloom, and in the streets, the smell of roses was in the air. The sun baked with a gentle heat, and all thought of winter was over, winter brief but beautiful, dark but not without its light.

Reev was glad to be in this blessed land, but over all was the sense that he would not be here long. Where would he go, and where would he travel, to tread Seymus under his feet? How would he fulfill the prophecies? Where would he go?

And where was Wrinn? He would trust the gods… Wrinn was alive when Amané had appeared to him in visions. Wrinn was capable, and the gods loved him.

The gods loved Wrinn… and they loved Gastreel.

Gastreel was at his door.

The Green Wizard, garbed in a green robe and carrying the black staff he had taken from a Red Robes wizard, looked smaller perhaps, slighter… weaker. But in his eyes was a blazing fire, and his spirit seemed stronger than ever. The fact he would not depart with Reev caused mixed feelings in him, for whatever travail lay ahead would be made easier with him, but Gastreel had lived a long and good life — and he needed his rest.

"Reev," he said, "come with me to the Elder Chamber. We have a surprise guest."

~

In the Elder Chamber, the elvenking stood beside an elven man of long silver hair. His skin, too, seemed silverish in the light. His eyes were gray.

"Sage," said the elvenking, "this is Hirvo of Non. He has brought the lost prophecies posthaste as we make our preparations."

Only then did Reev realize the gray elf was holding something, a pile of papers, that though yellowed with time, were untouched and immaculately cared for.

"For all time, the location was known to two people, the Watcher of the Tower of Arbonnon, and the elvenking regnant," the elvenking continued. "If anyone else was told, both speaker and listener would be killed, and another would take their place. Such a law, even the kings of the elves were subject to, for the first Sage Antheleon had said, the law could be revoked by no one."

Reev wondered at Hirvo's majesty, the gray elf from the Land of Non. He eyed the papers.

"What do you wish of me?" Reev said.

"As we prepare to make our moves," said Hirvo, "as we ready our decision at the Council of the Last Time, we wish to enter in with all the knowledge and insights we can. For elves and humans were separate for these more than thousand years during the Time of Mankind, and knowledges diverged, and memories were separated and lost. Perhaps, some things, a human would know and an elf would not. For some things elves know, which humans are ignorant of."

Hirvo eyed the papers he held.

" *Darkness was from whence he came, and darkness is where he will go. In Shadow he was born, raised by ghosts and a spirit.'* " Hirvo eyed Reev after he had quoted the topmost paper.

"A prophecy of the Dark One's Hand," Reev said.

"So, it seems," said Hirvo. "But you knew neither father nor mother."

Could such a dark prophecy speak of someone whose fate was good?

Hirvo flipped the page.

" *'In the twilight the House of the Serpent gains sudden strength. Sudden speed is given to it, and it speeds to the ruin that was pronounced to it.'* "

Reev stared blankly ahead.

"Any insights, Gastreel?" said Hirvo.

"The Sage will be a Telantine, the Dark One's Hand of the House of a Serpent," Gastreel said. "But what the House of a Serpent is, and who the Telantines truly were, is beyond the knowledge of wizardry."

Hirvo frowned, seemingly disappointed. He turned the page.

" *'To darkness he speeds as the dawn approaches, light, glorious light unending. Darkness falls and he is overcome, but of strength he has little. Strength will be given to him.'* "

Both Reev and Gastreel stared blankly ahead.

"We had hoped you would know more," said the elvenking. "Our scholars and priests are poring through this hidden knowledge. Some prophecies we will not unveil until the gathered parties arrive at the Council of the Last Time, and the final coalition is formed, the final coalition against the Dark One and his servants."

"I will ponder," Gastreel said, "I will think and ruminate. Reev, you shall ponder as well. I am sorry I do not know."

"Do not be sorry," said the elvenking. "We know, it will all be made clear to us, someday."

"Clarity," Gastreel said softly. "We shall not leave until we are armed with knowledge."

"You shall not leave with the Sage, anyhow," said the elvenking.

"Yes, yes," Gastreel said, and eyed Reev. "You are correct. But he shall be in good hands."

The festivals in Danarion were unending, and so many feast days occurred Reev wondered when the peasants in the villages abroad could ever afford to work. Yet in the markets there was always food, and in the palace an endless number of recipes ready to be made. No elf seemed to lack anything, even as reports of trouble began to swirl.

When Reev walked the streets of Danarion, people spoke of a rebellion in the land of Tharvané and its capital, Harkon. Reev could not forget the leader of Tharvané, Lord Albenhas, and his fiery clash with the elvenking, nor could he forget the vision of Reev's friend Xan turned to darkness and leading the bitter Tharvanians astray.

Reev had not disclosed the vision to anyone. Something in his heart seemed to prevent him from speaking it aloud, or telling anyone of the visions and dreams he had witnessed.

Reev knew the Six Servants of Seymus were loose in the Elf Lands, and they neither slept nor ate, never resting in their desire of the ruination of the elven people and in their desire to harm Reev. Where had they gone? It was a mystery, and the fact that it was a mystery was enough to cause panic.

Tharvané was in rebellion, or lurching toward it, and Reev did not know what that meant. Tharvané and Lamdar had ever been at odds. Now, it seemed, the consummation of the hostility was at last here, stirred by the Six Servants of Seymus and their newfound ally, Xan.

Part of Reev wished to confront Xan here and now, but again something stopped him, something inexplicable prevented him from making his move.

"Tharvané tona luné, xanoren xanen," Reev said under his breath, as he found the market he was looking for, and purchased for himself a bottle of new wine.

~

Days passed by in the spring light, and the news of the rebellion in Tharvané was only growing. The elvenking was monitoring the rebellion from afar, and strengthening the number of his troops, but he refused to invade.

Rumors swirled about, that the rebellion was not just against the king but against something far higher. And by the time the month of Sindjé passed into Sorjé, and the gentle warmth had become heat, messengers said that Lord Albenhas had closed the borderland roads of Tharvané altogether, and no one was allowed to enter or leave.

All Reev had, then, were his visions of Xan leading the people of Tharvané into darkness, and memories of what the Sibyl had told him, that a wall of smoke and ruin stood between him and the completion of his quest.

Chapter Thirty-Three: Abon Bet Belas

Spyke had learned quite a bit, but not enough.

And as the city warmed, and summerlike heat had returned to Danarion, he vowed he would not stop until all the truth was known.

The Sixth Anthanian Legion, considered cursed, had been disbanded for almost a thousand years. Now, in this modern age, the memory of it was returning, by way of visions in the elven city of Danarion.

But here, there were few ways to uncover the truth.

So Spyke was, instead, pacing in the grounds outside the palace, wondering how he could uncover just how to learn what he did not know, without the help of a nation who now was turning the investigation back on him.

They now wanted to know about his friend Fortunato of Ríva, who had led the Gallian armies against the Empire. They now wanted to bring him to trial, and bring him a swift sentence of death.

But Spyke would have no part in betraying his friend. Spyke would not tell his superiors in the Imperial Army what they wanted to know. For Spyke too had fought for the Gallian army, on behalf of Reev Nax. He had fought for a higher cause than the Empire. And now that higher cause had brought him to this foreign place, to the land of the elves, called Elders by his fellow Imperials.

Knowledge would have to come from elsewhere. But where would he begin?

In the Empire, the Conciliar Library was considered the largest library in the ecumene. Any book of note throughout the ages, and many books of little note, were found there. For every nation in the

Empire's knowledge, every important book of theirs was copied, and to that was added a record of all the deliberations of the Imperial Council, for all of the Imperial Council's history.

Yet the elves were possessed of libraries of their own, and though the records of other nations were not as much of interest to them, the books they possessed had been acquired for all their history, a history much longer than the Empire. From the earliest years of the elves, far earlier than what they termed the human era, until now, the knowledge of the ages was stirred up. Could something of the Sixth Anthanian legion, far away, be stored in one of those ancient repositories?

Spyke knew only a little Elvish. But most learned elves, when they learned a human language, learned the Imperial tongue.

~

Spyke did not quite know where to begin, and when he asked the steward where the library was in Danarion, the steward asked, "Which one?"

The steward's long brown hair, his green eyes, sparkled in the light of the starstones beyond the palace vestibule.

"The one, most active, in the 3rd century Y.E.," Spyke said.

By dark roads they traveled, and the area they traversed was growing more and more roughshod and dilapidated, until they reached a wall, and through the wall a gate. They were in the far northeastern part of the city, not far from Amanddon. And amid the ramshackle homes and lean-tos, there was a bit of grandeur — a large building shaped like a basilica with a faded dome, and two great doors, and guards posted at them.

"Here," said the steward, "the library most active near the start of the Time of Mankind. Tell the librarian I give you access to all documents, on behalf of His Majesty the king."

With the aid of the librarian, Spyke made note of the books and parchment scrolls on the library shelves, and what amazed him was not so much the content of the books, but the breadth of the subject matter. They recorded what to Spyke's mind was banal, the weather on certain holidays and minor eclipses of the moon, whether the harvest on a certain year was good or bad, even the time that the leaves in the city changed color. To Spyke the elves seemed insular, not caring about what happened outside their borders, considering such thoughts beneath them — living, as they were, in such a blessed place. The third century by human reckoning seemed an uneventful time in the history of the elves, but with the librarian's aid, he found something.

In the basement of the library, three levels below the ground, was a record marked "Disturbances in the year 527."

Spyke stood in the dim light of starstones as the librarian read the work aloud.

"The text reads, 'The harvest was poor in the year 527 of the Time of Humanity. The Sibyl reported a sacrilege taking place, but the priests made offerings, and seers were inquired of, and nothing that the people did was reported to have displeased the gods. There was an outbreak of illness among the children of Danarion, and offerings were made to the poor. Toward the end of the year 527, red skies were seen. More offerings were made and the king was ritually cleansed. The Sibyl said she is fearful.'"

It was baffling to know, and even more difficult to understand. Perhaps, it meant nothing. But Spyke wondered.

The year 527 according to the elves was the year 211 according to humans, and Spyke knew that the Sixth Anthanian Legion was disbanded at the end of that century.

"There is something written in the margins," said the librarian. "It says, *Abon Bet Belas*, 'the Omen that Desolates.' "

It was something… but it could be nothing.

It was something, and strange things were reported in that century, according to the elves.

Could the two be connected, the Sixth Anthanian Legion's crimes and the scattered reports in the elven kingdoms, thousands of miles away?

It was an affront to the skeptical man. But to the one who took heed of omens and signs, it was something to remember.

Omens.

"What is 'the Omen that Desolates?' " Spyke said.

"You will have to do more research," said the librarian.

Chapter Thirty-Four: A Great War

Feast-days came and feast-days went. The Council of the Last Time was more than a discussion of strategy, it was a final determination of the coalition against Seymus, of who would battle the Dark One and who would serve him.

To Gastreel's mind, who fought who was of less significance than the method of Seymus's defeat, but to the elves, the question of who would fight alongside them was most significant.

The elven tribes had been invited: the vampires, whom obligation demanded an invitation but whom the elvenking already treated as de facto rejects… the Lord of Non, who had already sent emissaries ahead of his arrival… the Umen or Forest Elves, who lived in the rainforests west across the sea… and the Lonen or Dark Elves, who heeded no god and proclaimed ironically the Lady Nihil, or Nothing. The Kahren, or Plains Elves, were considered protectors of the borderlands and so their participation was already affirmed.

Others were invited, too. For in ancient days, before the Empire was in existence, there was a tribe of humans bound in allegiance to the elves. They lived in the far inestimable east of the world, near the Dweorg. In fact, they were allies with the Dweorg, too, and traded with them often. So far were they from other human kingdoms, they had lost contact. But now they would be brought near, if they ever arrived.

Gastreel was performing his breathing exercises in his private room, and though he was not in as dire a state as he had been, he had reached a plateau far lower than his prior height. He would never run as swiftly, or strike with his sword as strongly, as he had before.

Yet his powers of magic remained strong, and while his body was weaker, he felt his mind was sharper, and he possessed boundless mental energy. Whether such energy would ever be used again was in doubt, but he was in agreement with the king's request that he stay behind. His pupil had been affirmed by the Sibyl to be the Sage, and Gastreel had raised him, kept him out of danger, and delivered him to the Elf Lands. His task was done.

Reev would venture — where? He would crush Seymus and his followers underfoot — how? That was now out of Gastreel's purview. No longer the pupil he was, but the Sage full and true. Now was the final battle. Now was the last conflict. Now no longer the student Reev Nax was, but the fighter.

What now? Gastreel did not know. He was with the elves, and with the elves he would remain.

The door to his room opened, and a familiar face stood there, one who filled his heart with inestimable love, one closer to him than a brother.

Fortunato of Ríva was not smiling. Something seemed to be on his mind, and whether Gastreel could draw it out of him was unclear. For Fortunato was not one to be manipulated, not by anyone.

"Fortunato," Gastreel said, "heart of my heart, sword to my spell. Welcome."

He strode into the room without speaking any more, a certain sign he was upset. But Gastreel would not pry. He knew all too well it was a futile endeavor, if there was something Fortunato was truly against.

"Green Wizard," Fortunato said, "when will the dawn arrive? And who will bring it? And who brought the night?"

Gastreel wondered what Fortunato truly wished to speak of, for it was clear something else plagued him. But an opportunity for education was something Gastreel never let slip by him, an opportunity to instill in a great warrior something other than skill with the sword, for perhaps in the war ahead, knowledge would inform Fortunato's moves.

"Who brings the dawn?" said Gastreel. "The gods. Who brought the night? I do not know. But it is not night we lie in, but dusk… the first Sage, Antheleon, struck Seymus a mortal blow."

"Not night you lie in," said Fortunato, "but perhaps, I do."

Now Fortunato was attempting to manipulate Gastreel. Gastreel knew him all too well. He wished Gastreel to ask what bothered him, and Fortunato sought an opportunity to lash out, and to lay him low.

"A war lies ahead," Gastreel said, ignoring Fortunato's words, "a great war that will consume the world. The Shadow has fallen, and the elves will not escape the trouble ahead. Crises will mount, and woe betide those who refuse to fight."

"What of Gallia?" said Fortunato. "What will befall our friends?"

Our friends… Fortunato wished to know what had happened to Ambrass, but Gastreel did not know. He still thought of her, the one he loved most.

Gastreel knew all too well of Nenré and Fortunato's rendezvous. Though Gastreel had tried to thwart the elvenking, the elvenking had already begun an investigation of what was considered unspeakable, unthinkable. The idea that an elven princess would have relations with a human would have been preposterous, but Fortunato's charisma was great, and he was held in such high esteem by the elves, there was enough to room to doubt.

"I don't know what happened to Ambrass, Fortunato," said Gastreel.

"Don't speak of her," Fortunato snarled. "That story is no more."

"Is it?" Gastreel questioned.

Fortunato's eyes turned to the window outside, to the warm

springtime. What had stirred him to speak? What caused his pain? What was getting to him? Gastreel had a thought, but that thought would lead to the deaths of Nenré and Fortunato and another. He prayed that such a thought was untrue, that Fortunato was not so reckless. But courage and recklessness was a fine line, and in some there was both.

"Ambrass," Fortunato said softly, and the pain in his eyes seemed to dim, the stress that was eating him seemed to fade away. "Is she where the Shadow has fallen?"

"Only in Lamdar has the light remained," said Gastreel. "Only here, seers say, will the Shadow never fall."

"My mother, my father," Fortunato said. "Alessa and Petro… the Shadow will fall over them. It's not fair."

"But you have a task," said Gastreel. "To bring the light wherever you tread. And you will go where I do not, to accompany Reev to Seymus's final defeat. An honor for Alessa and Petro."

"Do not speak of them, either," Fortunato said.

Here he was, a battle of wills. He wished Gastreel to ask what was truly upsetting him. He wished to lash out, and lay Gastreel low. But Gastreel was not one to be manipulated, either.

There was silence a little while. Then Fortunato spoke.

"My mother said I was a Telantine."

Gastreel looked at Fortunato in wonder. He questioned why, in all this time, Fortunato had not told him.

"I did not know that," said Gastreel. "So you are of the same blood as Reev, at least in part. Yet the elves, the wizards, they know nothing of Telantis."

"Do you believe it?" Fortunato said. "Do you believe I am a Telantine?"

"Mothers often know best," Gastreel said. "The Sage shall be a Telantine. But perhaps, he is not the only Telantine."

"Where was Telantis?" said Fortunato. "A forgotten kingdom, wiped away in one cataclysmic moment. Yet some of them remain."

"Some," Gastreel said. "Many, it seems."

"I am a Telantine," Fortunato said. "My mother was a Telantine, too."

"How fitting," Gastreel said, "for a friend of the Sage."

The fiery storm was quieted, and Fortunato ceased his struggle for the verbal lash.

~

As the heat built, and winter was a memory, and the feast days continued unabated, Gastreel continued to try his best to recover his strength. The Chief Healer's visits were becoming less and less frequent, and the visits to the Elder Chamber were becoming more so.

One day when Gastreel was in the garden, with Maderias in hand, he was slicing and stabbing the air with weak strokes. It was then the elvenking made his presence known.

"Gastreel," he said, "I think it best if you not try to recover your strength. It will not return to you."

"Is that why you have come here?" Gastreel said.

The elvenking shook his head. "No," he said. "The Sage arrives, with him other humans. Two elf-friends, but not all of you are elf-friends."

He spoke of Spyke, the participant in the Pan-Vardic Games that Gastreel hardly knew.

"The one of you who is neither a *dra'datsi* or an elf-friend has been making a stir in the palace of late," the elvenking said.

"Really?" Gastreel said, and he continued to thrust at the air despite the elvenking's presence, he who would demand all other elves bow and shudder at his appearance.

"He has been inquiring of *Abon Bet Belas*, of 'the Omen that Desolates.' "

At the elvenking's words, Gastreel sheathed his sword and

gazed into the elvenking's eyes, at last giving him the deference that was due him.

"A demon of the ancient world, thought forgotten," said the elvenking. "A foe of the ancient elves when they were at the height of their strength, a memory now or so we had thought, before Spyke brought him to our attention again. Why he inquires he will not say, but the name being mentioned again has brought to us alarm, and at such a time as this."

"Why does it alarm you?" Gastreel said.

"A dread foe," the elvenking said, "we cannot vanquish at our current strength."

"Never say you cannot," Gastreel said. "You have the Sage, now."

"And we have the Green Wizard," said the elvenking.

"At your service," Gastreel said, "always."

Chapter Thirty-Five: Words

Nenré had gone to the tailor and fashioned new robes and dresses to hide her growing form. Still, she refused to tell her father.

She said her father were forgive her, but her actions said he would not.

And Fortunato was afraid. He did not want to die. He did not want the child to die, either.

He had strategized with her, he had given her his best counsel, and he had given her his all. But what happened to him, and to her, and to their son — if the seer was to be believed — was not up to him.

For the first time in many weeks, Fortunato and Nenré were apart. In the springtime, building toward summer, as he made his way through the palace, he realized he did not like being apart from her, after all. Perhaps, he really did love her most of all.

But one he remembered with flowing dark hair, eyes bright, lips lush. One he remembered, whom he could not find in the streets of Galiope, one he wondered if his heart belonged to.

He would not speak her name in the Elf Lands. He would try not to think of her.

Now was not for her. Now was not for Nenré either. As twilight turned to night, and he wished to escape the palace's heat, he found himself amid the garden in the coolness of the air, and he thought of what mattered — the dawn, the coming war.

~

The bushes of the garden appeared to be made of silver, and the only sign they were not the work of some divine metalsmith were the juicy — though inedible — berries that grew in their branches. The waxy leaves glittered in the moonlight, and as a crescent moon arose in the skies above, Fortunato realized he was not alone.

The cause of his troubles and his high honors was before him, the boy turned young man, Reev Nax.

The amulet, fixed with a coin of both their homelands, was around his neck. He was still wearing the blue tunic that the elves had made for him.

"Fortunato," he said. "I can't think of the last time we were alone."

Fortunato didn't remember, either. But they were alone, amid the splendid bushes, the metallic silver garden — or so it appeared — the leaves that gave the appearance of winter and Yule even in late spring.

"Nor can I, Reev," Fortunato said. "But here we are, in the garden, alone."

"And what is next for us?" Reev said.

Fortunato looked beyond Reev. "First came the Prince of the Dusk, and after him came night… the dawn shall not come easy."

"But it shall come," said Reev.

There was silence a little while, and Fortunato wondered if Reev wanted something. Then he spoke.

"The Prince of the Dusk… the Prince of the Dawn… there is so much I don't understand," Reev said.

"When we leave, we'll have a better idea."

"I don't want to leave."

"Who would want to leave this place?" Fortunato said. "I think, however, you had best get to bed. You are not a boy, anymore, but you're young. You have a big task ahead of you."

"Yes," Reev said, "I suppose you're right." And he walked away, disappearing into the darkness.

~

For a while, Fortunato was alone, and he was thankful for the solitude. He thought of Nenré, and of their son. He prayed silently that the child would survive, whether or not he and Nenré lived.

And something stirred, the silvery leaves rustling, too harshly to be wind. Through the garden appeared one Fortunato had found he had never liked, one with whom he had always felt at odds.

It was Vélerion, the Crown Prince. His long hair was the color of driftwood. The sword he bore, Nagaró, was of *estirion*, as valuable as many kingdoms. Fortunato felt a stirring of envy at the blade, and fought against it.

"Was the Sage just here?" Vélerion said. "Have you seen him?"

"Why do you ask?" Fortunato said.

"He has something of mine," Vélerion answered. And Vélerion turned his bright yet dark eyes to Fortunato. "Why are you in the garden at this hour?"

"The same of you, I could ask," Fortunato said.

"Where is my sister?" Vélerion said. "She is always with you, or so it seems."

"Apparently not," Fortunato said.

And Vélerion stalked off, in pursuit of Reev perhaps.

Fortunato thought of following him for Reev's sake, and making certain no harm would come to him, but why would Vélerion the Crown Prince bring harm to the Sage? How could any member of the elvenking's family bring harm to Reev?

Chapter Thirty-Six:
Two of Light

Where were the rokahn coming from? Wrinn only knew, they were everywhere.

In a part of the forest that hardly any elf ever visited, in a part of the world that — Wrinn guessed — no one had lived before now, rokahn wandered under the hemlocks and spruces in their multitudes. Wrinn and Iradahon had taken care to hide themselves as they conducted their investigation, as they tried to uncover what had happened, and what nefarious task the rokahn were engaged in.

Several times, Wrinn and Iradahon had witnessed rokahn warbands transporting elven captives to parts unknown. Other times, they had witnessed rokahn sawing down trees, or fashioning swords and axes in newfound forges. And Wrinn had at last remembered the source of the name he remembered, Lothan, the enemy that had almost destroyed Gallia, whose Forge Fortunato had destroyed years ago. Could Lothan again be at work? Was it possible?

Fortunato had not slain Lothan; he had slain the Fell Smith. And now Lothan's name was mentioned again, in utterances by the rokahn.

Crouched in the brush, ears listening for rokahn, waiting beside Iradahon for his next instruction, Wrinn uttered prayers under his breath for success and quick feet. Unlike Iradahon, Wrinn did not know the rokahn's harsh, guttural tongue, only heard how perverse it sounded as it was spoken. Iradahon's knowledge of it had been invaluable. They knew the trees were right, that the rokahn had come from the north. They knew the master the rokahn spoke of was the one called Lothan.

"I hear… I smell…" Iradahon began to fall back.

And a desperate voice wailed in Wrinn's mind, *"Rescue us, Son of the Forest!"*

Another voice said, *"I am dying!"*

Said an ancient spruce, *"We have no arms or legs, no axes! You must defend us from this impending death!"*

And something was on the wind, Wrinn smelled, something he thought he knew. The smell awakened a memory he could not place. He knew the smell on the wind, but he didn't know what it was.

They were on the northern periphery of the Forest of Daron Hen. The trees and the brush were growing less cluttered, and where they stood, entire hours passed without rain.

"Come," said Iradahon. "We go. We go north…"

~

Beyond the woods were rolling hills, and beyond the rolling hills there was smoke rising. Amid scrub pines and brownish-green grass, a cloudy sky was above-head, and when Wrinn gazed at the landscape they had found themselves in, he sensed doom.

They were not alone. There were camps on the hills, and fires burning, surrounded by rokahn. There were crude fortifications — dark-holds — in addition to stone towers hastily built. Here, far from any elven tribe, there was enough secrecy for rokahn to operate without notice.

But Wrinn and Iradahon had noticed them. And Wrinn — if not Iradahon — would make it his goal to tell the king of the enemy gathering on his doorstep.

"So many," said Iradahon. "An army on the northern marches. They are gathering for war."

"We must tell the elvenking," said Wrinn.

"We must learn, first, what they are doing, and why they are transporting all those elves to this place. We must not be fools when we meet His Majesty."

But how would they learn, and how would they get close to the camps? How would they learn anymore, when they could get no closer?

"How can we investigate?" Wrinn said aloud.

"I have an idea," Iradahon answered.

~

For days, they laid in wait in the forest's eaves, and Iradahon told Wrinn little. Rokahn passed by, of all species and kinds, but Iradahon instructed Wrinn not to strike.

So many times Wrinn's hand went to his longknife, so many times his hand was stayed. And he was growing angry, thirsty for blood, at the sight of so many rokahn where they did not belong.

It was early morning in one of those days, and Wrinn and Iradahon were hiding in the trees. Through the gloom three figures came walking, kehrad in heavy armor and crude black helms, carrying swords and spears. It was then Iradahon gave the signal that had been promised to Wrinn, the one he had craved, one thumb up. And Wrinn took to his task with relish, showing his face and displaying his hatred for all rokahn-kind.

A kehrad struck with his spear, and with a flourish and strike that Iradahon had taught him, Wrinn sent the spear flying out of the kehrad's hand into the distance. He pummeled the helpless kehrad twice with his quarterstaff, then pierced him in the heart with his longknife.

Iradahon rushed forward to the stunned remaining kehrad and bowled them over in a swift charge. He rammed his quarterstaff into a prone kehrad's head, then drew his longknife and slit the other's throat in one swift motion.

The three kehrad were dead, and Wrinn wondered why Iradahon had at last allowed him to execute his wrath.

"Rokahn are too tall," said Iradahon. "Toltar are too small. Kehrad are just right."

They removed the armor from two of the kehrad.

"We leave one for Narenvi," said Iradahon. "I spit on him."

They washed the armor in the waters of a stream. Then they donned the armor. When Wrinn looked at his reflection in the stream, he could not tell the difference between himself and a kehrad.

"You do not speak the language of these beasts," said Iradahon. "If any approaches you and tries to converse, say '*luntokk rhorkudu.*'"

"*Luntokk rhorkudu,*" Wrinn repeated after him.

~

They walked toward the camp in their clumsy armor, Iradahon assuring Wrinn that their quarterstaffs and longknives would not attract the rokahn's dull-witted attention. Wrinn fought against his nerves, worried his gait would somehow mark him as an impostor. But Wrinn tried to remember he was risking all this for a higher cause, for the promise of the dawn.

And so, when they broached the camp, and entered into the unspeakable filth, Wrinn did not tremble. When Iradahon made his way through the ranks, speaking freely, Wrinn did not flee. And when a monstrous rokahn walked up to Wrinn in all his hideousness, and when that rokahn spoke to him in his hideous tongue, Wrinn answered, "*Luntokk rhorkudu.*" And the monstrous rokahn departed from him.

Chapter Thirty-Seven: The Arrival

As spring and summer converged, no news did not seem like good news to Reev.

None had yet arrived for the Council of the Last Time, though the Council of the Last Time approached. And there was no news from Tharvané, but that was because Lord Albenhas had assured it. The roads to Tharvané were blocked with Tharvanian soldiers. No one entered, and any outsiders were thrown out.

Whatever went on in Tharvané, whether Reev's vision was true or not, was unknowable. Some had asked the elvenking to act, but the elvenking refused. Long had the Lord of Tharvané and the elvenking been at odds. Now, it seemed they were true enemies. Their hostility had been spurred by Reev's arrival, and the fact that the news of Reev's entry into the Elf Lands had not been relayed to the Tharvanians.

Reev had lost track of the feasts and the festivals, but at the elvenking's insistence he had taken a ritual bath, donned the orange robe called a *laeras*, and undergone an inscrutable ritual in Old Elvish. He had dropped one silver penny into an offering bucket and he was passing through the gates of the city district of Pelladdon for a festival called Henanhir's Day.

Above head, there were blue skies. Behind him walked the elvenking and Gastreel. And ahead of him, there was unspeakable splendor.

There were stone buildings that stretched to the heavens, their roofs crowned in red tiles. There were braziers at every street corner, and in every brazier a blazing fire. Priests walked the streets, garbed in orange robes, with shaved heads or with ponytails, carrying staves that resembled shepherds' crooks. To them were added soothsayers, wearing two-pointed hats and whose shoes were curled at the ends.

"Who is Henanhir," Reev said, "and why does he have a day, all to himself?"

"He was said to be the luckiest elf who ever lived," said the elvenking, "and on his feast-day, good things are said to happen to they who follow the gods."

"What good will happen to us, then?" Reev said.

~

The temples of Pelladdon were growing grander and larger as Reev, Gastreel and the elvenking walked. As they approached the wall, they passed under a green *wari* and entered into a temple complex.

There was a stone courtyard the size of many Galiopean city blocks, and there was a pillared colonnade flanking either end. On the far edge of the courtyard was a temple larger than any temple Reev had seen in Pelladdon, with a curved roof crowned in blue tile, and festooned with many pillars and emerald colored windows.

"The House of the Fire of Imon," said the elvenking. "A center of the priesthood. My son, Avernathi, is a candidate to join the priesthood. He is the house-watcher here."

Beyond the peristyle, they broached the temple. Dozens of priests in orange robes wandered the temple grounds. As Reev passed through the doors of the temple, he felt his heart shudder.

~

Within the temple was many rooms, and within the rooms were many fires. Other than the fires, the temple seemed bare. There were no portraits or paintings, or statues to be seen. The many fires gave the temple a brightness that hurt Reev's eyes. And Reev felt himself begin to worry, inexplicably.

The number of rooms and chambers was bewildering to his mind, and they all seemed identical. As they passed through the identical rooms, one after the other, a sense of confusion and disorientation dawned in Reev's mind, and the inexplicable worry grew into fear, verging toward panic. So many rooms — all the same, and for that reason they seemed to make no progress as they passed through the temple.

Reev did not complain for fear of seeming weak, but his hands were growing clammy, and on his skin there was an icy sweat. As he fought the fear, he prayed under his breath. The elvenking stopped his walking, and they were in a room Reev thought he had seen a thousand times already. Yet now someone else was within it, an elven figure standing near the flame, one he had seen before in a different guise.

Avernathi was wearing orange like the priests, but his orange robe had two white marks to mark him as a candidate and not a full priest. Unlike the priests, he had a weapon by his side, a dagger. And in the light of the fire, his long silver hair seemed aglow.

"Sage," Avernathi said. "King. Green Wizard. Welcome. Welcome, on this Henanhir's Day. Stare into the fire, and see truth. *Avela!*"

Avernathi's words were like a command from heaven, and when he spoke Reev's eyes darted to the fire, and fixed on it. Reev felt himself sinking downward toward the depths, and as it dawned on him he was about to see another vision, he gave up resistance.

~

He was in Tharvané, in the town square of the capital town of Harkon. Lord Albenhas was amid the crowd, and Reev was amid the crowd, present but unseen.

Like before, Xan was the central attraction. His tunic and

trousers were pitch black, his hair was black, and his eyes were black. He was a dark figure with dark charisma. But now he was not alone.

Though Xan remained the most striking tableau, behind him was a giant. A statue far taller than any building in Harkon now dominated the town square. It was made of bronze, with three steps leading up to its main body, the torso of a man with hands upraised, the head of a chthonic bull. In the center of its chest were seven chambers, and at the bottom of the torso near the steps was a cavity in which was dry logs and kindling.

Though lifeless, the citizens of Tharvané and Lord Albenhas were gazing at it in reverence.

"As I have instructed, you have made a portrait of your new god," said Xan. "His enemies call him the Desolator, but he shall surely not desolate you."

"We shall treat him with reverence," said Lord Albenhas, his voice radiant with devotion.

"Will you?" said Xan. He paused an eyed the crowd. "Will a devoted worshipper of this new god fetch me a torch?"

There was a mad scrambling amid the crowd, arms and hands wrestling against each other, and in the end many torches were brought. Xan grasped hold of the first one.

It burned in his hand, and his eyes had an infernal gleam as he turned and tossed it into the statue's bottom cavity. The twigs, logs and kindling burst into a blazing inferno, and then the statue itself began to smoke, and to glow reddish, burning and raging with heat.

The gathered Tharvanians gasped and remarked in awe.

"The gods you once served demanded coins of silver and gold," said Xan. "Money to make the priests rich. They did not allow your offerings of wheat and apples. They refused to cherish your abhorrence of wine. Your new god, though, demands something more than coin, and also more than wheat and apples. Tell me, Tharvané, what is most precious of all?"

"Strength!" shouted one in a crowd.

"Honor!" said another.

"Close," said Xan. "The most precious of all is life. And what is the most precious life of all?"

"The life of a king," said Lord Albenhas.

"No," said Xan.

And at last a woman in the crowd, with a babe at her breast, said, "The life of a child!"

"You are correct," said Xan. "The life of a child, is what your new god demands."

"We shall give him what he demands," said Lord Albenhas.

~

Reev was back in the temple rooms, overcome with emotion and fear. He wondered if he should tell the elvenking and Gastreel what he had seen. But couldn't have the vision have been a delusion, a product of the sum of all his fears?

Avernathi was looking at him. Gastreel and the elvenking seemed caught up in thought.

"What did you see?" said Avernathi. "*Locta!*"

"Xan, leading the Tharvanians astray," said Reev.

But the elvenking did not seem to hear, though Reev spoke, and Gastreel was seemingly caught up in a vision of his own.

"What did you see?" said Avernathi, turning his attention to Gastreel.

"A sword in my hand," said Gastreel, "piercing the heart of my most hated foe."

Avernathi's eyes turned to the elvenking, and the question was implicit.

"I saw the gates of the city opened, and horns blowing, and welcome news spreading through all Danarion's districts," said the elvenking.

"Truth on Henanhir's Day," said Avernathi. "Gods be with you. *Illuné vadila.* And now, *ananda.*"

He spoke, and it was like a command from heaven. In unison they turned and left through the doors of the temple, past the peristyle, and at last beyond the district of Pelladdon itself.

~

The South Gate was open, and horns were blowing. They were not elven horns, nor were they Imperial or Gallian, but pure and crisp trumpets of a fine make. Crowds were gathered in the street, crowds of elves, and they were watching new arrivals in wonder.

There were hundreds of them, perhaps thousands, humans such as Reev had never seen. They were fair, with hair of blond or light brown, tall and muscular, with healthy complexions that hinted of a lifetime in the sun with an ample diet.

Some wore leather and others chainmail. Some rode on horses and some walked. All had swords at their hips, and all had two features in common: their hair, whether blond or light brown, was tied up in a knot that hung to the side of their head; and their faces were handsome and comely. At the sight of them, the elves cheered and hollered. The sight of them spread joy wherever they walked.

The elvenking, the Sage and the Green Wizard were now a sideshow, apparently outclassed by the outsiders.

"Our treaty allies, the Viegs," said the elvenking, "from the Eastern World. Look! Here comes Theudo, their leader, and his sword-thanes."

At the end of the train of the new arrivals rode a man on a brown charger. He was dressed in a suit of chainmail, and by his side was a sword marked in gold leaf with floral patterns. His hair was a shining gold, and on his hair was a gold crown studded with rubies and emeralds. In the bright sunlight he appeared as one favored by the gods, and on all sides he was surrounded.

His sword-thanes wore thick plated iron armor, and their winged helms allowed ample space for their bright eyes to be seen, and for their handsome countenances to be displayed. They were the servants of Theudo, Reev guessed his closest confidantes and finest warriors.

Behind Theudo came the women of the Viegs, of the same complexion and beautiful countenance as the men. They had all arrived for the sake of the Council of the Last Time, and they had arrived first.

From Luaddon and its forested avenues they were progressing north, and now Reev was caught up in the joy, glad to be an onlooker rather than a recipient of attention. The elvenking and Gastreel too were following the Viegs as they progressed down the road, cheering as they passed from the forested avenue toward the great road and the monuments that preceded the palace.

Vélerion was at the gates of the palace with a cold look. Nenré was with him, and Fortunato. She and Fortunato gazed at the Viegs in wonder, and as the Viegs halted their procession, Theudo and his sword-thanes made their way up to the front.

Theudo looked at Vélerion. "Is this the cause of our long journey? Is this the Sage?"

Vélerion had a look of quiet fury as the elvenking made his way around the vast crowd. "No, no, good Theudo, he is here — behind me. A human, as was promised."

The fury in Vélerion's eyes threatened to become no longer quiet. But Theudo's blue eyes fixed on Reev, and wonder filled them.

Here it was, and Reev bristled. Reev did not want adoration. It was the last thing he wanted.

And reacting to the adoration he feared was coming, he dropped to one knee and bowed his head. "An honor to meet you, Your Majesty King Theudo."

Theudo smiled, and his smile was bright. His teeth were white like snow. "Sage," he said. "Long have we traveled. But it was worth it. Some have lost their lives along the way. But now is the final conflict."

~

King Theudo was given a room in the palace across from Reev, and across the city, elves shared their quarters with the men and women of the Viegs. At dusk a feast was declared, and that night the Viegs gathered in the palace's feasting hall.

Fortunato and Nenré was seated together, and Reev was seated with Spyke. All Reev's fears and the lingering terror of his vision had dissipated on the arrival of Theudo and his fighting Viegs. His fears no longer seemed possible. His terror no longer seemed near. As they began to pour the wine, he tried to cling to that feeling, to that joy. For danger would surely come near, and the Enemy would not stop their efforts to harm him, until their final defeat.

Reev took a deep sip of his wine.

"Theudo, King of the Viegs," said the elvenking from his seat. "The first to arrive, the first to announce his participation in the war against Seymus. He is a week early. More soon shall surely come."

The steward, Reev noted, was sitting near Avernathi. Vélerion was in the corner alone, and had a bitter look.

"Theudo, tell me, how many have come with you," said the elvenking. "You seem to have brought all your people."

"No," said Theudo. Reev noted, Theudo was sitting at the table of honor next to the elvenking's seat, and a starstone was on the table so that all could see his face. "My people are a countless throng. I have brought my nobles and their children. And you have not seen us all, for our wolves and our wolf-keepers, we thought, would be rude to take past the borderlines."

"It is black wolves we fear, not brown wolves," said the

elvenking.

"All black wolves save Tyra!" shouted Fortunato from his table, and there was scattered laughter among those gathered in the feasting hall.

At an early age, Gastreel had taught Reev of the great wolves and their great varieties, the black wolves who lived among the rokahn, the white wolves who lived in the snow, and the brown wolves who were thought lost to history. All were larger than regular wolves, and all possessed of a greater intelligence, though their intelligence was lesser than humans or elves.

"Now, we shall entertain you in the Vieg way," said Theudo. "You have been so gracious in your hosting of us. We shall repay the favor."

Young Vieg men arose from their table, carrying spears in their hands. They began to toss the spears to each other across the room, and the elven partygoers at first seemed uncomfortable, perhaps even offended. But so strong were their arms, and so sure was their aim, that the elves began to trust them. They caught their spears, and then they caught their spears with their backs turned. They caught the spears sitting on their seat, and then standing upon the table. They caught their spears blindfolded, and then blindfolded when their backs turned. When the elves' fear had evaporated, and the spear-throwing had become a source of unabated entertainment, the Viegs stopped the festivities.

Reev noticed Theudo's queen sitting next to him, bright-eyed and bright haired. He noticed that Spyke had departed from the table.

He scanned the room as platters of chicken and mashed tubers were brought, as wine was poured and wine glasses clinked. Theudo had more entertainment planned for the night and now Reev feared it. But he would trust Theudo, and all the Viegs, with his life.

"Now," he said, "our bard, Freki."

A brown-haired man strode to the feasting hall's stage, dressed in leather armor and wielding a spear like it was a walking stick. "Thank you for giving us your houses, people of Danarion. It is a wonder to live in this place, in these stone houses it would seem are the work of cunning giants."

Freki spoke his verses, and at the end of each verse he struck the stage with his spear. He spoke of winter snows, of "oar-steeds," and battles with "jotuns" in high mountain passes. Then he departed into the dim light of the room.

Reev realized why he had been scanning the room all this time, sensing something missing. The seat of his helper and friend, across from him, was empty. Wrinn was gone from the feasting hall. Reev prayed his friend would come back soon.

Chapter Thirty-Eight: Closer to the Truth

Wrinn was among the rokahn.

He was amid filth. Elves called humans slovenly, and considered their cities inadequately clean. But to Wrinn, the rokahn's filthiness was otherworldly.

Trash piled up all throughout the camps, and discarded scraps of meat and refuse was left out in the open. The filth had attracted mice and flies, and maggots were growing in every stinking pile. To the smell of excrement was added the smell of the rokahn themselves, who never bathed or washed or cleansed themselves. For the first hour, Wrinn had fought nausea. He had tried to endure the toxic environment as best he knew how. After all, he was learning things.

The rokahn who had taken over these hills had one mission, and that was to capture as many elves as possible. Where they were taking them, and what they were doing with them, was beyond Wrinn's knowledge. But Iradahon knew how to converse, and as they progressed through the stinking camps, Wrinn had little doubt that they would eventually uncover the rokahn's purpose. Whether or not they would survive was uncertain.

Iradahon, as always, was leading the way.

As they passed through a large camp with a blazing fire, a sickening smell assailed Wrinn's nose. He saw there were scraps of meat roasting in the fire. A monstrous green rokahn was standing by the fire, singing the meat's praises in his inscrutable tongue. And Wrinn looked to his right and then looked away, spying a glance of the body of an elf, dressed as if by a butcher.

Wrinn felt a swell of nausea. The filth, the rokahn diet, was threatening to undo him. The risky gambit had not yet paid off. And

Wrinn wondered if rather than investigating the rokahn presence, he should be fleeing back to the City of Light, to go where he belonged, to be who he was meant to be — a helper at the Sage's side.

"*Adari*," Wrinn whispered under his breath, so softly even he couldn't hear it. How lovely did Elvish sound amid the rokahn grunts and growls.

They were passing by a trash-filled avenue, and for a brief moment they were away from rokahn's ears. Iradahon, dressed in kehrad armor ahead of him, muttered quietly: "That rokahn said, 'gray elves taste best.'"

Wrinn was appalled, and he was sickened. He would be glad when these rokahn received the fate that was coming to them. He supposed he was helping in that regard, for perhaps he would learn a weakness, a way for the elvenking and his armies to thwart these interlopers.

Up ahead, there was a commotion. A meaty kehrad with a potbelly was leading a train of elven captives through the filth of camp. Some of the elves were men, others women, a few of them very young. They were weeping. Iron collars were about their neck, and chains were fixed to the iron collars, preventing escape.

Iradahon gave the signal he had explained to Wrinn — an index finger up, "Follow them!" And Wrinn and Iradahon followed them, under the gray-skied morning.

~

There were black wolves in cages, and though the rokahn used them as steeds, Wrinn saw little evidence that the black wolves were anything more than afraid of rokahn. The rokahn did not have the capacity to love their pets or the animals unfortunate enough to find themselves in their company.

Wrinn thought of Tyra when he saw them, and he winced when

toltar poked the black wolves with sticks through their cages. He thought of Fortunato. He uttered a prayer for his friend, under his breath.

The rokahn jeered at the elves as they passed them by, and as the disguised Wrinn and Iradahon walked after them in pursuit. Some eyed the elves hungrily, but the mightiest of the rokahn, the ones the others respected, those with large horns, would restrain any of their inferiors who got too close.

A blue-skinned rokahn approached Iradahon and uttered something guttural. Iradahon spoke something guttural in return, and pointed to Wrinn. The rokahn snarled and let them by, as they passed through mile after mile of camp, mile after mile of filth.

Wrinn's stomach was turning, and he had endured about as many hideous smells as he could bear, when the camps began to taper away.

The grass was yellow up ahead, and when Wrinn trod on the ground, his feet were beginning to sink and create cavities in the surface. There was the smell of sand and dry dust, of lifelessness. The grayness of the skies was turning a shade of ochre. They had passed a mile from camp, and the skies were red.

At that moment a violent stomachache assailed Wrinn, and the pain prevented him from taking a step forward. Iradahon, up ahead, was beginning to stagger rather than to walk. The rokahn holding the chain was now dragging the elves into the distance.

There were no longer any trees. Ahead of Wrinn were dunes of sand, dry dust — a desert.

But he had seen this before. It was the Blight that had come to Gallia, and now the Blight had reappeared in a new place.

When Fortunato slew the Fell Smith, Lothan's Forge had not been destroyed… it had reappeared in a new place. Humiliated, the vile Lothan had set up shop in a new place he thought Fortunato would not find, and in cowardice he had continued his work.

But what was that work?

A hundred-and-three elves, Wrinn had counted, bound by chain to collars.

And Wrinn noticed, as he stood — unable to penetrate the newfound Blight, unable to continue on —that a hundred-and-three dark figures, exactly, were walking in from the west, a number of rokahn to match the elven captives perfectly.

They were headed to Lothan's Forge.

Lothan… Wrinn cursed him under his breath.

Chapter Thirty-Nine: The Final Coalition

The joy of Theudo's arrival had not waned. No, Theudo and his fighting men had brought new life to the elvenking's palace, and on the faces of the elvenking's courtiers there were more smiles than Reev had ever seen.

The Council of the Last Time was imminent, and Reev was in the feasting hall, when the doors opened.

Theudo turned to look, and everyone else followed after him.

A messenger had stridden in, a Lamen elf with long gold hair. His face was covered in bruises, and across his cheek and across his bare forearms were scars that looked newly formed. He had a black eye and it was clear he had received a beating.

"Your Majesty the King," said the messenger. "A letter from Londor and its leader."

The elvenking arose from his seat in the feasting hall and walked to the messenger. The elvenking's eyes radiated grief, for it seemed he knew what all this meant, though none others did.

The messenger was holding a letter, and the elvenking took it from him and broke the seal. The letter unfurled, and the elvenking read the letter aloud.

" 'To the king of delusions and superstitions, steeped in madness: The Council of the Last Time is a product of myth. Seymus has no bearing against Londor, for Seymus is a pious fiction. We shall not send our sons and daughters to die for created stories. We curse you and yours, and so we always will. Lady Nihil we serve, but she is nothing, too.' It is signed, King Mordenal."

The elvenking began to weep. "The Dark Elves have chosen their lot. It would be better for Londor to sink into the sea, and all the sons of Loni to drown in the bottomless depths, than for them to have made this choice. *Iramon iramoren! Londor abolliu…*"

The treaty-allies had arrived, and they had arrived first. The Lonen, called the Dark Elves, had refused to join the final coalition against Seymus. Reev recalled Gastreel's lessons that during the First Shadow War the Lonen had fought alongside the elvenking's armies. Yet in the current age they no longer heeded the gods, and they revered nothing and no one.

"*Londor abolliu,*" Reev repeated, after the elvenking, under his breath.

The elvenking continued his weeping. Yet Theudo continued to spread his joy. Reev was glad he and his nobles were among them. What a despairing place the feasting hall would be without their light.

~

On the twenty-second day of the month of Vlesti, the South Gate again opened. Reev was among the crowds as the Umen king rode down the way. On his head was a wreath of leaves and vines and over his body was a green robe of elvencloth. His hair was a long brown, his eyes a keen blue. He was riding on a white charger and a scimitar was clipped to his belt. He was called "Parthas."

Behind him came his warriors, the wildblades, with free-flowing hair of brown or gold, bare-chested and wearing leggings. On each of their right ankles was a silver anklet, what Reev remembered was called a *sindon.*

Behind them were archers with bows and quivers and full of arrows.

The Umen, or Wood Elves, would be participants in the final war against Seymus.

~

On the morning of the twenty-third day of Vlesti, the South Gate opened again, and the Lord of Non came riding in on a stag. Behind him were other stag riders, cloaked in full plate. But the Lord of Non was bare to see.

His hair was dark gray, his eyes were light gray. He had a silverish-white complexion. At his side was a lance.

The Nurnen would be participants in the final war against Seymus.

~

It was late, and it was almost dusk, on the twenty-third day of the month of Vlesti. The gate was shutting, and in the feasting hall, the elvenking had already considered the final coalition assembled. The Nurnen, the Umen, the Lamen, the Kahren and the treaty-allies were the final coalition against Shadow. But Reev was stirred in the shifting light, and as the palace servants served a meal to the feasting hall — now packed with people — the doors opened.

In walked the Captain of the King's Guard, Keras. At his side was his sword, called Helvenhari, "Bull-Cutter."

"Your Majesty the King," said Keras. He looked to the elvenking on his seat. His eyes scanned the room, and found Reev. "Sage. The gate is about shut. Two figures have arrived, wishing to be let in. But according to our regulations, the day is done. The sun has set. It is the twenty-fourth day of the month of Vlesti."

"In human lands," said Reev, "the day ends at midnight."

The elvenking looked to Reev. Reev stood up, and the elvenking followed moments later. Together they exited the doors of the feasting hall and made their way to the city below.

~

The gate had almost shut, but its closing had been halted. In the twilight, two figures on horseback stood outside the city. Reev realized he had seen these two in a dream. It was the Drazzandori, the King of the Vampires, and his queen. They were both riding on white chargers.

They had the black hair and cadaver-white complexions of Nocturne back in Galiope.

"Sage," said the Drazzandori.

"Zarial," said Reev.

"How do you know my name?" said the Drazzandori.

"Yours I know," said Reev, "but I do not know your queen's."

"Banwé," said the Queen of the Vampires.

Behind Reev, he could sense the elvenking's domineering presence.

"I am sorry," said the Drazzandori, "we are late. We rode ahead of our party so as to make it in time. We failed. We have faced blizzards and arctic snows, and wildmen, and hunger and disease. Many have perished, but we traveled as fast as possible. And here we are, alone."

"It is the twenty-fourth day of the month of Vlesti," said the elvenking behind Reev. "You shall not participate in the coalition."

And Reev in that moment remembered that according to elven law, the Sage was a higher authority than the elvenking. He sensed in the elvenking a disdain and a hatred unbecoming, an unwillingness to forgive that was an abomination. And perhaps not for the last time, Reev decided to overrule him.

"It is the twenty-third day of the month of Aurelios," said Reev. "Welcome to the City of Light, Zarial and Banwé. You are accepted into the final coalition."

There was nothing more to be said.

But tears of joy formed in Banwé's eyes, and in Zarial's eyes was relief, the relief of a thousand years of a curse lifted, and a people being welcomed back into the light.

~

Other Vampire Lords arrived later in the night, and they joined in with the other elves, eating and drinking copiously. It was the eve of the Council, and decisions would be made. Here was the final conflict. Here was the final battle.

Was Reev ready?

Chapter Forty:
Together At the Beginning

At dawn, Reev entered the Elder Chamber. He realized he was the last to arrive, and the others had been seated before dark.

The seats in the massive circular chamber were all filled except for two. One set aside for the Lonen King was empty, and the smaller seat next to Reev, for *adari* his helper was empty. One was *abolliu*, but Wrinn's seat was empty for a good cause.

Reev took the seat set aside for him, and he was thankful there was no adoration in the room for him, only stern focus and purpose. As he took his seat, another figure left hers, the Sibyl.

The elven seeress and prophetess stood among those gathered. "Welcome, members of the coalition. May the gods guide us. May the gods guard us. May the gods lead us to victory. May the gods bring the dawn."

She left and returned to her seat, and the Council of the Last Time began.

~

"Let us start," said the elvenking, "at the beginning, before the Sage was born.

"For trouble preceded him, with the theft of the six iron masks from their place of safekeeping. It was the first sign of things to come. They were stolen from the vault in *Vadras Henion,* in the Shield Mountains, and for decades they were unaccounted for. Eventually, it became known that the necromancer Jerek had returned the Six Servants of Seymus to life, but their time was not yet. They wandered the earth in their weak state, and dealt damage to the elven people. Eventually, the six phantoms fixed their attentions on human lands, for in the land of Alonar, in the city of Galiope, the Sage had been born.

"What then happened? Perhaps, the Green Wizard will tell us more."

Gastreel walked before the gathered dignitaries. "Your Majesty," he said. "The day after Reev was born, the glyrn Drayfin had been sighted in Galiope. His birth was widely known in the city, for his father was a famed hero and his mother was known for her virtue. I knew that if he was allowed to remain in the city, the outcome would be his death. I took him from his mother's arms, and did not tell her where I was going. I, after much deliberation and research, located a town in the Empire that almost no one had heard of, in a part of the Empire that was sparsely populated and little thought of, where two outsiders moving to town would not make a stir. That town was Norwood. With the aid of the Woodsmen of Brill, I settled into Norwood, and among those Woodsmen was a fifteen-year-old boy, Fortunato of Ríva, who had been recently captured wandering in the Woodsmen's grounds. Fate seemed to have brought Fortunato, and I, and the infant Reev, together. The rest, I suppose, is history."

Gastreel returned to his seat.

"And so, the Sage grew up in the town of Norwood," said the elvenking. "But eventually, the secret of where he had been taken was learned. And Fortunato and Gastreel quickly sped to Norwood to recover the Sage before the Enemy found him. He was whisked away, in the nick of time."

Reev wondered why he had never been told this, why Gastreel had attempted so mightily to keep the truth from him. Fortunato, present in his infancy? What harm would it have brought to him if he had known?

"Reev destroyed the Six Servants of Seymus. Their time was not yet," said the elvenking. "But eventually, the phantoms were restored to their ancient strength. Mighty foes they are. Mighty foes they remain. Even now they wander Lamdar, somewhere, in parts unknown. They have not been seen since last year."

"The phantoms are not far?" called out Theudo.

"They are not," said the elvenking. "I did not wish to alarm you. They are strong, but they are not yet strong enough to breach the city's defenses. It would take them, and an army of rokahn, and something much more, to lay us low."

Theudo frowned. He seemed a bit angry that the dark news had not been disclosed to him. Reev assumed all gathered here, had been told all.

He saw in the vastness of the room, in the countless seats, Mikal the Half-Fey was present, and his rainbow hair was brilliant in the light of the windows up above. Reev was glad at the sight of him, Mikal who had brought him to the Sibyl's door.

"What happened to the glyrn, Drayfin?" said Theudo.

"Fortunato of Ríva slew him," said the elvenking.

And Reev realized that Fortunato was not present, nor was Nenré.

"And why is such a man not here?" said Theudo.

"There are many heroes," said the elvenking, "many contributors to the cause. They cannot all be present at the Council of the Last Time."

~

At noon they broke for lunch, and for Reev's part, the only thing he gained was anger that so little had been told to him. Yet he knew personal feelings of hurt and bitterness were secondary to the task ahead, to tread Seymus underfoot, and for the gods to bring the dawn. So when he saw Gastreel alone in the garden with Theudo, he did not bring up his feelings of anger that he had been told so little, and that so much had been concealed from him. There was something higher, something more important, and he vowed to keep his focus on that.

Not all had been a waste, for he felt that the more he knew, the better he would be able to fight. Fortunato had been with him when he had been a babe. What would Fortunato remember? Wherever Reev went, wherever he would depart, Fortunato would surely come with him. Wouldn't he?

And where was Fortunato now?

Chapter Forty-One: Opposites, Opposed

Nenré had not stopped her sobbing for hours. In a dark corner of the palace, Fortunato did his best to comfort her.

She had tried to broach the subject with her handmaids, but as she tried to reveal the truth, she had stopped herself as it dawned on her what she was telling them would lead to her death.

Not just her death, and not just Fortunato, but also their son.

"My father will not have mercy," said Nenré, "I was a fool."

"You do not know that," Fortunato said. "You do not know just how deep his love goes."

"Perhaps, he loves me," said Nenré. "Oh, Fortunato, we should flee. In the Southern Reaches there are places to hide, valleys where no one would think to look. We will raise our child in secret."

"A half-elven child would stand out," said Fortunato. "And I have not come all this way, and fought as hard as I have, to abandon my quest. I will see the Dark One defeated."

"Then we will all three of us die!" Nenré wailed, and her sobbing became uncontrolled weeping, tears flowing, and she buried herself in Fortunato's chest.

Her belly had grown larger with the child growing inside her, and Fortunato wondered at how deep the elves' disbelief ran, the thought such a crime was so unspeakable, it could not have possibly taken place.

But it had taken place, and a child was in Nenré growing stronger, and growing more ready to be born. The deed had been done, and it could not be reversed. The three of them would die, or the daughter of the elvenking would give birth to a half-human son. It was Fortunato's goal to make sure the latter was the outcome. But he was not so strong as to change fate.

He could not change fate. But fate had brought this child to them. Would the gods allow the three of them to die? They had allowed worse injustices.

"We cannot hide this forever," Fortunato said.

"Don't tell me what I know," Nenré said.

"You should tell your father, and ask his forgiveness," Fortunato said.

"I will not be a fool," Nenré said. "Let us flee! Let us flee!"

"No," Fortunato said. He had dedicated his life to something. Even now, he could not abandon it.

~

"Tell me, Green Wizard, when the Sage was born, did you know it was he?" said Theudo amid the silvery bushes that appeared crafted of metal in the sunlight.

"I had my beliefs," said Gastreel, "but not until he wrote in the Script of Sages did I know for certain. Only two can write in the book, the Sage and the Dark One's Hand."

"And what happened to the Script of Sages?" said Theudo.

"Reev destroyed it," said Gastreel.

"I recall," said Theudo, "the Script of Sages, a wonder crafted by the Dweorg. But there were two parts. The book with gold pages, and the quill. The Quill of Varda, and the Script of Sages, are bound together by Dweorg wonder-craft. What happened to the quill?"

Gastreel somehow felt insulted by Theudo's words. Yet he pondered the stirrings of his heart, and felt a sense of conviction. He did not know what happened to the Quill of Varda after Reev had written into the Script of Sages the Script's destruction. What indeed had happened to the quill?

"I confess," Gastreel said, "I do not know."

Reev had written into the Script of Sages its destruction. They had learned in the span of a moment that Reev was the Sage and that Jerek the Necromancer was not the Dark One's Hand. They had fled the accursed tower, and who knew what had happened to the Quill of Varda? The Quill of Varda was equally an artifact of evil, crafted by the Dweorg at the behest of the Dark One. Perhaps, Gastreel felt insulted by Theudo's words because he had been uncharacteristically reckless.

"I do not know," Gastreel repeated more softly. "I do not know where it has gone."

~

Gastreel returned to the Elder Chamber, his mental faculties close to exhausted. Perhaps, opening the Gate of Tedron had injured more than just his physical body.

Reev entered late, and Gastreel wondered if he was making a show of being insulted, and attempting in a backhanded way to make his hurt feelings known. He was learning things about himself and his childhood he had not known. He had not asked about his mother's fate. Her fate in Varda had not been good, but she was with the gods now. Where was his father? Only the gods knew. He had disappeared and was likely dead.

The Sibyl invoked the gods and announced that the Council of the Last Time had resumed.

"Friends, fellow fighters," said the elvenking, "We have begun at the beginning. We are working our way toward the end. Now, toward the middle of our tale, we uncover something new. In the ancient prophecies, it reads the Sage will be *telantari*, and the meaning of that word was unknown until now. We said earlier, that the elves and humans have lived separately for these thousand years, and knowledges have diverged, though elven knowledge has been superior."

Gastreel would disagree with that.

"Superior, but different, and in the human world lay the truth of the word *Telantari*. There was a people forgotten by elves, called by humans the Telantines. There was a kingdom the elves have no record of, called by humans Telantis. Where it was, we do not know, but the Green Wizard has informed us, there is an island off the coast of the human empire, now completely depopulated, that was referred to in times forgot by the name 'New Telantis.'

"A rump state of survivors, survivors now disappeared. But there must have been survivors that endured, for the Sage is alive, and he is with us. His existence bears witness to the fact that that the Telantines live."

"At last, a mystery solved," said the king of the Umen Elves, called Parthas. The wreath of leaves and vines on his head was a soft brown in the light of the windows above. "For our wise folk puzzled over *telantari*. They ate the roots of the *sarvas* tree, and drank the milk of the *hilvó* plant over the centuries, and spoke in ecstasy, but their answers were nonsense and we knew it as soon as they spoke."

"*Telantari*," said Gastreel, "Telantine in the human tongue. And Reev is not alone among the Telantines. Fortunato is a Telantine, too. Who knows how many sons and daughters Telantis bore, that live among us?"

"Perhaps, you are a Telantine, Gastreel," said the elvenking.

"All things are possible," Gastreel said.

"Telantis fell in one cataclysmic moment," said the elvenking. "But in the end it triumphs over its enemies. The Sage shall be a Telantine, the Dark One's Hand 'of the House of a Serpent.' The Telantines, and 'the House of a Serpent' are thus opposites of each other and totally opposed. *Telantari* was a mystery, for it was a word that was tied to no meaning. 'Of the House of a Serpent' has meaning, but it is an equally a puzzle, for what is this house, and which serpent does it speak of?

"I believe, like *telantari*, the answer lies in human knowledge.

But our investigators have prepared for months for this Council, and inquired of every witness including Gastreel and all the Sage's party, and the meaning of 'the House of a Serpent' is unknown among those gathered. But I believe it shall be made known."

"What makes you believe that?" said the Drazzandori, King of the Vampires, Zarial.

"Because Reev will defeat the Dark One's Hand," said the elvenking.

That meant Reev would come into contact with what the prophecies called "the House of a Serpent." Gastreel shuddered at the thought, and anew was filled with regret, that he would not be there to protect him.

And Gastreel also regretted not uncovering the meaning of all these ancient mysteries. He had pondered them all his life. But it was up to others now. This council, and the giving of all his wisdom, was his final act. He would accompany the elves, and await the dawn.

"And how shall he defeat this House of a Serpent?" said Theudo.

"That is the entire purpose of our council," said the elvenking. "That is why we have gathered here, to uncover what must be done. We must be swift, for I fear that danger is crouching at our door."

Danger… Gastreel knew, the Six Servants of Seymus were at work. And they were at their full strength. They had all the powers they possessed in the ancient world. They would not hesitate to wield them.

~

Days passed, and the Council continued to deliberate, taking breaks for feast days and certain days of the week for rest. They pored over the writings about the first Sage Antheleon, and the blow he dealt Seymus at the close of the prior era. They had not yet unveiled all of the lost prophecies, and the bulk of them, to Gastreel, were not known. What they were to do, and how Reev was to act, was still beyond them.

For to defeat an immaterial enemy, an immaterial weapon would have to be formed. That was Gastreel's thinking, as the council continued to think and deliberate, as the knowledge of the ages was revealed day by day and piece by piece, as the truth was at last uncovered — or what truth was available to them.

The identity of the Telantines was partially uncovered. They did not know who the Telantines were, but they knew that *telantari* was a people and a nation. What the House of the Serpent was, would not be uncovered at the Council of the Last Time. Perhaps, Reev would not know until he met this House of a Serpent face to face. The thought troubled Gastreel and vexed him. But though Gastreel would not go with Reev to where his destiny lay, others would, others he trusted.

Fortunato came to mind. But Fortunato was gone from sight of late. So was Nenré. He feared why. He feared the worst outcome for them both was ahead. For the punishment, and the method of punishment, for such a grave crime, had been anciently prescribed.

Gastreel uttered prayers under his breath that such a horrible punishment would not befall someone he loved more than a brother.

"Heart of my heart, sword to my spell," said Gastreel, to himself, to a friend now gone from his sight, in the solitude of the palace garden.

Chapter Forty-Two: The Grim Truth

When Wrinn ventured into the rokahn camps, following Iradahon's lead, he had thought they would spend the better part of a day within and no more. He had hoped they would uncover the rokahn's purpose and then swiftly make their way back into the security of the forest. But it was not so.

Iradahon and Wrinn had lingered amid the camps, and Iradahon had insisted they stay, as a quiet horror slowly dawned in him. And as a day turned to two days, two days to a week, and now a month had passed, he seemed to be learning things Wrinn did not know.

Wrinn was beginning to learn rokahn phrases, *"Lubluk"* — "Leave me be." *"Tarko"* — "over there." And they had made a tent amid the filth where they would retreat and occasionally remove their armor, and converse amongst themselves. And Wrinn had tried in the quiet of the tent, in the dark hours of the night, to tell Iradahon what he did know, namely, that he had seen the Blight once before, and that Lothan was no rokahn or villainous human, but a creature of another world.

Another world…

Hell.

For Wrinn's part, he had swiftly moved up the ranks in rokahn society, and the toltar and rokahn around him would obey whatever commands he dealt them. Not even Iradahon commanded so much respect, though he too was considered a rokahn of high rank, in so short a time.

When opportunity presented itself, Wrinn would venture to the edge of the Blight and observe, and more often than not, he'd see groups of elven captives and groups of rokahn in evenly matched pairs walk off into the Blight and its red-skied desert.

Wrinn felt he was gaining the rokahn's trust. He was also learning about them. He learned that they operated by violence in all ways, that the best of them were considered those whom none other could touch. The toltar were the lowest rank because they were small and weak. The rokahn respected horns because horns were weapons in and of themselves, and were an advantage, fighting rokahn to rokahn.

It was a baking hot day, and from the trash of the camps was arising such a stench that even Wrinn's conditioning was proving too weak to overcome, when the first sign of truth appeared to the two investigators.

The first sign… and what Wrinn realized he had unconsciously suspected all along, a horror and a crime so grave, his mind had not allowed him to consider.

Dozens of figures were walking south through camp, from the direction of the Blight. They were not rokahn. They were not elf. They were something else.

They were tall and slender, muscular yet not bulky. Their skin was shades of blue or tarry green, and their ears came to sharp ragged points. Their faces were harsh and angular, and their yellow eyes had a diabolic gleam. They were elf, they were rokahn, the worst traits of both species combined, into one abomination.

This, all along, had been the purpose of Lothan's Forge, to mix the unmixable, to join together what should not be joined.

"*Agh, Kobold!*" said a rokahn stone-layer Wrinn knew as Sorka.

"Look, the kobolds," Sorka had said.

Kobold, that was what they called these monsters, and Wrinn's heart was filled with grief. The elves had been led to the Blight, to Lothan's Forge, for this fate, and now the changed elves — or what was left of them — would fight for the Dark One's armies. Was there anything worse?

One of the kobolds, possessed of feminine features, eyed

Wrinn standing in the camp in his armor. And for the first time since he had arrived, there was not a look of stupid ignorance, but instead suspicion. The half-rokahn, half-elven abominations, were not stupid. What other powers did they have?

Chapter Forty-Three: Some Restored

For weeks the council had met, and the lost prophecies had not been proffered. Gastreel feared there was no longer any time.

For the Six Servants were at work, and there was scattered rumor of trouble abroad. Gastreel had a sense of impending disaster as the month of Kelvé moved into Kaudé, and the summer's end approached.

The council had at last finished the questions regarding the first Sage, the Prince of the Dusk. They were at last approaching the time of decision, on what would happen, and just what the coalition of Seymus would do. The answer was still beyond them.

It was before dawn in the royal apartments and Gastreel had just donned his green robe and took hold of his newfound black staff.

There was a knock on his door, as outside an uncharacteristic summer rain was falling lightly, and there was a flash of lightning, and a call of thunder. He crossed the room and laid his hand on the knob of the door, and opened it.

The elvenking stood there in the light rain, dressed in his royal robe. He was not guarded by the King's Guard or surrounded by servants. It appeared he wanted privacy, as if he feared detection.

~

In a room in the far corners of the apartment, the elvenking spoke openly.

"Green Wizard," he said, "alarming news from Tharvané. For we have learned that during these past months, the former warlock in your company has taken up his trade again. And at the behest of the Six Servants of Seymus, he has led the Tharvanians into evil."

Gastreel felt a cold gasp. "What do you mean, Your Majesty?"

"The Tharvanians have made a brazen statue, and in it they are sacrificing their young, by the hundred, by the thousand. They are casting their babes into the fire. At first my spies thought they had returned to the elves' former religion before they knew the gods, the Celestial Mother and the Terrestrial Father, who also demanded the sacrifice of elves. But then I realized, it is something far worse."

"Far worse?" Gastreel said, and felt himself grow faint.

"The warlock has a darker purpose than leading Tharvané *abolliu*. He is attempting to contact far darker forces. A demon of the ancient world, whom elves called *Abon Bet Belas,* 'the Omen that Desolates,' called by certain human tribes Shahg Bahag or by others Belpheor, has always desired the sacrifice of human children. To weaken his chains, and bring him back into Varda, the sacrifice of elven children — rather than human children — would have to be on an industrial scale. And that scale is close to being reached."

"We shall send armies to slaughter the Tharvanians, and stop them in their tracks," said Gastreel.

"I'm afraid we cannot," said the elvenking, "for my spies have also reported an army in the north, a vast army of rokahn that is growing by the day."

"We must speed up the deliberations of the council," said Gastreel.

"That, I am in agreement with," said the elvenking.

~

It was dark outside Reev's bedchamber. It seemed still night. He was awoken to a knock.

He scrambled out of bed and donned his blue tunic. He laid the coin amulet of Telantis around his head. And he hurried to the door.

Standing there in the doorway was one Reev thought he knew, an elf of long dark hair and green eyes, the hostler, Imrari. For the first time in what seemed like months, there was a smile on an elf's face.

The smile on Imrari's face was indeed bright.

"What is it?" Reev said.

"Come with me."

~

They passed beside Amanddon and came to the East Gate, which had just opened for the morning. There, in the morning cool, was a creature Reev knew, a creature Reev loved. And his heart was filled with relief, and love.

At the sight of Reev, Cobalt reared up on his back legs. His tawny coat glistened in the sun. His bright eyes seemed to shine. "Cobalt!" Reev said, and rushed up to his steed, and embraced him by the neck.

"This is your Elvish horse, correct?" said Imrari. "He traveled from Gallia to here by foot, so great was his love for you. We know better than to put him up in the stable. We shall let him wander freely."

~

The council convened, and now Reev was smiling. He was the only radiant countenance in the room. He supposed, of all those gathered, it was best for the Sage to be in good spirits, for the task of treading Seymus underfoot was his. Or so it seemed.

Yet as the Sibyl gave the invocation and returned to her seat, it was apparent that this council, on the twentieth day of Kaudé, or eighteenth Sextil by human reckoning, would be unlike any other council day before.

For as soon as the Sibyl had returned to her seat, the doors of the Elder Chamber opened and gray elves strode in carrying scrolls in their hands.

"At last," said the elvenking, "the lost prophecies."

"What we've been waiting for," said rainbow-haired Mikal.

As the gray elves began to read, members of the council stood up, and Reev followed.

The chief of the gray elves began to read. " *Darkness was from whence he came, and darkness is where he will go. In Shadow he was born, raised by ghosts and a spirit.'*"

"Who does this speak of?" said Mikal.

"That will not be determined," said the elvenking.

The gray elf reader continued. " *In the twilight the House of the Serpent gains sudden strength. Sudden speed is given to it, and it speeds to the ruin that was pronounced to it. '*"

"Someday, we shall know what this house is," offered Theudo.

" *To darkness he speeds as the dawn approaches, light, glorious light unending. Darkness falls and he is overcome, but of strength he has little. Strength will be given to him. To the Dark World he goes, and the gods guide his feet. He knows where to tread. He remembers his kinsmen.*"

The gathered members of the council paused and ruminated in silence. Reev pondered it as well.

" *'Having remembered, he treads. The serpent is dead at his feet. Dawn breaks over the hills, and the gods come with the dawn.'* "The gray elf reader set the scroll aside.

"The Sage goes to the Dark World," said the elvenking. "What does this mean? Clearly, it is where he must go. And perhaps it is not what the Sage wishes to hear, that he shall go to this Dark World and trust the gods to tell him what to do, and trust their guidance to tread Seymus underfoot."

Reev was willing to go there blindly. "I am willing," said Reev. "I am not afraid. But what is this Dark World?"

From his seat, Theudo's face had twisted to a grimace. "We

have come all this way, all these miles. We have put our hopes in these prophecies for these thousand years and they tell us nothing."

"The Dark World," Gastreel ruminated aloud, as emotions in the council threatened to spill out, the terror that came with the thought that they had been led unto futility.

"The Dark World, the Dark World," the Drazzandori, Zarial, said aloud, and to Reev it seemed he was in a panic, wondering if he had thrown his lot in with the wrong side.

"Do you know, Sibyl?" said the elvenking.

But in the Sibyl's eyes there seemed the beginnings of panic as well.

But there was no panic in Reev. As he stood amid the frenzy, and members of the council began to shout at and lash out at one another, he felt a moving in his heart. He had an inkling, a sense, like a memory from a dream he had forgotten.

He said, "What is 'the Dark World' in Elvish?"

But his words were swallowed up in the panicked shouting and arguments.

He shouted and they were silenced. "What is 'the Dark World' in Elvish?"

The elvenking said, "*Naron Da.*"

And then it dawned on Reev, what he had to do, and where he had to go. If he told anyone where he was going, they would send an army to stop him.

"I know what that place is," said Reev.

The panic was quieted. The members of the council looked at him in awe.

He quoted the Lady of Danyen in his vision. " 'Your greatest ally will surprise you. For there is none so lost as cannot be found, no darkness so deep the light cannot touch. There is none fallen that the gods cannot restore. And perhaps in the spirit of one laid low, you can find the torch to light your path.' "

He looked to Gastreel and then he looked to the elvenking.

"I am going on a journey," said Reev. "Whatever I do, wherever I go, do not hinder me."

Chapter Forty-Four: The Figure

Reev had heard the words *"Naron Da"* once before.

For when Reev drove the first dark spirit out of Xan, Xan had recalled his former life as a warlock. He had ventured to a place called *Naron Da* to receive hellish powers, and instead he had been betrayed. Would he remember?

Now, he was a worker of evil again. But the gods could drive out all vestiges of Shadow from him. The gods could cause him to return to the side of good. And Reev knew, of everyone in Lamdar now, only Ivan Xandrast would know the way to *Naron Da*.

Outside the South Gate, Reev put his fingers to his lips and whistled an undulating song.

Cobalt came galloping from the wheat fields, and Reev swept himself onto his back. Without Reev's urging, Cobalt began to trot southeast, down the road, in the direction of Tharvané.

~

A late summer wind was blowing when Reev reached the toll post of Tharvané. In a panic he remembered that the roads had been blocked, that it was said that soldiers were preventing anyone from entering the borders.

But no one was guarding the toll post and he wondered why. And as he rode, he realized that the houses of Tharvané on the outlying hills were empty, and farms were becoming overgrown by weeds. The Tharvanians were no longer sacrificing just children anymore, but also adults. The land was becoming depopulated.

Under the breath, Reev uttered words that flowed from his heart, *"Num Tharvané tona luné. Tharvané abolliu…"*

~

In the town square was the statue, and standing in the shadow of the statue was Xan, a worker of evil now in his prime. The morning's sacrifices had occurred, and the town was empty.

"Xan," Reev said, and Xan screamed.

The town square was exactly like in his vision, but now there were few people. South of the town were the Dragonteeth Mountains, and a jungle of low-lying trees and thick vines, sweltering in the summer heat.

Xan began to back away. Reev dismounted. He felt something overpower him. He felt peace. He felt light.

~

Xan screamed, standing in the town square of Harkon, beside an abominable statue. Last he remembered, he had been standing in the borderlines of the city. He wondered what he had done now. He realized he did not want to know.

About him was the smell of burning flesh, a sense of degradation and unhallowedness. He wanted to flee.

He saw the warlock's kit at his feet and his gut clenched. Had he made the statue, or ordered others to make it? Why was it burning and molten?

The figure standing in front of him filled him with love. Xan had been rescued again. He did not deserve it. And now… now, he felt, there was no darkness remaining. He saw the Skeleton Key was clipped to his belt. He grabbed the vile implement, cast it to the ground, and uttered a curse.

But the figure standing before him, the figure he loved, raised his hand, and light appeared about that hand, brilliant soft light. The figure said, "Oh, Xan, you like the Skeleton Key, don't you? Some things that are fallen can be restored."

AJ COOPER

things that are fallen can be restored."

Chapter Forty-Five: Waiting

The council had convened, awaiting Reev's return. Their deliberations had been few.

Gastreel had just taken his seat, and the Sibyl was about to descend to make her invocation, when the doors were thrown open, and Vélerion the Crown Prince rushed in, his face red and contorted with incalculable wrath.

"My sister! My sister!" he screamed. "Your daughter, father. The very blood of Solendir. The Light's firstborn. And that rogue… Fortunato of Ríva. We found the two abed, making love. And what's worse, she is large with child. She hid it well…"

The hour had come, the hour Gastreel feared. He said a prayer for Fortunato, and for his child, under his breath.

~

First, they separated Fortunato and Nenré. Then they stripped Fortunato of his clothes. They lashed him with a whip in a dark corner of the palace and spat in his face. Then, they forced him into a loincloth made of horsehair.

Elves cinched his neck in a rope, and then they led him outside of the palace, to angry crowds shouting over and over, "Shame! Shame! Shame!"

The king's men who had done this to him dragged him through the streets. The sky up above was cloudy, but the sun was threatening to break through. And Fortunato regretted that he had done this to Nenré, and above all regretted that he had done this to his son.

From the palace to Luaddon they traveled, and then they headed west in a procession toward Pelladdon. The stone buildings were growing more dilapidated, yet more ancient, as they progressed westward. At last, they arrived at a small crumbling stone building, covered in vines, square in shape with a flat roof, that had the look of a tomb.

There, the two lovers were reunited. Nenré's head had been shaven, and she was wearing a horsehair shift. Her pregnancy now was bare to see, and her belly was large. She was weeping, but when she beheld Fortunato, some of her mad terror seemed to quiet, and to her panic when she saw him, in her eyes was added love.

Then Fortunato wept at the sight of her, at the sight of the babe growing within her belly. And he rushed forth to embrace her, and the elves did not stop them. Yanenré and Fortunato wept together as they embraced, but the king's men pulled them aside, and then forced them into the tomb.

~

Together, almost naked, weeping in the dark, as sand began to fall into the tomb to bury them alive, Yanenré began to speak amid her weeping.

"What shall we name him?" she said.

"Now?" Fortunato said. "Really?"

"Yes, for he deserves it," said Nenré. "He deserves it, before he dies with me."

"I do not know," said Fortunato, and he did not know what to be most sad about. "I do not know. I do not think I am capable…"

"What was your father's name?" said Yanenré.

"Petro," Fortunato said. "Petro… it means 'rock.' "

"Rock," Yanenré said. "Alondir. Alondir of Ríva is the name of our child."

And Fortunato, Yanenré, and Alondir waited in the tomb, as the sand filled the dark cavity.

Sand covered Fortunato's feet, and then his ankles. It seemed his Telantine blood wouldn't get him out of this, though his mother said it had gotten him out of many dangerous situations before.

He searched in vain for a way out, but the door had been sealed shut, and the hole above head, from which the sand was pouring, was too small for his hand to fit through.

Under his breath, he said a prayer for Alondir.

Chapter Forty-Six: Alondir

Reev rode into the city on Cobalt, and Xan rode behind him on a white charger.

He rode, and remembered the urgency of his task, as he galloped ahead down the main avenue.

He had broached the palace when Gastreel came sprinting out. When he eyed Xan, something else seemed to be on his mind. "Fortunato," he said. "Fortunato…"

~

When Reev reached the Tomb of Varas where Fortunato lay, having ordered the halting of the execution, he saw no sign of his friend. The tomb had filled with sand, and Reev recalled what the elvenking had said, that in the elven kingdoms there was no higher authority than the Sage. Could he, then, order the execution of the elvenking, who had so betrayed his trust and ordered the killing of his friend?

It took crews of elves with picks and pickaxes to remove the stone ceiling of the tomb. Reev waited with his heart racing, beside the former warlock, uttering constant prayers under his breath. An icy sweat covered him as he waited, as the tomb was unearthed, and as there was the sound of coughing, and as Fortunato and another emerged from their sandy prison.

Fortunato and Nenré were alive, and Nenré was large with child. Nenré's brilliant red hair had been shaven, and the elves had attempted to shame her before the sentence of execution. But when she emerged from the sand, she carried herself like a victor.

A victory had been had, by the Sage's intervention. And now, Reev realized… the child would be born.

There was the sound of stamping feet. Reev turned.

"Iramon iramoren!" said the elvenking. Behind him was his steward and the Captain of the King's Guard, Keras. "The fall of the House of Iradahir. And the Sage has brought the warlock into the city itself. But I will not question his judgment."

Reev was still a bit shaken, still a bit angry. But Fortunato was alive. And so was his child.

~

"Sage," said the Sibyl in the Elder Chamber, "according to elven law you are of higher authority than the king. But I believe we deserve an explanation for why you have brought a worker of evil into the City of Light."

"All last bits of evil have been driven from him," Reev answered. "He has been purified. And I recall, and Nenré would too… he knows the way to *Naron Da*. He will be our guide."

"Nenré," the elvenking howled, and tears were forming in his eyes.

"Nenré, your daughter," the Sibyl said.

"She is alive," said rainbow-haired Mikal.

"She is alive," the Sibyl said, "rescued by the Sage. She will bear Fortunato's child. But she will not witness the Dark One's defeat. This, I can clearly see…"

Chapter Forty-Seven:
An Old Enemy

Fortunato had returned to his room in the royal apartments. Nenré was with him, now bare-headed.

Fortunato had donned his tunic and trousers, and he had clipped Danenhir and Glyrnslayer to his side. He had washed his hair and his face. He felt like he could fight all night, and into the day. Perhaps, he would have to.

And Nenré was smiling, and the sunlight shining in from the window cast her face in joyful colors. She was singing an inscrutable song under her breath. "Oh, Fortunato, I shall bear your child. And you know, now that the law has been voided, that our child will be a member of the royal family. He will be a prince. Imagine! Alondir of Ríva, half-elf and half-human, ruling over his fief in the Southern Reaches."

"Perhaps, he will be king," said Fortunato.

"Let's not get ahead of ourselves," said Nenré.

She was clearly overjoyed.

"Oh, I shall buy him the best clothes, and the best toys," Nenré said. "I will hire him the best tutors. He will lack nothing. Oh, I cannot wait to be a mother. There is nothing I want more."

But Fortunato had walked up to the window, and was staring outside. He was thinking and ruminating. He had heard bits of rumor from the council. He had heard, it was Xan the former warlock who would lead them to *Naron Da*. He did not like it.

"Fortunato, aren't you excited?" Nenré said, and cracks were beginning to form in her joy.

Fortunato continued to stare out the window. "I must prepare, Nenré. I am going on a journey."

"You will leave us here, alone?" Nenré said.

And Fortunato continued to think about the journey ahead and what it would entail. He was thinking, and he could not stop pondering the fact he would be following a former warlock into *Naron Da.*

"There is another you love," said Nenré softly.

She spoke of Ambrass.

"At the beginning of the Time of Mankind," Nenré said, far-off it seemed though she was standing right behind him, "the priests announced the king could be wed to only one wife. The king chose the one he loved best and sent the rest away. There was one wife, Bagaré, who could not bear it, and drowned herself in the sea…"

~

When Wrinn stood in camp in kehrad armor, the rokahn were credulous and ignorant, but the kobolds were suspicious. And so Wrinn had taken to avoiding the kobolds, and walking away when one drew too near.

Iradahon, however, did not seem to sense what Wrinn did, that kobolds were as intelligent as elves and as wicked as rokahn.

On a hot summer day, Wrinn notice disturbances at camp, and the rokahn multitudes were shifting and changing formation. Wrinn tried his best to disperse, but he could not avoid ending up next to a kobold.

A horn blew, blaring and blasting. Wrinn saw Iradahon in his kehrad armor several yards across from him.

And Wrinn felt his stomach begin to sink, his mind to twist and turn, as through the filthy camp emerged two kobolds holding staves, and behind them, a man… but it was not a man.

If a human, he was the tallest of all humans. Yet he was not human. His skin was colored gray, and his eyes were white and looked sightless, though he could clearly see. He was dressed in a black vest. His fingernails were long and pointed.

And Wrinn had a thought, and a fear.

And he heard a tree from far away where the Blight had no claim, a spruce crying out from the forest of Daron Hen, *"It's Lothan! Run!"*

"Kobolds, you are my most beloved creations," said Lothan, "and well shall you undertake your work. For you possess not just sword or spear, or physical might, but also magic. You possess not human or elven magic, but the magic the Master loves best."

The kobolds were parading before him, and to Wrinn the rokahn seemed jealous.

Lothan smiled, and Wrinn saw fangs. A tongue lolled from his fangs, and the tongue was forked. "But I am afraid some intruders have come, to interrupt your debut party," Lothan said. "They serve the one I hate."

"Run, Son of the Forest! Run!"

And Wrinn ran, obeying the voice of the trees, as spears seemed to appear out of thin air, and impale Iradahon straight through, then pierce the dust where Wrinn had been standing.

And Wrinn ran, and he ran, and he ran, amid the confusion of the rokahn camp.

"Tell the Prince of the Dawn," howled Lothan, "the dawn is not coming! Tell the Prince of the Dawn the kobolds will cut out his heart!"

As Wrinn bowled his way through the rokahn bodies, there was a new kind of commotion, rokahn screaming and being tossed aside, and the blood of rokahn spraying up in the air. An Elvish horse, colored silver with a white mane, was hoofing the rokahn and spearing them with its horns.

And Wrinn received a message, *"She is yours!"*

And another message from the trees, *"We sent her to you... she will have a better master!"*

And Wrinn swept himself onto her back, and allowed her to carry him forward, shooting fast like lightning through the stinking camps, and then away from them.

Before the sun had set, Wrinn had removed the kehrad armor piece by piece. Before the sun had set, Wrinn was riding in his white shift, with a quarterstaff and a longknife and nothing more — all a warrior should ever wield. And before the sun had set, he had entered the Forest of Daron Hen, riding with all due speed to bring to the Prince of the Dawn tidings of war.

Chapter Forty-Eight: On A Sunny Day

"To *Naron Da* you go," said the elvenking. "I do not trust you."

"I would not trust me, either," said Xan, standing before those gathered in the Elder Chamber.

Reev saw that the Skeleton Key clipped to his belt was no longer emitting heatless black smoke, but instead shining with a soft white glow. What had happened?

"Who else will accompany the Sage?" said the elvenking.

"Fortunato," Reev said. Then, after a moment, "Spyke."

"Anyone else?" said the elvenking.

"Yes," Reev said. "There is another."

~

The trees guided Wrinn's steed to springs of water in which were the nutrients of the ages, granting the Elvish horse strength and sustenance wherever she went.

And as they traveled, countless miles every day, south by southwest, through the mossy forest, the trees continued to converse. It seemed that conversing was what trees liked best.

"The one whose steed you ride, Iradahon knew…"

"Innuvi, he was called…"

"But Iradahon saw in him the workings of Narenvi. Iradahon was ever paranoid…"

Wrinn was wearing Innuvi's shift, and wielding his longknife.

"Paranoid, Iradahon was. Iradahon saw Narenvi in Iradahon's eyes. Iradahon committed murder. Innuvi was innocent…"

"Ah, Narenvi… he was proud when he walked these woods, and he was deceptive. The gods walked these woods too. And they examined Narenvi, and

they saw... evil was found in him."

What were these trees speaking of?

"*Judgment was pronounced to Narenvi... unquenchable fire. We shall not fear Narenvi...*"

And then Wrinn realized, Narenvi was the Dark One. The Dark One had walked these woods.

"*During the Age of the Gods, this tract of forest was present. It was untouched by the cataclysm. Some of us remember the gods and their speech, and their faces — yes, their faces.*"

Wrinn had traveled a hundred miles.

"*We love the gods. But Narenvi, we hate.*"

~

It was a cool Harona morning when Spyke received the news he feared most.

The steward was outside his room in the royal apartments. "Spyke," he said. "A ship with red and gold sails has docked in port. They demand to see you in person."

What could he do now? If he refused, the magistrate in Imperial City could draw up papers for his arrest. He could not resist meeting with Imperial investigators. He would have to use all the glibness of his tongue, the minor fibs and exaggerations that made his second cousin the emperor famous.

He would not resist. He would tell as much truth as he could afford. Above all, he would protect his own hide. But he remembered — the Prince of the Dawn.

It was afternoon, in the warming air, when Spyke arrived at port astride a horse that had been provided him. The port at Danarion was surprisingly small for a city its size, but its docks were large enough to host many ships. There were about two dozen houses and shops surrounding a market square, and beyond a pier. At that pier, a sleek Imperial craft was tied. In that craft was someone he thought he knew.

She was dark-haired, the investigator, fair of face, wearing a neat brown gown. Behind her on the ship itself were Imperial soldiers, wearing helmets with red horsehair crests. To their numbers were added sailors, and marines with swords.

"Greetings, Vitto," said the investigator.

"Please, call me Spyke," Spyke replied. "Everyone does."

"Very well," said the investigator.

Spyke stirred, as an ocean breeze ruffled his hair and the whitecaps crashed in on the beach. Beyond was blue and only blue. Blue — a color he knew so well.

"You are a distinguished soldier of rank," said the investigator. "You would not want to lose your pay or be dishonored."

"It is the thing I fear most," said Spyke. He supposed it was true.

But he had fought against the Empire in Gallia. He had come all this way with the traitor Gallian general Fortunato. So was it true, in all?

"Would you take an oath to the god Imperium and state that Fortunato of Ríva is not with you, at punishment of discharge and potential prosecution?" said the investigator.

"I would not," said Spyke.

And his words seemed to confirm the truth to the investigator, the truth unsaid.

The investigator seemed to know it. And she smiled. "Very well, Vitto Khandulis," she said, using the name he had insisted against. "You will enter a plea of silence. And… I suppose… we both know what that means. But Fortunato of Ríva is for another day.

"And there is something else." The investigator made a signal, and one of the green-garbed marines walked up behind her, carrying a paper.

"The archivist at the Imperial Library overlooked a document regarding your inquiry on the Sixth Anthanian Legion," she said. "All qualified users of the cursus publicus are entitled to a thorough completion of official requests. I think, Vitto Khandulis, you will find it tantalizing reading."

~

Back in his room in the king's apartments, Spyke disrobed to his civilian clothes and began to read the paper.

(ADDENDUM). AFTER THE EXECUTION OF SERAPO REX, THE FINAL LEGATE OF THE SIXTH ANTHANIAN LEGION, THE IMPERIAL COUNCIL UNDERTOOK A YEARS-LONG INQUIRY ON THE NOW-DISBANDED LEGION. THROUGH INTERROGATION OF EYEWITNESSES AND ON-SITE INVESTIGATIONS, THEY UNCOVERED EVIDENCE THAT THE SIXTH ANTHANIAN LEGION COMMITTED AN ACT OF BARBARISM, A CRIME SO HORRIFIC IT CRIED OUT FOR JUSTICE. DURING THE UGAR WAR OF 210-211 Y.E., HIGH-RANKING MEMBERS OF THE SIXTH ANTHANIAN LEGION ARE BELIEVED TO HAVE COMMITTED A HUMAN SACRIFICE TO THE UGAR BARBARIANS' GOD, BELPHEOR. THE CREDULOUS BELIEVE THE BARBARIANS' GOD GRANTED THE LEGION INFERNAL POWERS OF DESTRUCTION, BUT THE IMPERIAL COUNCIL PASSED A RESOLUTION OF ADVICE AND CONSENT REJECTING THIS, AND RESOLVED TO STRIKE OUT ANY MENTION OF THE SIXTH ANTHANIAN FROM THE HISTORY BOOKS. ALL

STATUES AND MONUMENTS AND ANY MARKER HONORING THE SIXTH ANTHANIAN LEGION WERE DEMOLISHED AND DISPOSED OF ACCORDING TO THE LAWS OF DAMNATIO MEMORII. SACRIFICES WERE MADE TO ACQUIRE THE TRUE GODS' FORGIVENESS. THE IMPERIAL COUNCIL PASSED RESOLUTIONS CONDEMNING AND OUTLAWING THE WORSHIP OF BELPHEOR OR ANY BARBARIAN GOD.

A human sacrifice… a lost legion. And Spyke thought, *Abon Bet Belas,* the Omen that Desolates, and Belpheor, were one and the same.

Spyke would no longer call himself a skeptical man.

~

The day was sunny when Alondir of Ríva was born. The day was warm.

It was the twenty-second day of Harona, but Fortunato was in the Elf Lands. The midwife would call it the twenty-fifth day of Oré, but Fortunato would not, not so long as he lived.

Alondir was happy and he was healthy. He had his father's dark brown hair and his mother's bright blue eyes. His ears came to the slightest of points.

In the natal chamber, Nenré soothed the baby boy.

And Fortunato thought… would he really leave his son for the Dark Land?

After all, the Council of the Last Time was ending. The Sage's party was readying its departure.

Would he go with them, in truth?

Chapter Forty-Nine: Messenger

"And where will you go? And how will you leave?" said the elvenking to Xan.

"By ship we will leave," Xan said, "to a port on the Empire's southern coast. I remember this port, and I remember the desert road I walked, the road that led to *Naron Da.*"

"So we must ready a ship at once," said the elvenking. "Who can pilot it?"

"Spyke knows how to sail," said Reev from his seat. "I can learn."

"Spyke, Fortunato, Reev… who else? Who else?" the elvenking said.

And Reev said, "There is another."

~

Wrinn galloped from the borderlines to Danarion's northern gate. He could see the palace. He knew the news he brought with him would not be welcome.

The journey had been dangerous; the journey had been long. From the far northern parts of the world he had traveled, and his mare, whom he still did not have a name for, had grown tired.

When he arrived, the soldiers on the gate made a signal, and the gate began to crank open. Wrinn cried in delirium, "The rokahn are coming! The rokahn are coming!"

An elf was standing in his path with dark hair and green eyes. Wrinn thought he had met him before, though he did not know his name.

"*Adari,*" the elf said, "welcome back. We know, indeed, the rokahn are coming. But we did not expect you to come riding in on an Elvish horse of your own…"

At the mention, the Elvish horse reared up on her hind legs and Wrinn struggled to gain control of her.

"What have you named her?" the elf said, and then Wrinn remembered, this was the elvenking's hostler, Imrari.

"She does not have a name," said Wrinn.

"To an Elvish horse, that is a grave dishonor. You shall not enter the City of Light without naming her, if you have claimed her as yours."

Wrinn remembered his horse back in Galiope, a horse of the standard species, Noble. "What is 'Noble' in Elvish?" Wrinn said and struggled to think of it. He remembered. "*Asti.*"

"She is a girl," said Imrari, "so, *Asté.*"

Astride Asté, Wrinn rode into the city, bringing tidings of war. Reev would be glad to see him. Would he be glad to see him when he knew the truth?

~

Gastreel watched as Wrinn finished his speech in the Elder Chamber, bearing the garb of a *dó kentari.*

No longer the ruffian he looked, no longer the pit fighter or slave, but a warrior of the gods. And Gastreel could not help but be impressed.

"Kobolds," said the elvenking, and he seemed a man defeated. "*Iramon iramoren!* What shall befall us?"

Gastreel thought such talk was not fit for a leader of his people.

Lord Calion, whose hair was so fair it was almost white, whose hand gleamed with many rings, spoke from the dark corners of the Elder Chamber. "Rokahn cannot wield magic because as a species, they cannot create, only destroy. The Dweorg alike have no magic in them, but that is because their powers of creation are in the crafting of wonders.

"Kobolds, though, could wield magic. And imagine what foul magic would arise from such a soul."

The figures in the Elder Chamber shifted as they pondered and ruminated.

"We must send the Sage's party away at once," said the elvenking. "The city, and the elven people, are doomed… and Gastreel should seek safe haven elsewhere."

"Nonsense," said Reev from the Sage's seat. "We will defend the city. The soothsayers have declared the City of Light will never fall."

"But it will fall," said the elvenking, "and our people will perish."

"Quiet," Lord Calion dared say. "The Sage has made his command. He and his party will not depart. We will defend the city and we will defend Lamdar. So defend it. *Sinta!*"

The elvenking, it seemed to Gastreel, was a man defeated. It was up to Reev to lead the defense of the city. It would take courage and wisdom he would have to muster. But the City of Light, and the land of Lamdar, would be defended.

~

As the month of Harona turned to Brightleaf, and the summer lingered into autumn, the city was ablaze with smith-fires, of swords and axes being forged. And as Reev managed the number of troops, and called forth a mustering of every elven man across Lamdar, news continued to trickle in from the region's far corners.

"Sage!" said one of the king's spies in the palace garden, one of the king's spies who now reported to him. "Though Xan the warlock has given up evil, and departed, the Tharvanians have only continued to make sacrifices to their abominable statue. What's more, those sacrifices are increasing."

"Tharvané abolliu," Reev said in response.

~

Brightleaf had turned into Anthanos, and the winter winds in the port outside the city were kicking up the waves. Reev's sleep was becoming troubled. It seemed he was seeing visions he was not remembering on waking.

Chapter Fifty:
The Battle of Daron Hen

In the dark of the palace garden, Reev had retreated to pray. Every citizen of Lamdar had called himself a warrior, and the city's population had doubled. He was convinced he had made the right choice, to stay behind, to fight.

Wrinn had said he wasn't so sure.

But Wrinn was gone… He was alone.

No… he wasn't.

Reev looked up from his prayers to the sound of footsteps, of military boots crunching against the frost-licked grass. And there in the dark was one he feared, one who had shown him only enmity.

Vélerion stood there, and he no longer hid his hatred. His eyes were black like the abyss.

"They call you the Sage," he said. "You took the kingship from my father."

"I did no such thing," said Reev, "your father still reigns…"

"You dishonored my sister," said Vélerion.

"That was not my doing," Reev said, "and will you rue such a thing, when a child has been born?"

Vélerion grimaced. In his now-black eyes was wrath, in his now-black eyes was the height of pride. And as Reev stood amid a blowing winter wind, he realized, he was no longer afraid.

"You came here to bring ruin to the House of Iradahir," said Vélerion. "How can such a person be the Sage?"

Reev only looked at him in the dark.

"If I were the Sage, I would do no such thing," said Vélerion. "I would use my powers to benefit the ones the gods love best, not harm them."

But did the gods love the elves best? Reev did not think so.

Vélerion swept Nagaró from its sheath. "If I were the Sage," he said, "the glory would be mine."

"Perhaps, that is why you are not," said Reev, "for I want no glory."

"You want no glory," said Vélerion. "You lie. Everyone wants glory."

"Not all are snakes like you."

The wrath and the pride in Vélerion's eyes was building to an apogee. His grimace seemed infernal in the light of the moon above head. He swept Nagaró back, then pushed the point to Reev's heart.

"If I cannot be the Sage," said Vélerion, "no one will be…"

Reev said, "Seymus lives in you."

And as Vélerion fell back a step, his murderous intent did not seem to lessen, but horns were blowing, horns both Reev and Vélerion knew.

Shouting voices confirmed what was happening.

"The rokahn are here! They are pouring through the Forest of Daron Hen!"

And Vélerion lowered his sword, then turned his murderous black eyes back to Reev. "Duty calls," he said, "but I said what I would do. I am not finished with you, Reev Nax."

~

Wrinn rushed to the stables to mount Asté, as signal-fires burned and horns blew and all the men of Danarion scrambled to don their hauberks, their vambraces and their breastplates. Wrinn, though, would enter into battle armed only with what a warrior needed, armed with only what a warrior *should* wield, what honor and justice demanded.

He mounted Asté and galloped forth, into the dark streets, and was joined by others, a massive movement of warriors and arms and armor, heading north in the shadow of Mount Daró to where the enemy lay, amid spruces of green and blue, and avenues of lichen, and halls of mosses, he knew so well.

A cold wind was blowing, icy in its character, and a frosty rain was beginning to pour, as Asté breached the North Gate, and surrounded by his fellow citizen-soldiers, Wrinn rode forth to face the enemy.

Light was appearing in the sky when rokahn met elf, in the eaves of the Forest of Daron Hen. Wrinn dismounted as through the darkness the growing light reflected on yellow eyes and monstrous bodies, as the two mobs crashed into each other like waves crashing into rocks.

A blue-skinned rokahn hooted and howled a war-cry and heaved his spear, impaling an elven warrior right next to Wrinn. Wrinn struck with his quarterstaff and hit the rokahn's iron collar, then spun about and slit his throat with his longknife.

As blood gushed from the wound and he sank into death, Wrinn looked up, and sensed the elves' spirits strengthening. For in the growing light of dawn, an elven figure rode in on a white charger, and behind him the standard-bearers carrying the blue flags of the House of Iradahir. It was the Crown Prince, Vélerion, dressed for battle, and wielding in his right hand his purple sword, Nagaró.

"Who wishes to slay rokahn?" Vélerion called out, and the elves about him cheered.

But the sight of Vélerion did not cheer Wrinn's heart. Something seemed off. Something seemed misplaced.

A black wolf came rushing through the front lines, ripping the throat of an elf and slamming her to the ground. Ten kehrad came stamping in amid the mosses armed with crossbows and instantly loosed the bolts, killing scores.

Wrinn knew hesitation was death. He charged forth at the

crossbow-wielding kehrad, and when he did, others were inspired to take the charge as well. He speared a kehrad in the head with his quarterstaff, then twisted about, and in one swift emotion, tripped three more and sent them flying to the ground.

Vélerion had charged forward on his horse, and with mighty strokes was felling rokahn in rapid succession. An ash-skinned rokahn was pierced straight through; a green-skinned rokahn he beheaded in one swift motion. Masterful were his strokes, and his *estirion* sword cut through common iron like it was paper.

Vélerion was legendary as a rokahn slayer, so much so the sight of him caused rokahn to flee. But these rokahn were not fleeing, and Wrinn thought he knew why.

There were so many more of the rokahn than there were of them. And perhaps, there was another reason they were unafraid.

As the sun rose, rokahn were spilling out of the forest in a never-ending multitude, and as soon as reinforcements arrived for the elves, countless more rokahn would appear. Their number was only increasing.

Vélerion's horse hoofed a gray-skinned rokahn in the head and sent him flying into death. Vélerion pitched back Nagaro and slew two kehrad in one motion.

And Wrinn did battle with a rokahn of mighty horns. The rokahn was driving him back, and though he had killed several — ten last he counted — he had received a cut on his arm and a bludgeoning of his head, and he was growing weaker, and more fatigued. He pitied those in armor, whose strength was far less, who did not wield the weapons or the garb that honor and justice required.

Vélerion was carrying the entire effort on his shoulders, and he was the only one making any progress into the forest. Bit by bit, he was dragging the elves forward. He slew rokahn like he was a wild animal, beheading them and stabbing them, and casting them down when his horse did not bludgeon them with his hooves or impale them with his horns.

But as morning turned to afternoon, and exhaustion and confusion reigned, Wrinn looked back, and he saw the elven lines had retreated, and they were beginning to fall backward.

A mighty stroke by Vélerion… a rokahn slain. A strike of his pommel and a black wolf whined and fled away.

But as a fog arose, as often happened in the Forest of Daron Hen, obscuring sight, Wrinn realized the moment he had dreaded all along was coming. Lothan's abominable creations had arrived.

The sight of the kobolds approaching put in Vélerion's eyes a look of bottomless despair, for he recognized what features of theirs were elven. He seemed to see himself within them, and he could see how they had been distorted.

His fighting strokes became weaker. He seemed to fight as one who was already dead.

And the kobolds were wielding staves. They were mages. What sort of magic would they work?

~

The air in Daron Hen grew cold, and at the same time, it seemed to grow hot. The wicked kobolds' eyes gleamed with an eldritch spark. And Vélerion seemed to freeze, his body to stiffen. He gasped. He was no longer fighting.

Then his face began to change, turning a bright shade of red.

He clutched at his chest and fell from the saddle, and in mid-fall, holes burst in his skin, and blood spurted into the air in frothing streams.

The elves wailed, and turned and ran.

They were running back for the city.

Wrinn did not want to follow them. If the gods wished him to die fighting the Shadow, he was willing to accept it. But he remembered Iradahon's words. He remembered what the path of the true *dó kentari* was. He was to serve legitimate authority. He was to serve the elvenking, but he was also to serve the Sage.

He could not lay low these kobolds.

Amid the panicked retreat, Wrinn saw that Asté was right behind him, and she was bucking and braying, ready to take him home.

Chapter Fifty-One:
The Battle of Danarion

The retreating elven warriors were pouring through the North Gate, and a defeat had been dealt in the Forest of Daron Hen. As Fortunato rushed forward, trying to rekindle in the elves' bravery, trying to force them out of their panic, he heard other tidings too, "The Crown Prince Vélerion is dead!"

The elvenking had already been beside himself. He had already been barely making any preparations whatsoever, and the Sage, Reev Nax, was leading the defense of the city.

Fortunato thought of Alondir and of his mother, now hiding away in the palace. Nenré was a lightbearer, but she was in no shape to work her magic.

And so the defense of Alondir rested in him.

"Steel yourselves!" Fortunato cried to the retreating elves, as the elves rushed inwards, he charged outwards, out of the protection of the gate, to make sense of things, to gain an understanding of the terrain, and of the enemy they faced.

Soon, Danarion would be a besieged city. Would its walls hold?

The elves had a small fraction of their former strength. They were not what they once had been. But the Enemy was stronger than in its first iteration.

Perhaps, Reev had been wrong… perhaps, he and his party should have left for *Naron Da* months ago. But then Fortunato would be gone, and Alondir would have died.

Amid the rush of elven bodies, he sensed love. He felt something — a sense he knew.

And amid the warriors making a panicked retreat, a defeat for the sons of Lumas and Luvé, was a black wolf rushing in with her tail wagging.

Fortunato smiled at Tyra Jade and saw that she had brought her master a present. In her jaws was the head of a kobold she had clearly torn off. Perhaps, it would please Nenré.

On second thought, it would not.

"Good girl," Fortunato said, "but drop it."

Tyra Jade dropped the kobold's head, and it bled on the ground. The gift had not made Fortunato as happy as she had hoped, but he scratched her head just the same.

~

As the North Gate began to shut, Reev drew Doomblade and rushed outside the palace grounds. He had demanded that he and the others in his party remain behind and fight, for he did not wish the City of Light to ever fall.

Yet Vélerion was dead, and the Battle of Daron Hen had been a defeat for the elves.

It was on Reev's shoulders. And so, on the front lines, he would fight.

With Doomblade held aloft, he rushed ahead, as the light of the afternoon hinted at dusk. Some elves were fleeing in the opposite direction, but at the sight of him running to danger, some slowed their pace and others stopped their flight.

Reev was not the best of warriors, but he had taken command of the defense, for the elvenking's spirits had been broken.

"Forth!" he shouted. "Forth Solardi!"

More warriors were retreating. More warriors were slowing their retreat, and some were turning around.

"Forth Solardi!" Reev shouted as loud as his lungs would carry, and amid the chaos he saw that his command was obeyed, and standards bearing Solardi were raised and carried forth, aloft — the sun and tree symbol that was the insignia of the city of Light and Life.

When he reached the wall, and the South Gate was closed, he sprinted up to the battlements, and saw the rokahn horde was like a sea.

Amid their faces were kobold mages. And Reev, for his part, felt a stab of fear, that perhaps the soothsayers had spoken untruths, and that the City of Light would fall.

As ladders fell onto the walls and rokahn shimmied up them like beasts of the jungle, there was noise behind Reev — and he heard a pure voice shout "Forth Solardi!"

Mikal was rushing up the steps to the battlements, wielding in his hand his two sabers like a wild man.

An unlucky rokahn leapt onto the wall, and Mikal's savage blow crushed his head on the pommel of the saber. More rokahn reached the battlements up ahead, and Mikal charged them, severing an arm and cutting off another's head in a savage frenzy, as he continued to shout with conviction, "Forth Solardi!"

Yet the rokahn were so numerous, and their ladders were built with such cunning skill, that it seemed the elves on the battlements were inadequate. And it was clear the forces of Shadow were focusing on the North Gate, to break it open and bring their darkness into the City of Light.

Reev looked back and saw Spyke, rushing forth, with his edged board in hand, and instantly began to bowl over the rokahn who had breached the wall. He swept his board in wild, mad strokes, knocking rokahn back off the wall to their deaths or slashing them to death with the edge of his board.

"Forth Solardi!" Reev cried, and he saw again he was obeyed, and now flag-bearers were rushing up the stairs, to perhaps strike fear in the rokahn and remind them of a time when elven strength was great.

A kobold had managed to make his way up the wall, and Reev fought panic as he charged him.

A strike of Doomblade and the kobold dodged with

amphibious grace. A stab of Doomblade and the kobold dove to the left. The kobold raised his staff to work his blood-magic on Reev, and Reev struck the staff. The *estirion* sliced the crystal and wood like it was paper. The staff exploded as it burst in twain and the kobold mage stood stunned, mouth agape.

From the shadows, Fortunato came running, and, with Danenhir, pierced the kobold straight through.

"Forth Solardi!" Fortunato shouted.

~

The sun set, and it was night.

The moon arose, and it was red.

The elves despaired at the sight of the full moon, colored like blood, considering it an ill omen. They could not afford to stop fighting, and on the battlements above the North Gate, where Reev fought, he vowed to fight all night, and ensure that the elves did not lose their spirits. He was growing tired, and with each cascade of ladders, and each strike of Doomblade, his bodily strength was waning. But he would live or die with the City of Light. If it fell, Reev would die.

It was clear the rokahn and kobolds had prepared. As the night deepened, underneath the blood-red moon, teams of black wolves began to roll trebuchets forward amid the sea of rokahn, and rokahn then began fling stones and boulders into the city. The sound of crumbling masonry and collapsing buildings further filled the elves with despair, if the blood-red moon did not already make them think the story of their people was over.

Yet Reev girded his strength and fought on, though he knew just how faint elven strength now was, how it was no longer at all what it had been in the stories Gastreel told him as a child.

Gastreel… where is he?

A rokahn was dead by Reev's hand, and a kobold. The elves

were growing weary.

Reev looked back and watched as a stone hurled from a trebuchet struck a tower of the palace, and the tower collapsed in a cascade of falling bricks. He was having a strange sense, that he had seen all this before.

"Forth Solardi!" Reev shouted, turning back to the battle ahead of him, the rokahn and kobolds below who were now wielding torches, and who still stretched into the distance, an inestimable sea.

"For Alondir!" Reev heard a cry, and darkness was transformed into light.

Nenré had ascended the steps, and her white lightbearer's robe was aglow.

The rokahn and kobolds below hissed at the light, for they hated light and life above all things. A staff was in Nenré's hands. She shot forth her hand, and a beam of pure light zapped a kobold below straight through, opening a hole in his chest.

"Forth Solardi!" Reev said. And then he repeated Nenré's words, "For Alondir!"

Yet the rokahn below in all this time had been assaying to breach the gate, and the strongest of the rokahn and kobolds had now brought a massive battering ram. They were beginning to slam it against the North Gate, and the North Gate was beginning to crack.

Underneath the red moon, Nenré seemed faint. Reev watched as she retreated as soon as she had come, back in the direction of the palace and her babe Alondir. She walked as if in a trance, as if she were caught up in a dream, as if she were sleepwalking and not waking, a brilliant white figure taking confused steps.

The gate burst in two.

~

The rokahn and kobolds were now pouring into the city, and Reev called out the retreat, not the Solardi.

Was the day lost? Were the soothsayers wrong?

How could they not be wrong?

Reev scrambled down from the wall and Fortunato followed a step behind, as now kobolds and rokahn engaged elves in the streets below. Sword against sword and spear against spear, the battle was now in the City of Light itself.

But as Reev joined the battle, he had a terrible sense. He looked at the red moon and thought something terrible was coming. He felt he had left something undone.

And as he rushed forth to fight a kobold swordsman in what once had been a peaceful alleyway, he felt a finger of fear touch his heart. Or was it a finger of something else?

Smoke? Ruin?

~

Gastreel fled into the southern parts of the city, south of Luaddon. The bodies of elves lay all about him, and the rokahn were carrying the day. Maderias shone in his hand, in the light of the red moon, an eclipse that the elves surely had predicted.

But they had not predicted such a devastating defeat.

His old hands trembled holding Maderias. Was it the end?

Could it be?

And then he saw — the body of Keras, Captain of the King's Guard, lifeless in the street, pierced straight through. Helvenhari, his *estirion* sword that was worth the price of many kingdoms, lay in his right hand's dead grip.

He had seen Keras. He looked in the direction of the South Gate and he saw something else.

Smoke was on the horizon.

Dark, gray, smoke.

Gastreel backed up a step and took in a sharp gasp. He did not know why the smoke so frightened him, why his heart was now pounding out of control.

The smoke cast in orange colors by the red moon, was a massive wall, and it was clearly visible despite the darkness of the night.

And there was something else.

The smoke had eyes.

Flames that were surely the size of city blocks or larger, burned like twin beacons in the smoke. And Gastreel knew they were eyes, for there was a head.

As he turned his panicked gaze from one side of the smoky horizon to the other, he saw in the smoke a chest, legs, and from the head, the form of two large horns.

He thought... *Abon Bet Belas.*

He thought... *Belpheor.*

The people of Tharvané had done such evil they had loosened the monster's chains, and now it walked in the mortal world. The monster was larger than the city itself, for it dominated the sky. It was taking smoking steps toward the City of Light. Its eyes were scanning the city, as if it were looking for something.

It roared, and its roar carried through the heavens.

The rokahn and kobolds in the distance were turning back to look in fear.

~

When Wrinn saw the monster, dominating the horizon, his heart seized up in fear. The elves beside him wailed and seem to know the day was lost. There was whimpering and there was crying, a sense the gods had abandoned them.

From where Wrinn stood, at the city's western gate, the

monster appeared close, for it was as large as the sky.

He saw Lord Calion walking through the streets in robes of white. Lord Calion took a nervous gulp.

And then, out of thin air it seemed, an Elvish horse came galloping, and Lord Calion was swept onto its saddle. He was riding in the direction of the monster.

~

Fortunato had been standing on the South Gate, and now he could scarcely breathe. The smoking behemoth that towered into the heavens was kicking up ash and cinders, and what elves remained were coughing wildly. And as Fortunato backed away, and thought better of facing down this monster, he saw below translucent figures approaching at the vanguard of the smoking monster, what appeared to be the ghosts of Imperial soldiers holding their eagle standards aloft.

Fortunato at last turned and ran, for he knew he was no match. He thought of rushing to find Reev and speeding away.

And then he thought, *Alondir…*

~

Wrinn could see the smoking monster's eyes darting from one part of the city to another. At last, they fixed on the North Gate. He realized in that moment who the monster was after.

The monster, *Abon Bet Belas,* was after Reev. And Reev was no match for him.

He turned to the building he was standing under and grasped hold of the windows. He pulled himself up and leapt up, grasping hold of the roof. He pulled himself to top of the roof, and wondered at the sight of the moon.

Then, as Iradahon had taught him, he used his quarterstaff to vault from rooftop to rooftop, speeding to where he knew Reev was, his post at the North Gate.

~

Gastreel's heart was pounding. His hands were trembling. He knew *Abon Bet Belas* wanted Reev.

As he stood alone in the street, watching as the smoking horizon took steps into the city proper, creating cyclones of smoke and ash, there was light up ahead, a light-garbed figure shining in the night.

It was the Lord Calion, riding on his horse.

"*Dibalsomnar, danen ira!*" Lord Calion howled.

And the head of the smoking horizon was growing close, though the monster was so large, Gastreel did not know how to make sense of just how close it truly was.

Lord Calion raised his right hand, and a ruby ring burst. A spear of fiery red energy shot from it and struck the smoking monster, and the smoking monster roared in pain.

Lord Calion raised his left hand, and an emerald ring burst, and a jet of brilliant green went soaring into the sky. But this time the smoking monster's hand caught the beam.

The smoking horizon roared in anger.

And then it was so close, Gastreel could see its feet.

There was ash, there was cinders, there was a poison cloud. And a finger descended from the heavens like a cyclone touching down, and covered Lord Calion and his horse.

Gastreel felt he would faint.

When the smoking finger was removed, Lord Calion and his horse were gone.

A figure came running through the street, a figure in an orange robe. It was Avernathi. Avernathi was looking up at the monster, and was craning his head.

Gastreel looked at his sword Maderias, and thought it would not do.

"*Gastreel! Evar Pellan Imen!*" Avernathi said, and then he fled.

"*Evaiu Pellan Imen,*" Gastreel repeated.

Gastreel had said, "I possess the Fire of Imon."

~

Reev knew the monster in the horizon was searching for him, but halfway into the city, it had ceased his walking. Reev knew he was no match for a creature of such might.

As he stood and watched in horror, a white figure was bounding toward him, leaping from rooftop to rooftop. It was Wrinn.

At last, Wrinn made a great leap, and he was at Reev's feet.

"Reev!" said Wrinn. "Let's get out of here."

"No," Reev said. "We must defend Lamdar. We must defend the City of Light…"

~

Maderias would not do, Gastreel's sword of common steel. But in front of Gastreel was the body of Keras, Captain of the Guard, and Keras's sword was in his lifeless hands.

Keras's sword was of *estirion*.

Gastreel stepped forward, trying to manage the racing of his heart and his growing fear.

He took Keras's sword, called Helvenhari, "Bull-Cutter," and let Maderias fall ringing to the ground.

What happened next was chaos, what happened next was cataclysm.

But by the end of it, buildings had fallen to rubble, and the earth was shaken, and in the night, there was terror; and the head of the monster was at ground level. Its monstrous eyes were much larger than many city blocks. Its mouth was the size of the palace itself.

Gastreel said, *"Kon Helvenharu, heru y helvon kidairu."*

The monster spoke in a voice that was hellish, one that carried for miles and caused Gastreel's ears to scream in pain: *"Buar num kidaira danenvon."*

Gastreel said, *"Num danenvi thó. Thó Abollari."*

And Belpheor's hand was about him, a storm of cinders and ash, and Gastreel could no longer see. But as the monster grasped him, a shield of fire gleamed, and he remained conscious.

~

Wrinn watched as the smoking monster again stood up on his feet. The monster was now holding something in its right hand, and as Wrinn squinted with his elven eyes, he could see what he was holding was either a human or an elf.

He made out a green robe and his heart clenched. "Gastreel!"

Wrinn turned to Reev in a panic.

But Reev was looking at the smoking monster, and there was a light in his eyes. He did not seem himself. He said, *"Avela! Tond kon aion."*

That meant, "Look! They are with him."

~

Gastreel was in the clouds, where he could not breathe, and where he lay, or was held aloft, there was a constant rain falling, and a constant peal of thunder.

Fire shimmered about him as Belpheor swung him about, a mile with each flinging of its hand, as Gastreel took a firmer grip with Helvenhari, and having taken a firmer grip, begun to strike.

He struck and the blade whistled through smoke. He called out curses. He could see the monster's eyes.

And then he repeated the words of Lord Calion: *"Dibalsomnar, danen ira!"*

"Child-eater, the gods rebuke you!"

And there was a flash of lightning amid the clouds, and Gastreel saw another face besides Belpheor in the storm.

He struck with Helvenhari as Belpheor's gripped tightened. The lights of the city below were like twinkling stars bunched together.

He hewed with Helvenhari, and lightning flashed, and there seemed to be another hand, enclosing his own.

He struck a third time, and a wound seemed to open up amid the body of smoke, and there was flame, and there was fire. Belpheor roared in pain, but Gastreel's ears seemed guarded by a shield unseen.

~

Once, Fortunato had fled rokahn. Now, he was fleeing ghosts.

The translucent Imperial soldiers had dark dead eyes, and were cutting swathes through the elven lines. Fortunato had come to realize they were invincible, and so he was fleeing them and not fighting. He turned back and saw their translucent standards, red and gold, with a numeral six written upon them. They numbered in the thousands, and it seemed what they were doing was not their will, but that they were possessed.

Some foolish elves had brandished swords, but no weapon could harm them. Their fate was tied to the monster who had enslaved them.

Fortunato uttered a prayer under his breath.

~

Gastreel struck a fourth time, and then a fifth. Every time he struck with Helvenhari, opening a wound in the body of smoke, there was a flash of hellfire.

At last, roaring in pain, the monster relinquished his grip of Gastreel.

But Gastreel, to his wonder, did not fall.

He was seemingly suspended in the air, and lightning flashed, and Gastreel thought he saw wings.

A sixth strike, a seventh wound, and now Gastreel knew he was not alone. He was not alone…

~

Reev watched as the smoking monster began to take dizzy steps, as its knees buckled. The fires in its eyes were blazing, yet to Reev they seemed the blaze of a fire burning out. Under his breath he prayed for the rescue of the City of Light, for the peace of Lamdar. But he thought… there would be a cost.

~

An eighth strike, a ninth strike, and the monster roared. Belpheor's body was now flaming in multiple wounds, even as Gastreel was growing weaker, expending the last bits of what physical integrity in his body remained.

And he saw that Helvenhari was now leaking liquid metal onto the ground below.

Carried aloft somehow, Gastreel struck a tenth time, and Belpheor's roar was so loud Gastreel's ears were deafened. He could no longer hear a thing.

Flame burst from all parts of its body, and Gastreel realized Belpheor was shrinking, and that both he and Gastreel were plummeting to the earth. Their fates were bound, but the Sage was rescued.

No, he heard a voice, *your fates could not be more different…*

The fire as Gastreel plummeted, as Helvenhari dissipated into liquid, leaving only a hilt, was turning to hues of green, and the green-hued fire was beginning to swirl about the ever-shrinking Belpheor, and as the green-hued fire swirled, it was beginning to take the shape of chains.

Gastreel heard a voice, *Well done…*

And as he plummeted to the ground, striking the street without pain, and took his final breath, he saw mountains and fresh water, and an orchard he hoped he'd never leave.

~

The Imperial ghosts were rising up into the air. Fortunato had ceased his fleeing. The Imperial ghosts' translucent bodies were turning transparent, and shades of blue, as over the hills dawn appeared.

"We are free, Rufus!" one of the ghosts shouted. "We're going home!"

The ghosts rose up into the heavens, and eventually vanished from sight.

Chapter Fifty-Two: Saying Goodbye

In the daylight, in the wake of the slaying of Belpheor, the rokahn and the kobolds met a new foe.

Theudo's warriors were riding in on brown wolves, on wolves large like Tyra, but with brown fur and blue eyes. Reev watched as the kobolds turned and fled, and as more of Theudo's soldiers came charging into the city.

Yet Reev had a sense that things had not gone as he hoped, though in the light of the dawn it was clear, the City of Light endured, and Lamdar was rescued.

~

Others were already crowded around Gastreel's body when Reev found it. In his hand was a hilt without a blade.

And Reev began to weep, though he knew death was not the end.

I should weep for us…

But now his mentor was gone from Varda, and if Reev wanted Gastreel to accompany him to the Dark Land, it was no longer possible.

"No!" howled a voice, and Nenré came running in. She was holding Alondir to her chest. "No! It cannot be! How can the gods be so cruel?"

"The city could not have been rescued without him," said Reev through his tears.

"Why? Why, oh gods? Why?" said Nenré, and then turned and ran back, in the direction of the palace.

~

As Reev continued to weep, he saw that the city largely lay in ruins, that the rokahn and the kobolds had slain countless elves, and that untold numbers of buildings had collapsed into rubble. Yet as Theudo's men drove the last of the rokahn and kobolds outside the walls of the City of Light, he knew the soothsayers had spoken the truth, that the City of Light would never fall to Shadow.

And Reev wondered… there was a City of Light. Was there also a city of darkness?

~

In the afternoon, they buried Gastreel in a tomb outside the city, where in prior times only elvenkings were buried. They would allow his body to turn to bone, and then he would be placed in an ossuary.

As for Reev, he fought feelings of guilt through his tears, for if he had abandoned the City of Light and the land of Lamdar, perhaps Gastreel would be alive.

But he was no longer, in the sense most people thought of life, and Reev wondered if there ever would be an end to his weeping.

"A good man, brave," said the elvenking. "In fact, there is not a word for how good a man the Green Wizard was. The City of Light is saved. And now, gathered friends, we move on to our next chapter."

Reev had never seen Fortunato cry. But across from him, as the tomb was sealed shut, tears were running down Fortunato's cheeks and he was weeping bitterly.

~

Though the Council of the Last Time had reconvened, it

seemed different now, and the mood was dour. The City of Light was saved, but some wondered, not least Reev, if it perhaps had not been worth the cost of Gastreel's death.

Yet Reev and others would have to find a way to move on. For the fight against Shadow would continue, and though the forces of evil had been dealt a devastating defeat, the elven kingdoms were in ruins, and the Enemy would only grow stronger.

"Five to *Naron Da*, five warriors of light," said the elvenking in the council chambers. "Five to *Naron Da*, in the shadows of the night…"

And the council had been concluded, on so heavy an occasion.

~

As preparations continued for the departure, Reev knew the days of Anthanos were growing late, and if they waited too long, the seas would be rough.

Yet the Shadow had been beaten back, and the rokahn and kobolds had retreated. Though all lay in ruins, there was ample time for the Sage and his party to leave prepared.

Victuals and foodstuffs were brought from the outlying farms, enough to last for a ship's journey of many weeks. And the last bits of guidance were offered to Reev, and to Fortunato, who was considered the planner and the captain of the effort.

How would Reev defeat the Dark One? He did not know. He would enter into *Naron Da* blindly. He would trust the gods.

The prophecies said he would be given strength, that he would know what to do.

The prophecies had said Danarion would not fall to Shadow. And it had not.

Prophecies were all they had, prophecies and each other. And as winter returned anew, the winter of 1154, not for the last time did Reev think of home, of Glenda and Aunt Ramona and his cousin Ash, and all the friends they had left behind.

Gastreel had been a good man, Reev's mentor and guide, the father he never had. Reev owed so much to him. And now, for a little while, he was gone. Reev did not know if he'd recover in this life from the severing of that bond. But *Naron Da*, and duty, awaited.

Duty… the treading of Seymus underfoot.

Blindly would he trust the prophecies, like he had trusted the prophecies that Danarion would never fall.

Chapter Fifty-Three:
The Ship

The dawn broke on the morning of the twenty-fifth day of Anthanos. The air was cold yet still. The elves now lived in a city of ruins, and there was a question if they would rebuild to their former height, if it was possible.

As for Reev, he had been packing everything he thought would be necessary for the long journey to *Naron Da*. As he was stuffing a tunic into his pack, it dawned on him he wasn't alone.

Fortunato was standing there in the sun's light.

Outside Reev's new room in the king's apartments, a holding place as they prepared to depart, Fortunato stood. For the first time in days, Fortunato had a smile on his face.

How could anyone smile at such a time as this?

"Are you ready?" Fortunato said.

"As ready as I think I'll ever be."

"Well," Fortunato said, "it's about time."

~

Reev strode out into the cold air, and he saw that crowds had lined the streets of Danarion. Some were uttering prayers, others throwing flowers before he and Fortunato's feet. It was time, time for another prophecy to be fulfilled, the Sage leaving out of the River's Gate in the company of his friends. The time had at last come for the five to leave for *Naron Da*.

Reev wished it were six, but now that could not be.

Where the Watercourse began, there was a carrack idling in the water. The ship was the finest he had ever seen, each dark board perfectly fitted. There were three sails, one vast, one large, and one small sail above, all painted with the Solardi, the sun and tree symbol of the Lamen elves. The sails were white and red.

Here it was, the point of the departure, and Reev saw that he and Fortunato were the last to arrive. Spyke was there with two suits of luggage, and Xan was waiting with his pack, and Wrinn was standing by. Along with them were Wrinn's horse Asté and Reev's horse Cobalt, and Tyra Jade, who was wagging her tail and beaming.

As Reev and Fortunato arrived, the elvenking strode out from amid the crowd and said, "This is the ship that shall bear you, Sage. It had been a merchant ship called *Benadhar,* 'Fair Winds,' but now we call it *Velatari*, 'Prince-Bearer,' in your honor."

But Reev was not a prince, unless they were referring to the Sage's title of Prince of the Dawn.

Spyke boarded first, and Xan, then Fortunato followed. In scurried Tyra Jade, and then Wrinn, eyeing Reev sidelong, at last walked aboard, leading Cobalt and Asté by the reins.

Reev then boarded the ship, the last aboard, the ship that would take them to *Naron Da.* And as he stood on the deck, through the crowd there was a commotion, an elven woman so beautiful she took Reev's breath away, Nenré.

Her red hair had begun to regrow.

"Come with us, Nenré," said Fortunato.

Nenré laughed. "And will I take our child with us to the Dark Land?"

Fortunato could seem to give no answer.

And there was a commotion, another noise, the sound of rushing waters. Reev looked up, and saw up above what looked like the gears of a watermill, now beginning to turn.

The wheels of water were kicking up froth, and the Watercourse was growing unstable. The waters became violent and churning, and the ship was beginning to turn this way and that.

The Watercourse seem to be rising, even as the waters became unstable. And then there was a rushing sound, as Reev heard the

River's Gate burst open, and the ship *Velatari* was borne swiftly out toward the sea.

~

They were quickly leaving Lamdar, the five warriors of light now venturing to *Naron Da*. They passed swiftly through the River's Gate, and the canal leading to the Great Sea filled with water ahead of them. Swiftly they were borne, toward "a port on the Empire's south coast" or so they intended, as the sails caught the wind, and Spyke seized the ship's wheel, and gained control of the ship called *Velatari*.

On deck, Reev saw that the elves had provided crates filled with ship's biscuit, and barrels filled with fresh spring water from Mount Daró. They would not starve. But Reev knew that there would be danger.

There would be danger, for not all questions had been answered at the Council of the Last Time.

What was the "House of a Serpent" that Reev would have to face?

And above all, who was the Dark One's Hand?

As the ship seemed to skim the waters under the blue-skied day, Reev felt a wind, a wind he knew, and a familiar feeling. A vision was coming. He gave up resistance.

Chapter Fifty-Four: Seeing Visions

"Wheels of water, wheels of time," said the elvenking in his private chamber.

The mills of the Watercourse had swiftly sent the ship to the sea, as had been prophesied.

He heard a cooing, and looked down from his seat.

The creature twisting his arms and babbling in the crib at his feet was like the opposite of the kobolds. The kobolds had the worst features of both rokahn and elf, but Alondir of Ríva had the best features of elf and human.

His ears came to slender points. His blue eyes radiated warmth.

And, the elvenking realized, he was next in line to the kingship. For the elvenking's son Avernathi had been made a full priest, and so disqualified himself. Vélerion…

"Oh, Vélerion," the elvenking said softly.

He could not afford to be controlled by his grief.

A handmaid in flame orange took hold of Alondir and lifted him from his crib. She rocked him, intending to put him to sleep.

A door opened and Nenré walked in. She took Alondir from the handmaid and held him to her chest. "Oh, my precious boy," she said.

And she walked across the room, closer to her father.

"Danarion," she said, "will never fall."

But Nenré was wrong.

"It will fall," said the elvenking, "but not to evil."

~

Behind Bala was an army of five thousand undead. They did

whatever he asked, and it was slowly dawning on him that he was not welcome in vampire lands.

The Vampire Lords had been sending armies to hurt him, and he had defeated them. He had given the bodies false life as Granny Yaga had taught him, and then the cycle had continued.

He wasn't sure what to do next. For now the vampires were abandoning their towns, heading south on horseback or carriage, leaving the land called Nardur altogether. And Bala was not entirely sure why.

Bala had been an accidental conqueror. He realized that Nardur was his. An entire kingdom belonged to a nine-year-old boy, if he wanted it.

Yet now, as he pushed east through the black pines, he saw he had at last come to the vampire capital, the town called Druenel-Hai.

The walls were of black stone, with spikes at the top. Along the walls ran skull reliefs. The gates were painted with twin skulls on either door. And Bala saw there were no guards on their posts.

But someone else was standing there.

Three someones, in fact.

Granny Yaga the hag, purple of skin, clothed in rags, was standing outside the city gate. With her was blue-skinned Jenny and her green-skinned sister, Anise.

"Balor," said Granny Yaga.

"Don't call me that," Bala said. "That's not my name."

"It is your true name," said Granny Yaga. "It is what your father named you. And you will call yourself that, by the end."

"I will never," Bala said.

Granny Yaga was looking at the army behind Bala. Was it possible for a hag to show fear?

"Oh, Balor," said Granny Yaga, "you have become a great conqueror. But there are greater things than conquerors. Let me show you."

And Bala and his army of thousands of undead followed Granny Yaga, away from the City of Druenel-Hai, through the snow.

~

They were passing far from the city, deep in the wilderness. Snow was blowing, and winter was deepening. They passed over a frozen pond, and through a few stands of pine trees. It was dusk when Granny Yaga stopped her walking.

She had stopped her walking before a forest.

Beyond her, black pines stretched into the distance. Between the black pines was a profound darkness, and though a harsh arctic wind was blowing, the black pines neither stirred nor swayed, their boughs remaining perfectly still.

Bala gulped.

And for the first time since he had come to the Land of Nardur, his heart was beginning to race, and his hands had grown clammy, and he wanted Mama.

"Balor," said Granny Yaga, "you have one last conquest before you can become king, the conquest of the self. For beyond me lies a forest so perilous that not even the undead soldiers who fight in your name will enter. It is called the Haunted Forest, and it was here the ancient druen performed their worship of the Dark One, the crime that caused their curse."

Now, Bala really wanted Mama.

"Balor," said Granny Yaga, "you have been working your magic, and raising your army, with only an apprentice's wand. But a true mage must fashion a staff. And in the Haunted Forest, there is crystal aplenty, and wood, for you to make a staff worthy of a wizard-king.

"Your army will not dare follow you. Will you dare enter in?"

"I will," Bala said, and the hags smiled. He felt a ghostly wind blow as he took his first steps into the Haunted Forest.

And he thought, his name was Balor, truly, after all.

~

Reev stirred awake from his vision, and he could now see the shoreline of Lamdar. The skies above him were blue, and the winds were fair, and Spyke said they would be off the coast of the Southern Reaches by dusk.

"No more visions," he said softly under his breath.

But he thought he saw the Lady of Danyen in his mind's eye, and he thought he saw her eyes of green and her hair of burnt gold. Words: "Just one more vision, *Velati Sonoren.*"

~

Ambrass and the gypsies had been rejected outside the gates of Bregantium. The gatekeeper had spat at them when they arrived, and said they would not accept their kind.

And so, they had made their way here, to the shoals in the south of the province of Gad, and as the ancients had done before, they had begun to disassemble their wagons, and reassemble them into ships.

Ambrass fought tears as she watched Gaius at work.

Twice she had miscarried. Her womb, it seemed, was a soil on which their child refused to grow. Ambrass feared she was barren, and she feared Gaius resented her.

The day progressed, noon to afternoon, and one by one the wagons transformed, from wheels to skids, from canvas coverings to sails, and then they began to push their sailing crafts out to sea.

She wept for herself, for a memory she had buried deep inside. Happiness was unrealistic, she knew. Joy was beyond her. There was no such thing. She could not expect it. She could not have it.

The gypsies had left Galiope, the city that had welcomed them, because the Empire had seized control of it, like they had seized control of the world.

Were all Imperials violent and wicked? She could no longer remember. She could scarcely remember her time in Galiope. She could only remember her married life. She could only remember this.

This… this was her lot.

And she stepped into she and Gaius's sailing ship, and helped push it to sea.

Soon and very soon, they would reach Vharat, the gypsies' ancient homeland. That was where Gaius, now chieftain of the gypsies, intended to take them.

But Gaius had confided to her privately that he did not know where Vharat was, and he did not know if he was leading the gypsies to doom.

Doom… was this not doom already, Ambrass thought, as the multicolored sailing crafts left their moorings, and headed south into the water?

On the ship, Gaius and Ambrass tried again to have a child. And in the midst of it, Gaius gasped, and was still. Ambrass allowed Gaius to slip off of her. She touched his wrist.

Gaius's heart was no longer beating.

Death had come to them… death.

And what would befall the gypsies now?

She felt something within her, a memory unbidden, straining to break free.

~

The vision was gone from Reev when the ship called *Velatari* sped westward into the sea. Into the Great Sea it sped, and it skimmed on the waters, carrying the five warriors of the light south with all due speed.

Naron Da awaited. The House of a Serpent awaited. Yet Reev could not afford to feel afraid.

"We'll be gone twenty miles before the sun sets!" cried Fortunato on the foredeck.

"More than that!" called out Spyke from the ship's wheel.

Gastreel was gone. Galiope was gone. And the Elf Lands were gone from Reev, but Reev realized, he did not belong there.

The Time of the Elves was finished, and it would not come back. Their strength had withered and it would not return. To the humans it was left to wage this war, this war against Seymus and his followers in the mortal world. Reev had a thought, that Fortunato and Xan as well, would tread Seymus under their feet.

"Goodbye, Danarion!" called out Xan, as he watched the coastland and farmland swiftly move by them, and as the winds blew stronger, and the ship skimmed the waters even faster — if it were possible.

"Goodbye!" called out Wrinn, more softly.

Where was *Naron Da*? Reev did not know. Xan said he knew the way. But Xan said a lot of things.

All evil had been purged from him now. Reev had a feeling they would have to rely on each other. Not just Reev, not just Xan, but all of them, working in concert, to reach *Naron Da*, and deal to Seymus his defeat.

"Wrinn! Do you want to try the ship's wheel a moment?" said Spyke.

"Why not?" Wrinn answered.

And the landscape continued to fly by, under the beneficent wind.

"Goodbye," Reev said, to Galiope, to Gastreel.

"Goodbye," Reev said, to the Elf Lands.

The danger they ventured to was great because it was still so unknown.

But Reev knew the Time of the Elves was over, now, and their part in the prophecies was finished. He knew that, though the City of Light would never fall to Shadow, it was up to others now, to fight this war, others who still had strength.

There was strength in humanity — Reev only had to look about him, to Spyke, to Xan. There was strength in the five headed to *Naron Da*. And Reev knew something else, too, that the Telantines endured.

The wind was picking up. The ship was skipping south along the coast at speeds Reev had not thought possible. And it seemed to his mind, because of that, that the gods favored this journey — even mandated it.

As the sun's light continued to strengthen, as the ship called *Velatari* sped through the blue waters, Reev felt a stirring in his heart. He wished he had said goodbye more thoroughly. He wished he could have bidden farewell to the Elf Lands more properly.

And so he said, to the crew, to the raging sea, "Forth Solardi!"

But that was the past.

So he said, "Forth Telantis!" and his voice carried, across the wind, across the waves.

And he knew in his heart, these five to *Naron Da* would crush Seymus under their feet.

THE END

Continued in Book Six, *Warriors of Telantis*…

Glossary

Times and Dates

Vardic Calendar		Julian Calendar Equivalent
1.	Albos	January
2.	Kaldsil	February
3.	Primrane	March
4.	Tidusca	April
5.	Brenua	May
6.	Aurelios	June
7.	Odens	July
8.	Sextil	August
9.	Harona	September
10.	Brightleaf	October
11.	Anthanos	November
12.	Candlebright	December

Elven Calendar (Lunisolar)		Julian Calendar Equivalent
5.	Gilné	Jan. – Feb.
6.	Sindjé	Feb. – Mar.
7.	Sorjé	Mar. – Apr.
8.	Ríal	Apr. – May
9.	Vlesti	May – Jun.
10.	Kelvé	Jun. – Jul.
11.	Kaudé	Jul. – Aug.
12.	Oré	Aug. – Sept.

1.	Yanenré	Sept. – Oct.
2.	Estion	Oct. – Nov
3.	Dorion	Nov. – Dec.
4.	Dandathon	Dec. – Jan.

Elven phrases

Danen vadilla… Illuné vadilla, Eldari: "The gods guard (you)… The Light guard (you), Sage."

Dra'datsi: Literally, "out-born," an elf born outside the Elven World.

Ridio: *"Awaken!"*

Locta: *"Speak!"*

Hirda: *"Arise!"*

Drubi: "Annoyance"

Dilari sonoren: "Servant of the Dawn"

Tiras pal Erdot: "He rules over ashes."

Velati sonoren: "Prince of the Dawn."

Tharvané tona luné, xanoren xanen: "Tharvané without light, unto the ages of ages."

Iramon iramoren: "Indignity of indignities!"

Tó Solarias: "Hail Solarias!"

Sí eldari: "I am the Sage."

Selen'veni: "Half-Fey"

Loctari: "Speaker"

Eldari: "Sage"

Eldaren: "Sages"

Abolliu: "Cast down to hell"

Avela: "Look!"

Ananda: "(You all) go."

Iramon iramoren! Londor abolliu…: "Indignity of indignities! Londor cast down to hell…"

Num Tharvané tona luné. Tharvané abolliu…: "Not Tharvané without light. Tharvané cast down to hell…"
Sinta: "Listen!"
Dibalsomnar, danen ira: "Child-eater, the gods rebuke you!"
Gastreel! Evar Pellan Imen!: "Gastreel! You have the Fire of Imon!"
Evaiu Pellan Imen: "I have the Fire of Imon."
Kon Helvenharu, heru y helvon kidairu: "With Bull-Cutter, I cut and I slay the bull."
Buar num kidaira danenvon: "You cannot kill a god."
Num danenvi thó. Thó Abollari: "You are not a god. You are an unclean spirit."
Avela! Tond kon aion!: "Look! They are with him!"

Rokahn phrases

Luntokk rhorkudu: "I am not of your kind."

Terms

Alonar: An Elven term roughly corresponding to Gallia and some surrounding lands.

Black wolves: Large, intelligent wolves of the Dragonteeth. They are often captured and forced into the service of rokahn. They are one of the three divisions of Great Wolves, along with White Wolves and Brown Wolves.

Brown wolves: Large, intelligent wolves who now live among the Viegs. They are noted for their intelligence and great loyalty.

Danda: Heaven, the domain of the gods and the gods' followers.

Dark One, the: A name for Seymus, the enemy of the gods, the king of the Abollaren or demons.

Doomblade: One of the original *estirion* blades, first called *Pelladrimas* ("Flame of Fire") and wielded by the elven warrior prince Camlon in the First Shadow War. Through many names and owners it eventually made its way into the hands of the human Simeon Nax.

Dó Kentas: Literally, "the Way of the Staff." The elves' most ancient martial art, focused on mastery of the quarterstaff. A practitioner of *dó kentas*, called a *dó kentari*, is mandated to only wield a quarterstaff, a longknife as a weapon of last resort, and a loose white uniform called a shift.

Dohorensi board: A traditional weapon of the nation of Khandara, an edged metal board used to slash and bash.

Dragonteeth: Large snow-capped mountains, stretching from Gallia in the east to the ocean in the west, forming the border of the northern kingdoms and the lands of the elves.

Druen: Elvish for "night people," a term for the cursed elven tribe known as vampires.

Dweorg: A race of metallurgists, smiths and tinkerers said to have been given powers of creation in ancient times.

Elves: Long-lived beings whose kingdoms and settlements lie in the north of the world. They are divided into several tribes, including the Lamen, the Umen, the Lonen, and the Nurnen. In recent years, the Lamen kingdom lost a war to the Kingdom of Zarubain and untold thousands of elves were brought into forced servitude.

Elf-friend: A term of legal and cultural weight according to the elves, it is granted to non-elves who have proven themselves steadfast allies and trustworthy friends of elvenkind. Elf-friends are allowed to dwell in the Elf Lands and participate to a lesser extent in elven society.

Elvish horse: A kind of warhorse bred by the elves for speed and bravery. They are known by the bony horns that grow on their noses.

Empire, the: A vast state composed of seven provinces, ruled by an emperor and an Imperial Council. It is considered the foremost military power in the world.

Estirion: "Star-iron" is the hardest and sharpest metal known to man. The means of the making of star-iron swords are lost to history; they were said to be forged by Danthelon, the so-called "Wonder-Smith." Only twenty are known to exist; they are considered priceless.

Galiope: A large city of the northern kingdoms, called by those that love it the Queen of the North.

Gallia: A region east of Zarubain and west of Kardir, a place of mixed forest and farmland. Its greatest city is Galiope.

Gypsies: A wandering folk who traditionally roamed the world in colorful wagons. In recent years, they were welcomed by the Gallian government and allowed to settle in Galiope.

Imperial: To those outside the Empire, a citizen of the Empire. To those within the Empire, a man or woman originating in the coastal provinces associated with its founding.

Hafri: Literally "love-band," a white cord, tied around a lover's left hand, a token of affection.

Kehrad: The most intelligent species of rokahn, they are thinner built than the other breeds, with angular facial features and often red or green skin. They often become leaders of rokahn war-bands by force of will; however, their smaller size makes them easy targets.

Kival: A ritual bath.

Laeras: An orange robe symbolizing ritual purity.

Lonen Elves: A tribe of elves known for their atheistic beliefs and their advanced technology in war. They are often black-haired and pale in complexion.

Longknife: A single-edged, sharp knife native to elven metallurgy, used for slashing or piercing.

Necromancer: A sorcerer with power over death and withering.

Non: A large region in the northwest of the Elven World, composed of a vast and mostly uninhabited steppe. It is known for the stag riders it employs in war and the spider caves from whence it derives silk. The silk is spun to fashion the Elven World's most precious fabric, called by humans elvencloth.

Norwood: A small village in the region of Noricum in the Empire, in the province of Gad.

Rokahn: Humanoid creatures known to dwell in the Dragonteeth, considered creatures of shadow. When their population swells, they will often raid the lowlands for food. Breeds include kehrad, toltar, and the standard species simply known as rokahn.

Servants of Seymus: Six beings in service of the Dark One. They wear iron masks and are clothed in black.

Southern Reaches: A strip of coastal land in the south of Lamdar, bordering human lands.

Sindon: An anklet forged of silver which Umen wildblades wear at all times.

Starstones: Shards of crystal, infused with magic to the point that they steadily give off light.

Toltar: Thin, diminutive rokahn of tiny stature. They are nonetheless eager in battle and will fight to the death. They are used as scouts or spies in war or sometimes eaten by hungry rokahn as snacks.

Vampire: In Elvish, *druen*—a tribe of elves cursed in ancient times with a thirst for blood.

Viegs: A tribe of humans who swore an ancient treaty of alliance with the elves. They live in the far eastern part of the world, near the Dweorg.

Wari: An Elvish ceremonial gate.

Wildblades: Elven warriors of the Umen tribe who are said to work themselves into controlled rages. They are trained to be ambidextrous and wield scimitars in both hands.

Wizards: Powerful magic weavers of the northern kingdoms. They are governed by a council and have their own nation-state within the walls of Galiope.

Wizard's staff: An implement of magic that wizards use. Without it, their skill at magic weaving is weakened. The first task a wizard who has achieved full rank undertakes is the fashioning of a staff. They are constructed of crystal and certain types of wood.

Zarubad: The largest city of the north, far west of Galiope, by the sea, the capital of the Kingdom of Zarubain.

APPENDIX 5: THE HOUSE OF IRADAHIR

Annenwé Iradahir (female, the youngest, born 9 Riál 1137)
Yanenré Iradahir (female, born 7 Yanenré 1127)
Avernathi Iradihir (male, born 11 Riál 1118)
Vélerion Iradahir (male, born 22 Vlesti 1102)
Fenendi Iradahir (male, born 18 Vlesti 1101)

Annenwé Iradahir is young and being tutored.

Yanenré Iradahir is a lightbearer of exceptional talent, and has quickly become second to only the Chief Lightbearer.

Avernathi Iradahir is a candidate to join the College of Priests.

Vélerion and Avernathi Iradahir are prized warriors who fought in the wars with the Dark Elves and with the rokahn in the east.

About the Author

Cursed at birth with a wild imagination, Andrew Cooper spent his youth dreaming of worlds more exciting than Earth.

He is a graduate of the Odyssey Writing Workshop. His stories have appeared in Morpheus Tales, Fear and Trembling, Residential Aliens and Mindflights, among others.

He is also a graduate of the Creative Writing program at Western Michigan University.

Visit **www.aj-cooper.com** to sign up for the newsletter and stay up-to-date on new releases.

Find him on **x/Twitter** @ajcooperwriter.